Shadow of
DOUBT

God bless!

Amy Morton Winterstein

Shadow of DOUBT

a novel

AMY MAIDA WADSWORTH

Covenant Communications, Inc.

Covenant.

Cover image, by © EyeWire Collection/Getty Images.
Cover design copyrighted 2003 by Covenant Communications, Inc.
Published by Covenant Communications, Inc.
American Fork, Utah

Printed in Canada
First Printing: Month 2003

10 09 08 07 06 05 04 03   10 9 8 7 6 5 4 3 2 1

ISBN 1-59156-211-2

Library of Congress Cataloging-in-Publication Data

Wadsworth, Amy Maida, 1970-
    Shadow of Doubt : a novel / Amy Maida Wadsworth.
        p. cm.
    ISBN 1-59156-211-2 (alk. paper)
    1. College teachers' spouses--Fiction. 2. Married women--Fiction. 3. Mormon
women--Fiction. 4. First loves--Fiction. I. Title.

    PS3623.A35S53 2003
    813'.6--dc21

                                                                    2002041768

This book is dedicated to my sweet husband, Jason, who teaches me daily about love and commitment as we continue to build our temple marriage. I always remember.

Special thanks to Orson Scott Card for inspiring me and supporting writers' groups on his website, to Kathleen Dalton-Woodbury for assigning me to such a wonderful group, to Terry Montague for being my mentor, to all the ladies of ANWA (American Night Writers Association) for their detailed, insightful critiques, and to Rose Ostler for encouraging the poet in me. God answers prayers through people. You were all instruments.

The Letter

———————————

I pushed the last of the windows closed with a grunt. Ten A.M. had rolled around, and the air conditioner was still off; sweating that late into the August morning should earn me some sort of award.

"I'll feel better once I have cold air blowing on my face." I spoke into the cordless phone pinched between my ear and my shoulder.

"Do you miss Jon?" My mother spoke on the other end of the line. She was my best friend, and I called her every day.

"Not as much as I thought I would." I sat on the floor and waited for cold air to blow up through the vent, fanning myself with a copy of *Goodnight Moon*. "He was supposed to come home today, but he called last night and said his appointment with one of the directors fell through, and he was trying to reschedule for today."

"Has he liked the festival?"

"You know him and Shakespeare. If I believed in reincarnation, I'd think I married the Bard himself."

Mom laughed. "So if you don't miss Jon, then why do you sound like you just got home from a funeral?"

"You know what it's like staying home with kids all the time. I think I spend half my life in the laundry room and the other half in the kitchen. At twenty-six years old, I expected to know more about life than how to remove a banana stain."

"I know. It was hard for me, and I only had you to take care of. You've got three little ones running around."

"Speaking of my rugrats, I'd better check on them." I stepped out the front door with phone in hand and walked around to the backyard. Five-year-old Emily, three-year-old Jacob, and eighteen-month-old

Katie ran through the sprinkler, giggling loud enough for the whole block to hear them. Jacob tied his towel around his neck and held it out behind him like a superhero as he ran through the water.

"Jacob, how can you dry yourself off if your towel gets all wet?"

"Well, Momma, my towel's not as wet as Katie's."

Katie's towel lay in a soggy heap near the sprinkler head. She heard my voice and ran toward me with her arms held up. Her blond curls dripped water down her baby-smooth back. I let her hug me even though she soaked my clothes.

"I guess I need a change of clothes for me." I kissed Katie's cold cheek.

A doorbell rang at Mom's house.

"Oh, hang on, Lia, the mailman's here. He needs me to sign something."

I overheard Mom open the door and greet the mailman. Katie's cold body chilled me better than the air conditioner, but my clothes began to stick.

"Come on, Katie, let's go get some towels."

"Wow, I never get registered mail. I wonder who it's from. Oh boy," Mom said.

"What, Mom? Who's it from?"

"Well, it's not for me. I shouldn't have signed for this. I should have made them send it back."

"Then who's it for?"

"It's for you."

"Oh." I couldn't imagine who would send a registered letter for me to my parents' house. "So, who's it from?"

"It's from Derek."

"Derek?" I asked.

"Sullivan." I could almost hear Mom hold her breath after she croaked out his last name.

Derek Sullivan was my high school sweetheart. We were engaged until he decided he didn't care if we got married in the temple or not. He cared about other things more than the Church, and I wanted a temple marriage and would settle for nothing less, so we broke up. It was the hardest thing I ever had to do.

I cleared my throat. "But . . . why would Derek send me a letter?"

"I don't know. It feels like there's a box in it or something. Do you want me to open it?"

"No, that's okay. Maybe he found something of mine he forgot to give me. I'll get the kids dressed and come get it."

My mind raced as I dressed Katie then changed my clothes. What little trinket of mine was so important that Derek would send it to me after almost eight years? I had a completely different life with a husband and three kids; I was a different person than the young girl Derek remembered. But thinking of Derek stirred memories in me I hadn't thought of in a long time: silly sentimental things like giggles in a prom dress, sipping bubbling cider, and stealing kisses behind a chaperone's back.

I drove to my mom's house a little too quickly; at least the cop let me off with a warning. When the letter finally rested in my hands, with his messy scrawl in blue ink, I remembered love letters, phone conversations at one in the morning, the earthy smell of his cologne lingering on my clothes at the end of our dates. I lifted the envelope quickly to my nose and sniffed just enough to catch the scent of him. After eight years, I held a piece of Derek in my hands again.

"Well, aren't you going to open it?" Mom played with her short, permed hair as she glanced back and forth between the envelope and me.

"Not in front of my mom! What if it's something personal?" I said in dramatic sarcasm as I rolled my eyes. Then I slipped the envelope in my diaper bag, pretending it wasn't a big deal.

Mom and I fed the kids lunch and sat around talking about Dad's retirement, Mom's new recipes, and the pitiful garden in my backyard. But my thoughts glanced at the letter, like a teenager flirting across a classroom during study time.

I turned onto my street with the evening planned. I would put the kids to bed and relax in a steamy bubble bath while I opened the mysterious envelope. It was silly to linger in the mist of innocent memories Derek's letter revived, but I wanted to remember the days when I got butterflies waiting for a phone call, when everything was new and exciting, when a simple, innocent kiss thrilled me to my toes.

But as I pulled in the driveway, my plans dissipated. Jon's Chevette sat in its usual grease-stained spot. It wasn't that I was disappointed to see my husband. I loved him and would rather have him home than not; but his work took him away from me, and we had grown distant.

"Hey, kids. Daddy's home," I called to the backseat.

Emily and Jacob ran to the door and threw it open, yelling, "Daddy!" I tucked the letter deeper in the diaper bag and zipped it closed, then lifted Katie from her car seat and went in the house to see my husband.

The Married Woman

"Hey, I remember you!" Jon walked to me with one kid in his arms and one kid wrapped around his leg. He lifted a stray strand of my hair and gently tucked it behind my ear. I always loved it when he did that.

"I remember you too. Welcome home." I kissed him.

"Thanks. It's good to be back."

Jon bent down and set Emily on the ground, then he lifted Jacob and squeezed him until he groaned. I was amazed by how much Jacob looked like his dad—tall and thin with blue eyes and short, dark brown hair. Over the years, though, Jon's middle had rounded a bit. His hair had thinned and gradually streaked with gray, more gray than I thought he would have at thirty-four. Every teacher I ever knew looked older than they really were. I guess Jon was no exception.

Emily, on the other hand, looked like me. Her light brown hair hung straight down her back, held out of her face by two blue clips. Emily's eyes didn't really have a discernable color. If she wore green, they were green. If she wore blue, they were blue. I had chameleon eyes too. Jon told me they were like mood rings.

"How was the drive?" I asked.

"It was really good. Getting that tape recorder was a great idea. I took tons of notes for the book, and I never had to pull off the freeway."

"Did you get the interview you wanted?"

"Yeah. He fit me in this morning during breakfast. He even paid for it. I ate so much this week, I'll probably only snack for a couple of days."

Jon was a professor at the University of Utah, and as part of his job he had to write a book every three years. The current project was on dramatic interpretation of Shakespeare. He was always writing in his head, on scrap paper, napkins, or the phone book, whatever was nearby that had room for a word or two. Jon's heart beat with the scratch of his pencil, and he read so much Shakespeare that he wrote in iambic pentameter without even trying. His mind wandered to his books so often that conversations with him were sometimes a chore.

I fixed tacos for dinner as Jon went on about the Shakespearean Festival in Cedar City. He talked about the plays, the actors, the costumes. One of the plays was set in modern Puerto Rico, and Jon was really intrigued by the twist.

"You should have met this director, Lia. He's fascinating. He's traveled the world and seen so many Shakespearean productions, you wouldn't believe it. And years ago, gee, it must be twenty years ago now, he went to college with my old high school drama coach. Isn't that a kick?"

Jon's right eyebrow twitched when he got excited, and at that moment, it wiggled enough to make me giggle.

"Anyway, Dr. Brad's prodigy is coming to the U this year. His name is Stratford, if you can believe it, and he's doing a production of *Much Ado* for the Babcock. He's asked me to sit in on the rehearsals with him and watch the process. I tell you, this is the opportunity of a lifetime. It's kismet. Man, I'm so excited my eyes hurt." He closed his eyes and pinched the bridge of his nose.

I popped a cherry tomato in my mouth to keep from laughing out loud.

"I think I'll teach *Much Ado* in my Shakespeare class this semester. That way I can refresh myself on the play and be more of a help."

Katie tugged at Jon's pant leg and he lifted her, covering her face with kisses.

"Ooh, I missed my princess. Did you guys have a good week?" he asked, turning to me.

"We ran through the sprinklers a lot," I said. "Ate a lot of ice cream. Went to bed early, for us."

I cleared Emily's crayons, stencils, and coloring books from the table and lifted the diaper bag from my chair. I remembered the letter tucked deep in the bag.

Katie wrapped her little arms around Jon's neck and rested her head on his shoulder. He patted her back as he rocked back and forth.

I missed him more than I thought, and the mystery letter didn't seem all that important. I put the diaper bag on the bottom stair so I would remember to take it up to my room. Even if I didn't care much about the letter at that moment, I was still curious. I couldn't throw it away until I knew what it said.

With the diaper bag out of the way, I walked up to Jon and hugged him.

"Do your eyes still hurt?" I rubbed his eyebrows softly with my thumbs.

He closed his eyes and grinned.

"I love it when you do that. It calms me down so much." If he'd been a cat, he would have rolled over on his back and started purring.

I laughed and put my arms around his neck. "Welcome home, Shakespeare," I said.

"You know, it really is my favorite place to be, even though I'm not here very much." He put his arms around my waist.

"I know."

"Well I hope you never forget it." He picked me up so he could hold me tight.

"I hope you never let me forget it."

After we'd eaten dinner and tucked the kids in their beds, Jon went back downstairs to start transcribing his notes. I sneaked down for a last kiss and took the diaper bag upstairs with me. The corner of Derek's letter stuck up from the open bag, but the joy of being with Jon had dissolved my earlier mood. Why long for innocence when knowledge was so good? So I tossed the envelope under my bed and set the diaper bag just outside Katie's room. The letter could wait for me with the dust bunnies.

Walking Out

———⟨≋⟩———

The Relief Society room buzzed with conversations and laughter. A woman whom I'd never seen sat in the back row, crossing her long legs. She was tall, probably about five-foot-ten, thin, and blond. With slight bags under her eyes and almost translucent skin, she looked like she'd been sick for a while.

"Hello, are you Jane Hinckley?" I sat down next to her.

"Yes, I am," she responded.

"Hi, Jane." I extended my hand. "I'm Lia. Anna told me about you. I hope she told you about me. I'm your new visiting teaching companion."

She smiled and took my hand with a surprisingly strong grip. "Hi. Anna did mention you."

"I have an appointment scheduled with one of our sisters for this Thursday. Do you want to come?"

"Yes, I'd like that very much." She looked eager to get started.

Anna stood to conduct the meeting. The buzz of conversation drifted to a whisper, and we all sat back, waiting to be edified. A huge bouquet of sunflowers sat on the table, filling the air with the clean, warm smell of late summer. The flowers seemed to bow their heads, and we joined them as the meeting began.

After the prayer Anna introduced Jane during the announcements. Jane stood, and with a soft smile and timid voice said, "Thanks for your welcome. No, we're not actually related to the prophet, except maybe distantly. My husband, Scott, is doing an internship at the University Hospital. He's in cardiology. I am a neonatal nurse, so when I'm working I get to hold babies all day. I'm not working now. Scott and I don't have kids yet." She smoothed her skirt as she sat back down.

She was so thin. I felt a twinge of envy. Giving birth to Emily and Jacob was hard, but Katie ruined my body forever, or at least until the resurrection.

"Sisters, our Super Saturday is only one month away. The projects are displayed in the hall. There will be a nursery, so don't be afraid to sign up for the project of your choice—you'll have plenty of time to work on it."

"As long as there's a nursery, I'll be there." I didn't say it very loudly, but the sisters close to me turned and chuckled.

After the song and the prayer, Alexis Smith glided to the front of the room, handing out pieces of paper and pencils as she went. Most teachers sat at the front when they taught their lessons, but Alexis liked to make an entrance.

"Today sisters, we are going to discuss the vitality of our calling as mothers." She stood at the front of the room, clasping her hands at her waist like a professor preparing for a lecture. She projected her voice as if she were on stage.

"On this piece of paper, please write your favorite thing about being a mother."

Alexis was always so serious. I wrote, "When my kids are asleep or with a babysitter," and hoped she would ask me to read it out loud. I've always thought a little laughter goes a long way.

Jane sat with her legs crossed away from me and tapped her foot enough that her leg bounced noticeably. After slipping the pencil behind her ear, she crumpled the paper and folded her hands in her lap.

"While the men in the Church have the priesthood, we, as women, have motherhood. It is our connection to God. It is the manifestation of the power of God in us." Alexis gave importance to the words by pausing dramatically.

Jane uncrossed her legs and shifted her weight a bit. I looked over at her lap. Her fingers busily ripped the crumpled piece of paper into tiny bits.

"Nothing can compare to our joy when we feel the first stirring of life, or see the first ultrasound of our growing child. I can't express my own elation when I discovered I was having twins. I knew I would have to put off my career for a while, but I also knew it was worth it.

Anything is worth it to hold that sweet baby and watch her sleep in your arms." Alexis wiped tears from her eyes as I rolled mine.

After gathering the bits of paper in her hand again, and picking up her scriptures, Jane got up and quietly left the room. I couldn't say I blamed her. After Jane left, Alexis compared in great detail the physical trials of childbirth and the trials of the Savior. I appreciated the point of it all, but—yuck. I got up to leave too, hoping Jane was just outside the door and we could talk.

Jane must have ducked out to the parking lot, because the only person in the hall was a young mother slowly lulling her baby to sleep.

Emily and Jacob waited for me in the Primary room, as usual. Jacob held a picture of the Book of Mormon and the Bible, scribbled on in red and blue crayon. His teacher wrote his name in the upper right-hand corner with black crayon.

"What have you got there, buddy?" I knelt and looked at his artwork.

"I will read the scriptures." He recited the words and pointed in the general vicinity of the printed words at the bottom of the page.

"Very good, Jacob. Is that what you talked about today?" I slipped the paper in my far-too-heavy Sunday bag and took his little hand in mine.

"We all talked about it, Momma." Emily ran up and showed me her paper, colored exactly inside the lines. It was dark blue just like her scriptures, with gold surrounding the letters on the book covers. "We need to read every day together. Did you know that?"

"Yes, hon. I knew that."

"But we didn't read yesterday, Momma." Emily folded her paper and placed it in her little purse. Since kindergarten started in a week, she figured she was all grown up and able to change the world. But not without a bag that matched her outfit.

"Ah, it begins." Jon walked up behind me with Katie in his arms. "I knew our kids would be smarter than us, but I was hoping they would wait until they moved out so they couldn't remind us of it every day."

"And, Momma, Jacob was bad today," Emily snitched.

"He was?" I looked down at Jacob, his little hand enclosed in mine. He hung his brown head in shame.

"Yes. He had to sit by Sister Philips at the front of the room."

"What happened, Jacob?" I squeezed his hand, encouraging him to tell the truth.

"I was noisy," he replied, hanging his head.

"And they made you sit at the front of the room for that?" I smiled. I had never met a three year old who could sit quietly for two hours.

"They told him to be quiet three times, and he wouldn't obey." Emily skipped through the foyer as Jon opened the chapel door and held it for the rest of us.

"Okay, Emily. Let Jacob speak for himself," Jon said. He hated it when Emily tattled. Since I was an only child, and had never been tattled on, I thought it was kind of cute.

Jacob still frowned. I squeezed his hand again, and he looked up at me with blue eyes and eyelashes like butterfly wings. I mouthed the words "I love you," and blew him a kiss. He smiled and blew one back.

We sat on a bench in the middle of the chapel and flanked our children. Jon liked to watch Katie so that he could take her out if she got fussy. It was his way of compensating for all the meetings I missed while nursing.

After the sacrament, Missy Wilson stood as the youth speaker. Her eyes teared up before she opened her mouth. Missy turned twelve when I taught Beehives. My kids were the first ones she babysat, and I hired her twice a month until she turned sixteen and started dating. There she stood in front of the congregation, a young woman on the cusp of her senior year in high school. She was beautiful, and glowed as she spoke.

"Brothers and sisters, the bishop has asked me to speak on temple marriage today."

She took a deep breath and tried to steady her emotions.

"I hope I can get through this. As a young woman in the Church, temple marriage is one of my goals. And I hope the Lord will make me worthy of reaching this goal."

Her face twisted with emotion, and tears coursed down her face again. She dabbed the tears with a tissue and took another deep breath. Missy stood there for a moment, looking through watery eyes at her notes. Then she shook her head and sobbed into the tissue. Covering her face as much as possible without obscuring her vision, she left the pulpit and speed-walked down the aisle.

Several people turned to watch her leave, myself included. Her mother, Mary, stood and followed her, putting her arm around Missy's waist as they disappeared through the double doors.

First Jane, then Missy. I wondered who would walk out next.

"I hope she's okay," Jon whispered in my ear.

"Yeah, me too."

"Another semester begins." Jon collected his note cards, keeping them in some sort of order and sliding a rubber band around them.

"Summer went by fast this year," I observed.

"It sure did. This will probably be the busiest semester I've had in a while. I've got Beginning Shakespeare, English Lit., Beginning Poetry, office hours, and the book." He sighed and shook his head.

"At least you're not teaching Freshman Writing anymore."

He grinned. "Oh, that class had its benefits."

I smiled back.

"I guess I won't be seeing much of you for the next couple of months."

He sighed. "Well, you know how it is."

"Yeah, I know how it is."

I was proud of Jon. He had a good job, and he was good at it. He found lots of satisfaction with his students and his subjects, but as the semester went on, he always became less involved with the family. At least we were active in the Church; that ensured I'd see him at meetings on Sunday and every Monday night for family home evening.

"I talked to my mom before you came home, and I told her that I didn't miss you as much this time. I told her I was used to being alone."

"Oh?" He kept his eyes on his briefcase as he filled it with notebooks and paperback copies of Shakespeare. He could never look me in the eye when I talked about how many hours he spent away from home. I couldn't figure out if it was out of guilt or anger. Or both.

"Yeah," I continued. "But, it wasn't really true. I hate college. I can't wait until Christmas break. If it wasn't for our Sundays and Mondays, I would go nuts."

"Lia, we've talked about this. Some women don't get as much time with their husbands as you do. Some women don't have husbands at all."

"What does that have to do with anything? I'm talking about my life, our life, not someone else's."

"What do you want me to do? I can't do everything."

"Well, neither can I. And when you're so involved with work, I run the whole house, from top to bottom. During school, nothing functions without me. I can't even get sick."

"If I wasn't so involved with work, I wouldn't have a job. Then where would we be? I'm a teacher, Lia. I have to be involved."

He still wouldn't look at me.

"You're a husband and a father, Jon. Be as involved with us as you are with your job."

"If I'm involved with my job, I am involved with my family. I'm earning money for my family, remember? And the better I am at my job, the more money I earn. Do we have to have this conversation at the beginning of every semester?"

He shut his briefcase and set it on the counter next to the door, then brushed past me.

"I'm going to bed. I'll see you tomorrow."

Jon always walked out when he felt he had proven his point. He hated confrontation. And maybe he was right. The family needed him to be good at his job.

So, I let him walk out. It wasn't worth the argument.

Temple Marriage

When I got up the next morning Jon had already left for school and the house gradually woke with Katie's squeals, Emily's songs, and Jacob's computer games. I vacuumed Katie's crushed dry cereal from the carpet and looked absently around me at the same old thing. Then, the picture of the temple hanging on the wall behind the couch reminded me of Missy's talk the day before.

I remembered being emotional about the concept of marrying in the temple. Derek's father made a fortune and divorced Derek's mom during our junior year, then he moved to New York. After the divorce, Derek visited his father a lot and after graduation he got a job as a model. Before I knew it, my boyfriend's picture was all over magazine covers. He traveled back and forth between Salt Lake and New York all summer, and he always came back to his mom's with expensive gifts for me. Jewelry seemed to be his favorite thing. Some of the jewels sat in their boxes in my cedar chest, mostly because I never went anywhere fancy enough to wear them.

One day he came home without a gift. We went hiking together, and I was very content in jeans and a T-shirt, bejeweled with only my engagement ring. We'd talked of him serving a mission, but he'd decided that his calling was in modeling, and he could preach the gospel in his professional relationships. And though I had a ring, we hadn't really set a date. I wasn't sure why.

That day, as we hiked to Twin Peaks, the sky was clear and blue, and the air was crisp. Derek and I sat to catch our breath and take in the beautiful scenery, and he took my hand in his.

"Let's just elope," he said. His eyes, the color of the aspen leaves surrounding him, seemed to search for my heart. "I love you, Lia, and I don't want to wait."

"I didn't know you could elope to the temple. You have to make appointments and stuff like that. We'd have to plan it."

"I don't want to plan a big party and have to stand in a line all night shaking hands with people I don't know. I want to be with you." He kissed me softly and brushed his finger lightly across my cheek, then down the side of my neck.

"We're only getting married once, Derek. Let's do it right. We have to involve our families. They'd be crushed if we shut them out."

"This isn't about them, it's about us."

"But it is about them, Derek. They're our family. I can't imagine getting married without my parents there in the sealing room."

Derek stood and walked away from me, running his fingers through his blond hair. "I'm not sure I want to get married in the temple, Lia."

His back was to me, and I wasn't sure I'd heard him right. "What?"

"What difference does it make? I love you so much, and I can't imagine a loving God would separate us, even if we got married in a courthouse."

I couldn't believe what I was hearing. "Derek, we have to get married in the temple. I don't understand."

"I want you, Lia. I don't want to wait. Besides, I couldn't take you to the temple. I haven't paid tithing for months and I'm not going to start now. I'd pay more in tithing than most people make in a year. Besides, the Church doesn't need my money."

The world spun and the wispy clouds sailed above me much faster than normal. I shook my head.

His testimony had all but disappeared. I'd seen it coming, but I'd ignored all the signs. During the previous months he'd become more lenient about the movies he'd watched, less interested in attending firesides and ward activities. We'd done more things apart than we'd done together because I wasn't interested in boating on the Sabbath with his friends or coed overnight camping trips where "nothing" happened. This was the last straw. This was something I could not abide. I pulled the ring from my finger and put it in his hand.

"I don't need your money either. I'm going to get married in the temple."

I started back down the mountain alone. Derek followed me and took me home while I cried and avoided looking at him. When he stopped the car in front of my home, I got out of the car without a word and ran for the front door. That was the last time I saw him.

Derek called repeatedly, but Mom intercepted the calls for me. He invited me to see him off when he left for New York, but I didn't go. Instead, I waited until I knew his plane was gone, then went to the airport and watched miscellaneous takeoffs. After that, I walked through Temple Square, praying in my heart for some guidance and comfort. The solid granite temple rose from the ground in front of me, stretching to heaven like a pillar of light. That was the goal. That was the place to start my life with my best friend and companion, a worthy man.

My mother told me to get on with my life as if marriage weren't an issue. She said that sometimes we find the best things in life when we stop looking for them.

In the following months, I took out a student loan and signed up for classes at the University of Utah. I declared astronomy as my major. I had no idea what I could do with a degree in astronomy, but I wanted to study something I loved. The curriculum for freshmen required a beginning writing class, and that year it was taught by Jonathan Tucker.

I had met Jon at my high school where he did his student teaching in sophomore English. I had a crush on him even then, but I never said a word, even to my friends. At least I was smart enough to know that having a crush on your young, single teacher meant nothing in the big scheme of things.

When I went to college that first day, he sat at the desk in the front of the room, organizing syllabi. The old crush came back. The three months of that semester solidified my feelings, though I didn't do anything about it while I was in his class. Instead, I watched him, soaked in every detail—like his soft blue eyes and the sweet, cedar smell of his skin as he leaned over my shoulder to help me with my syntax. Intoxicating warmth radiated from his body, and I did everything within my power to be near him.

One day during the next semester, I hung out at Orson Spencer Hall just outside of his classroom. I told him I needed advice for a paper and maybe we could discuss it over lunch.

"I don't usually eat lunch alone with students." He flashed a lopsided grin and blushed slightly.

At that point, I knew he was attracted to me. That knowledge encouraged me to pursue him.

"So let's meet at the Student Union. I think that would be appropriate," I said.

We met that day for lunch. The Union bustled with students ordering coffees of every kind and spreading their papers across tables. Study groups clustered around every couch and chair throughout the main floor. Some of them greeted "Dr. Tucker" as we walked by.

Jon found a small table near a window and sat down.

"Would you like me to order for you?" He leaned his face closer to mine and spoke in low secretive tones. "You'd have to pay for it, of course, because this isn't a date. It's against policy for teachers to date students. I just got *that vibe* from you, and I wanted to clarify."

I nodded, told him what I wanted, and gave him some money.

He went to get the food, and I watched him, knowing I would marry him within the year.

Summer semester I transferred to Salt Lake Community College. Jonathan Tucker proposed to me on the porch of my parents' home on an autumn evening just before my twentieth birthday.

We married in the Salt Lake Temple in December.

It all seemed so long ago. I read Jon easily then, as easily as Jon read Shakespeare. But the children came quickly. Jon became more and more involved at the university. Occasionally, I lost my feel for him. I tried to predict how he would react to certain situations, like my difficulty with potty training Jacob. He never reacted the way I thought he would. In fact, he was surprisingly uninvolved in the little things of our lives. I had my temple wedding, but at times I wondered if I had my temple marriage.

Maybe I just needed to focus on him more, try harder to relate to him and involve myself in his life. I needed to pursue Jon like I did in the early days of our relationship; I needed to convince him that I really was the girl he had waited for.

Jon scheduled most of his office work later in the week so he could be home in the early afternoon on Mondays. Usually, Jon watched the kids for me while I prepared for family home evening and did the shopping for the week. But this would be a special Monday. The kids helped me make cookies in the morning, and by the time I started fixing lunch, dinner waited in the fridge. I packed some snacks and loaded the stroller in the car so that we could take off and spend time in the canyon before we got hungry for dinner. I borrowed three simple games from my mom, figuring we could play them while dinner cooked. I rented Jon's favorite video to watch after the kids were in bed. Before I knew it, two o'clock rolled around and he was an hour late.

Katie fell asleep in my arms as we sat and watched PBS. I laid her gently in her crib and figured I would let her sleep until Jon got home and the fun began. By two-thirty, Emily started asking about Jon. I called his office, but he didn't answer. I figured he was probably at a meeting or in the library working on his book. The afternoon dragged by slowly, and we all waited. I cleaned up the after-lunch mess and put in a small load of laundry. Then I changed the load to the dryer. Katie woke up and I got her out of the crib. Four-thirty came and went. The kids complained of hunger, so I put dinner in the oven. Surely he'd be home by five. Five passed. Five-thirty. The cheese on the enchiladas overbaked until it was crusty and brown. The house smelled like the burnt tomato sauce on the bottom of the oven. I tried to call his office again, but he still didn't pick up. At times like this, I wished he had a cell phone, a pager, or something. For all I knew, he'd gotten in an accident and was lying injured in a ditch less than a block away.

I put the enchiladas in the fridge and loaded the kids in the Civic. The English offices were three miles away. I kept my eyes peeled for his Chevette broken down on the side of the road as I drove those three miles. I knew that if he did break down, he would probably just walk home, but I looked for him anyway, a feeling of panic and worry rising in my throat.

Parking was free after six throughout the campus, but it was fifteen minutes till. I parked in the faculty lot just in front of the English Department building anyway. The thought crossed my mind that he might not even be in his office. Maybe he had fallen asleep in the library. It wouldn't be the first time.

I balanced Katie on my left hip and rushed Emily and Jacob along in front of me through the twisting corridors and up two flights of stairs. By the time we got to the third floor, Jacob and Emily both complained, and I felt a sharp pain in my lower back. I hushed the children repeatedly as we worked our way through the maze of offices toward number 356. When we found it, the door was closed. I leaned my ear to the door and heard the laughter of a young woman. Immediately, my mind filled with the image of a beautiful thin college student looking up at my husband with adolescent adoration. Jon had lost his wedding ring two years before, and we'd never had enough money to replace it. The giggling creature in his office probably didn't even know he was taken. What a surprise for her when she left his office to see his wife and three children waiting outside.

The only chairs in the hall sat just to the side of his door. I sat to ease the pain in my back. When he opened the door, he didn't even know we were there. I saw the girl, but couldn't see Jon. He shook the young woman's hand. "Yes, Ashley. I'm glad we were able to work something out."

"Oh, me too, Dr. Tucker. I love performing Shakespeare anyway, but to be part of a book about it! Well, I'm just thrilled." She flipped her long auburn hair over her shoulder and smiled warmly, showing dainty dimples and blinking her long eyelashes at him far too often. She practically curtseyed as she turned and left him. Her perfume wafted behind her, a sickening sweet smell like roses and fruit punch. I watched her bottom wiggle past me and then I turned to see Jon standing in the hall, watching her wiggle with that lopsided grin on his face.

"Hi, honey." I spoke loud enough for Miss Wiggle to hear me. "Where have you been all day?" I waited for eye contact from him, my head cocked to the side a bit.

"Oh, Lia—" He cleared his throat and looked at me with wide eyes. "She's going to be in my eleven o'clock Shakespeare this semester. I'm using her for my book."

"You're using her, huh?"

He nodded and I cocked my head to the other side.

"Well, I'm done here. Just let me get my things." He disappeared into his office again. I waited for him to come back out with his pile of papers to clutter up my kitchen table.

Jon rattled on about his day as we meandered to the front door. He walked a few feet in front of me, and I dragged the kids mercilessly behind him.

"Why did you come anyway? I was almost through. I would have called you if there had been a problem."

"You're usually home by one on Mondays, Jon. I tried to call you, but you never answered. I worried about you." I huffed out the door and down the sidewalk, still three feet behind Jon. Emily whined for me to slow down.

"I've been working on my book. You had no reason to worry anyway. I'm a big boy. I can take care of myself." He smiled at me, but when he saw my expression his smile melted. He could see that I'd progressed from worried to furious.

"I'm parked over there," he said. "I'll see you at home."

After he walked away, I let the tears burn my eyes and slip down my cheeks. "You could have called," I said to his distant back.

I fumed as we walked to our separate cars. All the car seats were strapped in my Civic, so I dragged the kids behind me. He could have called. How hard is it to pick up a phone? And the look he was giving that girl. Did he know she was flirting shamelessly with him? He certainly didn't seem to mind it. The fact that he watched Miss Wiggle didn't bother me half as much as the fact that I didn't know what he was thinking about while he watched her. Can men look without wanting? Did Jon commit adultery in his heart while his wife and children stood not three feet from him? The sound of her laughter reverberated through my head. And I couldn't help but wonder how many of the last four and a half hours Jon had spent in her company.

We got to the car and I spotted the all-too-familiar white slip of paper on the windshield. The parking Nazis got me again. They must circulate tickets through the campus at 5:55, looking for the run-down cars, which obviously belonged to the poorest students and faculty. My little Honda with its three car seats in back and its faded high school tassel hanging from the rearview mirror undoubtedly made a prime target.

I drove home a little more aggressively than usual. A redheaded driver in an old green car honked at me as I cut him off coming out of the parking lot.

After we got home, I pulled the kids out of the car and we all went in the house. Jon was already home. His papers covered the board games on the table and he lay draped on the couch.

"Oh, what a day," he sighed. "I'm beat."

I nodded as I stood over him, my arms folded over my chest. Tears burned my eyes again, but I refused to let them fall. I cleared my throat. "There's some enchiladas in the fridge. I don't feel well. Would you feed the kids? I'm going to bed."

"But it's just after six. Are you okay?"

Now he cared about my feelings? "I just need to be alone."

He just looked at her, I thought as I stomped up the stairs. *No big deal.* But I felt betrayed. And it wasn't just the way he looked at her. My hopes for the day, my expectations, all fell through. I collapsed on my bed and sighed. But I was too angry to sleep, or even sit. My anger grew as Little Miss Wiggle walked past me in my mind, stinking up my air with her cheap perfume and tempting my husband like a wicked siren.

Hard water spots clouded the shower door in our master bath, so I pulled my tub of cleaning supplies from under the bathroom sink. Those spots needed annihilation.

When my bathroom smelled lemon fresh, and my clothes lay rearranged and refolded in my drawers, I went to see the mess downstairs. Jon lay fast asleep on the couch, his dirty dishes on the floor next to him. Jacob slept on top of him, curled up in a sweaty little ball of boy. Emily sat at the kitchen table, coloring and singing. Katie still sat in her high chair, covered with enchilada sauce and surrounded with tomato splats on the floor and the walls. I cleaned everything up, bathed the kids, and put them to bed. Jon stirred a bit when I pried Jacob off of him, but for the most part, he didn't notice me. I had worked out my energy, but not my anger. I left Jon sleeping on the couch and went upstairs to bed.

As I dressed for the night, I looked up at an old frame with a picture of the Wasatch Mountains hanging on our bedroom wall. He needed a wedding picture in his office. If he wasn't going to wear a ring, he needed some means of letting everyone know he was mine. I reached for my box of wedding pictures under our bed, thinking of the picture where we embraced and looked in each other's eyes, the Salt Lake Temple gleaming in the background. But as I grabbed for the box, I felt the envelope resting on top of it.

When Derek and I were dating, he was the sweetest thing in the world. He always opened the door for me and brought a single long-stemmed rose to every date. He overflowed with compliments. I felt like a queen with him. Derek never would have been four and a half hours late without calling me.

My heart ached as I remembered my youth, and it was tied inextricably to Derek. He was my youth. All the best times I had in high school had something to do with him. Derek was the boy every girl dreamed about, and I loved being his favorite. He was gorgeous, funny, charming, and smart. He was never particularly active in the Church, but he had a testimony; I was sure of it.

Holding that envelope in my hand filled me with mixed emotions. I missed the boy who made me laugh, who made me feel like I was the best, most gorgeous creature on earth. But all the pain I felt at breaking up with him came back too.

I opened the envelope slowly and eyed my bedroom door. I didn't particularly want Jon to come to bed at that moment. I reached in and pulled out a small cardboard box and a single sheet of notebook paper.

Quietly, I read the note, scribbled in the same blue ink.

> *I found this the other day and thought you should have it. I bought it for you anyway, and I have no use for it now. Please forgive me if I hurt you all those years ago. I was selfish and foolish. If I could do it all over I'd do everything differently, especially my decision to leave the Church. I know that decision made me lose the best thing that ever happened to me.*
>
> *I hope you are happy.*
> *With love, D.*

A small, blue velvet bag nestled inside the box. I loosened the top of the bag and dumped the contents on my bed. It was my engagement ring.

Sugar-Free Muffins

———⌗———

I sat up and looked bleary-eyed at the clock. At 5:50, Jon ran the water in our bathroom. With a sigh, I turned on my side so I could watch him shave. Jon scraped the razor against his chin and cursed. He must have thought I was asleep because he never spoke like that in front of me. With my eyes closed, I listened to him frantically getting ready for work, muttering quietly about sleeping on the couch, a kinked neck, and a thoughtless wife. The drawer slammed shut as he put his razor away. He turned off the light and left the room, his footsteps pounding quickly down the stairs. I squeezed the small velvet bag in my hand as Jon slammed the front door on his way to work.

Later that morning Emily, Jacob, and Katie ate their breakfast. I put away the drip-dried dishes from the night before, glancing at the envelope lying on the counter as I worked. The envelope bulged where the box sat inside it. And inside the box sat the ring; a heart-shaped, two-karat diamond with small diamonds all along the band. It winked at me from inside the envelope. I couldn't stand it anymore.

I slid Derek's letter in front of me with my back to the kids. The ring willed its way out of the packaging and gleamed on the counter. I removed my simple gold wedding band and slipped the ring on. It was tighter than I remembered, but it did look good on me. I moved just enough for the diamonds to catch the light, but kept my back to the kids. It blinded me with color, dazzled me back to a night in the canyon when we sat under the stars. I pointed out constellations for him, and told him about new stars and how hot they burned. He said his love for me burned hotter, and he proposed.

The old feelings for Derek blazed inside me for that moment. I had to get rid of that ring. I couldn't even have it in my house. Not for another minute.

With some difficulty, I pulled the ring from my finger. It left a red crease in my skin. Quickly, I repackaged the small symbol of Derek's love and covered my creased skin with the wedding band from Jon.

"Come on, kids. Let's go to Grandma's."

Mom rinsed the last bowl clean and put it in the dish drainer to drip dry. She wiped the counter of her stuck-in-the-seventies kitchen and laid the rag on the long-necked faucet.

Mom and I had spent hours at this worn Formica table. I felt comfortable here, wrapped in the warm smell of whole-wheat muffins, my bare feet on the worn, orange shag carpet.

"Here's a muffin for my Muffin." She smiled and placed the steaming snack and a paper napkin in front of me.

"Yeah thanks."

"Eat it, it's good for you. And yummy, too. This even has carob chips in it."

I smiled. "You know that when it comes to 'yummy,' I prefer processed, sugary, and fattening."

"Yes, dear. And it's showing a bit too." She poked my soft belly. "Not that that takes away from your beauty, it just makes you more tired than you should be at your age."

"I may be tired, but I'm happy with my chocolate." I broke off a piece of the muffin and put it in Katie's mouth. She promptly spit it out.

Dad sat in the front room reading *Hop on Pop* to Emily and Jacob. His voice rose and fell with the story, just like it did when he'd read to little me. I missed sitting on his lap.

"I'm dying to ask you what the letter was, but I'd rather you brought it up." Mom sat across the kitchen table from me and sipped on a glass of ice water.

"It wasn't just a letter, Mom. He sent my ring." I closed my eyes and sighed. "Oh, I wish he hadn't done that. My heck, it was almost eight years ago. Let it go already." I pulled out the envelope, the ring, and the note tucked safely inside of it.

"Can you send it back as a bad address?" I asked. "Or tell him I'm dead?"

"I can't send it back because I signed for it. He'll know I got it, and then he'll assume you did too."

The envelope lay there in the middle of the table. We both stared at it like it was hazardous material.

"I don't want it in my house, Mom. I've got enough problems."

"What's going on?"

"I planned a great family day and Jon didn't come home from work. Then I caught him looking at a girl."

"Looking at a girl? Doesn't a professor have to look at his students once in a while?"

"Not at their little round behinds." I looked up at Mom and raised my voice a touch more than I intended to.

"Oh." She nodded and took another sip of water. "Is that it?"

"Isn't that enough to make me worry a little? He's never done that before."

"You mean you've never seen him do that before." She smiled at me with all the wisdom and patience of a mother who knows everything.

"He's not like other guys."

"What makes you think that?" She sipped her water again. I fought a sudden urge to grab the glass from her hand and throw it on the floor, just to see it shatter.

"Many good men look, dear. Not in a lustful way, you understand. It's almost like a reflex. They appreciate beautiful women the same way you appreciate the stars: amazing yet indefinable objects meant to be studied and figured out."

"The stars don't turn me on the way a beautiful woman does a man. And besides, even if it is a natural thing for a man to look, doesn't that mean he should fight the urge? Control himself? Fight the natural man?" Katie squirmed in my lap, and I let her down. She ran over to Mom's calico cat and chased it out of the room, trying hard to grasp its tail.

Mom reached over and patted my hand gently. "Dear, just because a man looks out of accident, curiosity, or some subconscious impulse, that doesn't mean he necessarily reverts to lust at that moment. There comes a time in every married woman's life when she realizes that her husband is not perfect. A while later, she realizes she isn't perfect either. Then she sees that the only way for either of them to become perfect is to wade through the imperfections together." She leaned back in her chair. "Welcome to reality."

My heart tightened in my chest. "I came here for comfort, Mom. You're supposed to tell me that it's all in my head and I have nothing to worry about."

"It *is* all in your head. But that doesn't make it insignificant. Talk to him about it. Tell him how you feel. Remember who he is and why you married him."

At that moment, I could only remember the apparent look of desire on his face and the fact that it wasn't aimed at me.

"Lia, do you trust him?" Mom asked.

"He's never given me reason not to, until now." The tears ran hot, and I bit the nail of my right index finger and inspected its cuticle. I hated crying. It made my face red, sticky, and swollen. If I didn't look at my mom, maybe she wouldn't look at me.

"He hasn't given you reason to not trust him, Lia."

"I just never thought he was capable of wanting someone else. Now I'm not so sure." I wiped tears from my cheeks.

"A look doesn't imply he *wants* her. Aren't you making a huge leap here? There's a big difference between looking at someone and being tempted by her." Mom looked at the ceiling as she thought of another example. "Remember David and Bath-sheba? His sin wasn't in looking at her, it was in looking at her *again* and thinking about her enough that he commanded her to come to him. If he had looked away and controlled his thoughts, history might have been completely different."

I shrugged my shoulders and inspected my nails again.

"Honey, we're all capable of doing whatever we choose to do. The important thing is the choices we make."

I knew she was right. She was always right.

"Jon may look at another woman. Sometimes it's impossible to not look; you'd have to walk around with your eyes closed. But what does he do with the information once it gets in his head?" Mom tapped her temple with her finger, then her face softened with love and surety. "You know Jon. He doesn't dwell on it. He doesn't *think* about how pretty she is. He certainly doesn't *want* her. He chooses, like all good men do, to think about his wife, his family, his covenants. Believe he will choose correctly, and treat him like you believe it too."

Mom drained her glass of water and stood to put it in the dishwasher. I sat at the table alone. I didn't mention that I wasn't sure what I believed Jon would do.

"Do you think Jon might like some of these muffins?" Mom set a plate of them in front of me.

"No, Mom, he's even more of a sugar freak than I am."

"Sugar's bad for you, you know."

"Well, unfortunately, some people like things that are bad for them."

The Faithful

Mom agreed to send the ring back for me. She asked if I wanted to send a note with it, but I didn't have anything to say to Derek that hadn't been said years before.

It angered me that he had the nerve to send the thing in the first place. I broke up with him because I wanted a temple marriage. Surely he knew I had moved on and gone after what I wanted. Was he so arrogant that he thought he could show up eight years after the fact and tear away my heart? Did Derek think I would run to his private jet and take off with him, visiting exotic places and meeting interesting people? Was he out of his mind?

Thinking about it all tired me. I needed to get out of the house, away from my kids, away from the home I shared with an absent husband. I looked forward to visiting teaching like dinner on fast Sunday.

Jon sat on our bed, transcribing his notes on his laptop. I tapped his shoulder. "I'm visiting teaching tonight, Jon, so the kids are yours."

He looked up at me through drowsy eyes. "Sure, hon, but we need to talk about my night schedule before you go."

Life had been dealing me blows lately. I felt another one coming on.

"Remember I mentioned they want me to advise on the production of *Much Ado* and I can use the experience in my book? Well, I'm going to the rehearsals starting Monday."

"You're so tired right now you can hardly keep your eyes open. You go to work at six and come home at six, then you lock yourself up in here and work some more. Don't you think you've taken on enough?"

"It's great research for my book, Lia. Plus, I've always wanted to do something like this. It'll only last a couple of months. You'll have the kids on Monday, Tuesday, and Thursday nights starting next week."

"What about family night?"

"Don't worry. We'll work something out."

I sighed as the doorbell rang.

"There's Jane. Come down with the kids so I can leave."

Jon folded his laptop and scooped up his notes, a look of irritation on his face. He followed me downstairs and spread his stuff on the kitchen table.

Emily ran up to him almost immediately, and he scolded her.

"Don't mess up Daddy's notes. I've got work to do. Just go put in a video for you kids, okay?"

I shut the door behind me, thinking I may as well have left the kids home alone.

We walked around the block to visit Mary Wilson's house. I couldn't stop thinking of her daughter's talk and tearful exit from the chapel. I hoped Missy would sit in on our visit.

Mary was the consummate mother. Her children had chore charts and allowances, set rules, and specific consequences for obedience and for disobedience to those rules. Her husband, Hyrum, worked as a teacher at a local elementary school. Even though money was tight, Mary did everything she could to stay home with her children and not work outside the home. Not only did her children do their own paper routes, she had a route of her own early in the morning. Mary worked as a seamstress for the high school dance, drama, and choir groups. Plus, she had a boutique in her home every November to earn their Christmas money. Her testimony of tithing was unshakable. If it came down to being late on a payment, she paid the tithing. If it came down to being without food, she paid the tithing. And though her family was by no means wealthy, they were happy, and they had everything they needed. Mary bore her testimony at least every other month, and she always mentioned their good fortune and testified that it was due to obedience. I really admired Mary.

After Jane and I prayed for the Spirit to guide us, we knocked on Mary's door. We heard her before we saw her. "Everyone get started on your night reading. Early to bed, early to rise."

I chuckled and said to Jane, "You'll love Mary. She's the queen of one-liners. She's very affectionate too."

Mary opened the door and smiled.

"Hello, hello! Come in! You must be Jane Hinckley! I'm glad to meet you!" Mary threw her thick arms around Jane. With all the sewing and crafting that Mary did, she had plenty of sitting time to put on weight, so she was twice the woman Jane was. Mary told me herself that if it weren't for the paper route she would need a "wide-load" sign.

Jane smiled and giggled a bit in Mary's embrace.

"So tell me about yourself," Mary said as she closed the door behind us.

"Oh, there's not much to tell, really. We're here for Scott's residency. I've been having some medical problems, so I'm supposed to avoid stress. That's why I'm not working. I read a lot." She nodded her head, and then shrugged her shoulders.

"Medical problems? Oh, I hope it's nothing serious?"

Jane shook her head.

"Oh, good. Come in. Good food, good company—that'll help you avoid stress." Mary led us to the kitchen and we sat down at the table. She set a plate of cookies in front of us and offered us each a drink.

"We're here to check on you, not eat all your food," I laughed.

"Oh, believe me, there's more where that came from. Go on, help yourselves."

She made the best cookies in the ward. Whenever there was an event that required food assignments, Mary filled her standing order of two dozen chocolate chunk.

"So how is everything?" Jane started in.

We talked about the weather and the new school year. Mary decided to help with the high school marching band's uniforms that year too. It would provide more money, but she would be sewing "every waking minute, burning the candle at both ends."

Mary went down the list of her children and told us what they were all up to. Jimmy was a very successful missionary, but he hadn't been feeling well the last few weeks. He had three baptisms, and was finally communicating in Spanish. Trisha started her first semester at BYU and would come home every other weekend. Missy had been dating one boy steadily for almost a year. Mary wasn't quite sure where their relationship was going, and it made her a bit nervous. Luke was thirteen and acting his age. Steve and Susan, the twins, were the joy of her life. They were just old enough to really talk with, and just young enough to still adore their parents.

Missy walked through the kitchen to the refrigerator. She wore only a long, baggy T-shirt. I remembered when I had legs like that.

"Missy! Would you like to join us?" Mary asked cheerfully.

"No thanks, Mom. I'm just hungry." Missy spoke as she rummaged through the fridge.

"You should at least put a robe on, we do have company."

"I've got shorts on." She walked to the table with a glass of milk and grabbed two cookies.

"Yeah, well they're short shorts," Mary mumbled.

"How you doing, Missy?" I asked.

"I'm okay. I'm really embarrassed about Sunday though."

"Oh don't be. Public speaking is difficult, especially when your topic is something you have strong feelings about. Lots of people cry when they bear their testimonies, including me. Remember that year at girls' camp? I sobbed like a baby."

Missy nodded, but avoided looking me in the eye.

"No one doubts your testimony after that, Missy. We all know you love the Lord. I think our tears mean as much to the Lord as our words do, you know?"

"Yeah, I guess. I'm going to bed. I'm really tired today." Missy nodded her head at Jane and walked away. Her slow, deliberate steps sounded hollow on the stairs to her room.

"Do you think she's okay? She doesn't have that old spring in her step," I said.

"Actually, I am worried about her. She doesn't seem herself lately. And when she fell apart on Sunday, I think that was more than the Spirit. Something was wrong. But she won't tell me anything. And I can't really help her if she won't open up to me."

"It must be frustrating," Jane said.

"Oh it is." Mary reached for the plate of cookies and took a bite of one.

"Well, let us know if there's anything we can do to help." Jane took a dainty bite of a cookie.

"I sure miss her babysitting," I said, trying to lighten the mood. "I think the last time Jon and I went out at night, she watched our kids. Katie wasn't even one then."

"Yeah, she's probably done with babysitting. You might be able to get her in a pinch if she doesn't have plans. Listen, I'm sorry about her little fashion show," Mary said. "I didn't even know she owned a pair of shorts that short."

"She's probably got a G-string," Luke spoke up.

"Oh, I didn't know you were in here too. What do you know about G-strings anyway?" Mary's face flushed.

Luke followed his sister's path to the fridge. "Give me a break, Mom. They show them on TV all the time." He grabbed four cookies and took a humongous bite from one of them.

"No more TV for you," Mary teased after him. "Oh, this is a terrible world to raise children in. Evil everywhere they turn."

"Just remember that the Lord saved the very strongest of His children to come in this day, to this world," Jane said. "If we can have faith and trust in His teachings, we can survive and live righteously, even though there is evil all around us."

I spoke up. "Boy, that was a good introduction to the lesson, Jane. Very good. I'm impressed."

Jane smiled bashfully as she continued with the message. "We're talking about faith this month. It's really hard to have faith sometimes. The world around us is so vivid, and so loud, and it's always there. Just like you said, we are bombarded with evil from all directions."

"Yes!" Mary set down the cookie she was nibbling on as she interjected. "I visited the school the other day to work out some problems with Missy's registration, and you wouldn't believe the language and the locker-room talk I heard in the hallways. It's disgusting really."

Jane nodded. "But you have obviously raised your children well. You have taught them the gospel, and they know right from wrong."

"Well, I've done my best. As a parent, you never know how much you say really sinks in," Mary added thoughtfully.

"That's where their agency comes in. You do the best you can to teach them. Then it's up to them. Sometimes they have to learn things the hard way, but the Lord stays with His people." Jane smiled gently at Mary and continued. "Have faith, Mary. Trust His words. By having family home evening, family scripture study, and family prayer, you are exercising your faith. You're doing what He has asked. And He is bound when we do what He says. Your kids will see you trusting the Lord. Eventually, they will come to trust Him too. They'll turn out all right."

I thought about how family home evening would be more difficult with Jon's new schedule. But I pushed the thought from my mind. No use worrying about it now.

Mary's eyes glistened. "I wish my children had heard you say that, Jane. You have the Spirit with you, there's no doubt." We sat in silence for a moment as Mary dabbed at her eyes. Then she offered us more food.

"Let's take the long way home, just for fun," I said.

"Okay. I need to work off those cookies." Jane patted her flat stomach. "I should be home by nine though. Scott's shift ends then."

"Thanks, I just need to walk for a bit."

"You okay?"

"Yeah, just . . . melancholy, I guess."

"We all get that way now and then." Jane picked a dandelion from Mary's yard and twirled it in her fingers.

"You look happy. Are you happy, Jane?"

"Yeah," Jane said as she gazed into the twilight. "I've been happy all day. I've been wanting something for a long time, and I think I just might get it."

"Really? What?"

"Oh, I don't want to say until I hold it in my arms. I'm encouraged, but nothing's positive yet. I don't want to jinx it or anything."

She rested her palm against her flat stomach and sighed.

If she was trying to keep a secret, she was doing a terrible job of it, but I kept silent about her possible pregnancy. The only reason a woman rests her hand against her stomach like that is to try to feel the extra energy a growing baby has. For me, it was as if I could feel all three of my babies almost from conception; it was like their spirits brushed against me before their little hands and feet could.

The moon rose just over the ragged mountains to the east. I looked up at its steady glow.

"Look how bright the moon is tonight." I smiled.

"Hmm. I love a full moon." Jane spoke melodically as she looked up.

"There was a time when I wanted to walk on the moon more than anything," I said.

"Really?"

"Oh yeah. I wanted to be an astronaut and study the stars. I even majored in astronomy."

"Did you finish your degree?" Jane asked.

"Nope. I had kids instead." I continued to gaze at the bright globe, glowing like a night-light for all the earth.

"Well, I think having kids is better than any other career." Jane clasped her hands behind her back as she spoke thoughtfully.

"Yeah. Being a mom is great. But sometimes . . . don't get me wrong, because I wouldn't trade my kids for anything, but sometimes I wish I could have a family and a career. It's too late now though."

"It's never too late to have a career. Childbearing years, however, are very limited. Be glad you have three. What if something happened and you couldn't have any more?"

I'd never thought about it. For the eighteen months since Katie was born I'd worried more about making sure I would wait for the next child.

Jane sighed as we reached her car. "Thanks for taking me visiting teaching. I like Mary. And I needed to make some new friends."

"I'm glad you came with me. I haven't had an active companion in a long time."

Jane gave me a brief hug then climbed in her car and drove away to her quiet little home to wait for her loving husband. I looked up at my house and thought of the three children inside. As much as I loved them and was grateful for them, I still hoped they were sleeping soundly.

I slipped through the front door and noticed how quiet the house was. Jon slept on the couch with his open laptop on his stomach. The screen saver flashed pictures of the kids and me.

I sat next to him on the couch and looked at his sleeping face. I missed him. I leaned in and kissed him softly, basking in the warmth of his mouth. Memories flooded my mind of when we fell in love—first kiss, first touch. I used to be his lucky charm, and he wanted me with him all the time. More than anything, I wanted to live that life again. I wanted things to feel the way they used to. His breath puffed softly on my cheek. After a moment, he returned my kiss and held my face in his hands as he had so many times before.

"Hey, I remember you." He opened his eyes as wide as his slumbering state would let him.

"I remember you too."

"Yeah, you're that little girl in my English class, the one who can't keep her eyes off me." He smiled and kissed me again.

"Yep, that's me. And you're all mine now, aren't you?" I smiled back, and didn't take my eyes off him.

He closed his eyes and kissed my neck. His breath tickled and sent chills down my spine.

He whispered, "I'm all yours."

I held his face in my hands until he looked at me. "You'd better be."

He smiled and got off the couch, setting his laptop on the floor. Without a word, he clasped my hand in his and led me upstairs to bed.

New Crayons

Emily's first day of kindergarten finally came. I equipped her with a backpack, a light jacket to keep at school, and a brand new big box of crayons. Everything had her name printed clearly on it. We were prepared.

Twenty little children lined up outside the kindergarten door, all of them shiny and clean and so excited they could hardly stand still. A few clung to their mother's hands, looking a bit scared. Then there was Emily. She stood on her toes at the front of the line and craned her neck to see through the window in the door.

"Mommy, look! My name is on that desk!" She pointed through the window to a desk near the door. Sure enough, her name was taped to the top of it, written in black marker on a slip of very wide-ruled paper.

Mothers around me wiped tears from their eyes and sniffled quietly. But I didn't. Emily had been ready for this for a long time. I was excited for her. In fact, I was even a bit envious. She stood at the beginning of a new adventure, anxiously clutching something she loved.

Emily's teacher came to the door. She was a short, stout woman with short black hair and a round face. She smiled. "Okay, sweethearts. Say good-bye to your parents and come on in."

Emily kissed me quickly and bounded into the room.

"I'll meet you right here when you're done," I called after her. Emily took her backpack off and tried to sit still at her very own desk.

I quickly took Jacob and Katie to Mom's. I'd filled a picnic basket with sub sandwiches and barbecue chips and two cans of pop. Then I covered it all with a light blanket. Hopefully this attempt at romancing Jon would be more successful than my last.

Mom greeted the kids with a hug and a melon-colored kiss.

"I thought I should tell you I got a notice from the post office that Derek got his letter back. I figured with a ring that big in there, I'd better send it registered. I thought that might make more of a point too. Maybe he'll leave you alone," Mom said.

"Yeah. Hopefully. Thanks for taking the kids, Mom," I said, and I was out the door.

I thought of Derek all the way to the U and wondered how he reacted when he got the letter back without a word from me. Surely he could tell it had been opened. I still loved my memories of him, but there was no room for him in my life anymore. I hoped that I didn't give the impression there was any interest by opening the letter in the first place.

Students dotted the hallways of Orson Spencer Hall. Some of them sat on the ground, studying; some stood in clusters talking about Kant and Plato. One boy sat on the floor and slept, his head leaning back against the wall and his mouth hanging open. Jon's classroom was on the main floor in the north hall. I could hear him talk through the old, drafty walls. I peeked through the window in the door.

Jon was born to be a teacher. He looked so natural standing in front of a group of kids, unfolding mysteries to them. These students looked up at him, mesmerized. Occasionally they took notes. But always their eyes came back to him, followed him as he leaned against the desk or meandered to the chalkboard. The students laughed in unison at something clever he said. He nodded and smiled. The chalk rubbed and the students copied Jon's notes in their books.

I cringed when I noticed Miss Wiggle on the front row. She seemed more mesmerized than the rest.

"So what do you think about this last couplet?" Jon pointed at what he'd just written. "'If it prove so, then loving goes by haps: Some Cupid kills with arrows, some with traps.' How does 'Cupid' work? How do we fall in love?"

A lanky boy in the back raised his hand. "I don't think we really fall in love. We have sexual attraction, and if we get along, we stay together. Every relationship is based on convenience."

"Yeah, male convenience." A mousy girl in sweats spoke as she slouched down in her chair and gave the boy an evil look.

"Women don't understand the concept of convenience," the boy retorted.

"Then why do you stay with them?" she snapped back.

"That's my point. I don't." A group of boys near him laughed and patted his back.

"So you've never been in love, Rick?" Jon asked the boy.

"No. Man, what's love anyway?" Rick stretched his gangly legs out in front of him and clasped his hands behind his head.

"Well, it's a lot more than a matter of convenience." Jon smiled. "Who in here has been in love?"

Most of the students raised their hands.

"Since so many of you have experienced this divine emotion, let me ask you this: do Benedick and Beatrice fall in love? For that matter, are Claudio and Hero in love?"

A pretty blond girl sitting in front of Rick raised her hand. "I think Claudio and Hero are in love, but I don't think Benedick and Beatrice are. They get together because everyone else wants them to. They're so weak that they can't make such a decision on their own."

The mousy girl shook her head in disgust. "If Claudio and Hero are so much in love, why does Claudio accuse Hero of infidelity? If he really loved her, he would know she wouldn't do anything like that. And the way he accuses her! In front of everyone, without even asking her in private first! Appalling!"

"I think Benedick and Beatrice are very much in love." Miss Wiggle spoke without raising her hand. Jon leaned back on his desk right in front of her. If she reached out her hand, she could rest it on his thigh. Her eyes locked onto his. "They've loved each other for a long time. But they're so afraid of getting hurt that they keep their feelings to themselves. Instead, they have this acerbic banter between them. When Benedick overhears that Beatrice loves him, he isn't afraid of getting hurt anymore, and he allows himself to recognize his feelings. The same thing happens with Beatrice. They're both really vulnerable. I think it's terribly romantic."

She continued to gaze into my husband's eyes. He didn't look away.

"Very good observation," Jon nodded and smiled. She smiled back.

Jon stood and walked to the chalkboard. She smiled softly and twisted her hair slowly around her pencil. She was a vixen. A demon sent to tempt my husband. I fought the urge to rush into the room and slap her perfect face.

"You've got midterms in two weeks, and this issue may be one of the topics addressed. So, in preparation, I want you to write an essay about love. Compare and contrast these two couples and their relationships. Discuss the question of love: how we fall in love, how we stay in love." He looked at his watch. "Oh, what the heck. I'm hungry, so I'll let you out a whole two minutes early."

Before the students rushed the door, I noticed Miss Wiggle wasn't in a hurry to leave. She stayed in her seat and scribbled something else in her book.

When the exiting traffic slowed to a drizzle, I entered the room. Miss Wiggle stood next to Jon as he erased his notes. She spoke to him melodically, trying to lure him to his death.

"I thought we could discuss the essay over lunch, since you're hungry." She smiled and shifted her weight.

"Actually, he's got plans." I practically sprinted to Jon's side.

"Oh, hi honey." He smiled and patted chalk dust from his hands. "What are you doing here?" If he felt awkward, he certainly covered it well. He looked completely comfortable.

"I thought I'd surprise you." I held the picnic basket up for him to see. As I stood next to Miss Wiggle, I wished I'd at least put some makeup on. And lost thirty pounds.

"Sorry, Ashley. Looks like I'm going out with my wife." I loved that he called me his wife, especially in front of her.

Miss Wiggle slumped her shoulders a bit and took a step toward her desk. I couldn't help but smile as I reveled in her loss. Victory was good.

"That's okay," she said. She looked at me and saw my smile. Her eyebrows furrowed toward each other and she grinned back at me. "Another time, maybe." She tossed her hair as she picked up her books.

"Thanks for class today, Dr. Tucker. You really gave me a lot to think about."

"Sure, Ashley. See you tonight." He gathered his papers and picked up the picnic basket for me.

"See you tonight." She smiled at me as she spoke to Jon over her shoulder. She wiggled out of the classroom. I felt like I'd been challenged. With the toss of her hair and the glint in her eye, she'd thrown a gauntlet at my feet and the competition had begun.

"You'll see her tonight?"

"Yeah, she plays Beatrice in the play."

"So you're with her three nights a week?"

"Yup." He held the door open for me and turned off the classroom light.

My mind raced. All the extra hours he spent at the university, the *self-appointed hours* he spent working on his book. He was with her the whole time.

"Oh look, it's Bob." Jon pointed at a handsome policeman parking his squad car in front of the building.

"He worked for campus security a while ago, and he helped me change a flat once. We figured out he's my third cousin or something like that."

"Really?" I asked. Bob came into the building and stood in the entryway while his eyes adjusted to the artificial lighting.

"Bob! What are you doing here?" Jon extended his hand toward the policeman.

"Just stopping by to see some of the guys. I'm UHP now!" He indicated his tan uniform. "My new ride is much more comfortable too." He nodded back at the Lexus.

"Good for you! The campus won't be as safe without you."

Bob chuckled warmly.

"Hey Bob, I'd like you to meet my wife."

Bob extended his hand, and I took it. His grip was warm and strong.

"It's great to meet you, Lia. Jon talks about you all the time."

"Good things, I hope," I said, giving Jon a teasing sideways glance.

"Of course." Jon and Bob spoke together.

"Well, I thought maybe we'd have lunch today if you were free, but you are obviously busy." Bob smiled and nodded at the picnic basket in the crook of Jon's arm.

"We'll have to get together some other day."

"Great. I'll see you later then. It was nice to meet you, Lia."

Bob climbed back in his Lexus and drove away.

"He seems like a nice guy," I said as we left Orson Spencer Hall.

"He's great. He just joined the Church a year or so ago. He and his wife were sealed during the summer. Look at the way he glows, the golden convert."

Miss Wiggle left the building with a couple of other girls. They passed in front of us and headed for the Student Union Building for lunch. She waved demurely at Jon.

"I'm glad you've got friends like him to keep you grounded while you're away from home," I said as Jon waved back. "It seems like there are too many distractions here."

Jon didn't hear me, or he ignored what I had to say. "So, where do you want to picnic? Do you mind walking somewhere?"

I cleared my throat, hoping it would clear my head too. "Um, no, I don't mind walking. But I only have an hour before I pick up Emily."

"Okay. Well, why don't you wait here, and I'll run this stuff up to my office. Then we can walk down to President's Circle."

Jon ran to his office building and I waited for him in silence. Miss Wiggle would have many opportunities to throw herself at Jon. And I knew she would take them.

Being the only adult in the house for so many hours in a row wore on me. I found myself longing for bedtime by six o'clock. I even tried it, but Katie cried with her lips pressed to the crack beneath the door, and Jacob jumped on his bed. Emily didn't mind because she was completely content sitting in her room with her crayons and a coloring book.

The minutes ticked by. To keep from getting angry and imagining Miss Wiggle flirting with Jon, I did my best to remember our good times. I remembered deep conversations about anything and every-thing. Conversations that made me laugh and cry, proving to me that I had married the most wonderful man in the world. He spoke to my soul. We didn't even have to use words to communicate and grow closer to each other. He spoke with his eyes when he looked at me, or with the warmth of his touch or the goodness that made him who he was. I closed my eyes once after staring at him for a long time. His image stayed on my eyelids, as if he was so filled with light and love that he had burned into me—a burn I prayed I would never heal from.

But as I closed my eyes that night, there was only darkness. Darkness and an empty pillow beside me. The kids eventually slept silently in their own rooms, and I put myself to bed even though it was only nine-thirty. I was tired, and without Jon there, I had no reason to stay up.

Derek stood on my porch with an envelope in one hand and a rose in the other. He ran his fingers through his blond hair and peeked through the window before he rang the bell. He looked handsome and mature in his sleek charcoal, double-breasted suit when I answered the door in my pajamas. My hair went in every direction possible, and a huge zit glowed red on my forehead, but I invited him in anyway. What could I do? Turn him away?

The house smelled like dirty diapers. Jon sat at the kitchen table, papers spread out in front of him, and ignored me completely. I asked him to take Katie and change her since I had a guest. But Jon told me he was too busy.

I cleared some laundry off of the couch and asked Derek if he would like to sit down. I sat next to him. He smelled fantastic— musky and clean.

He brushed the rose against my cheek as he handed it to me. Then he opened the envelope. He dumped the contents on my lap and smiled warmly as he scooted closer to me and put his arm around my shoulders. In my lap sat a new box of crayons with my name printed neatly on it.

"Leave with me," he said. "It will take a lot of courage, but it will be worth it." Then he leaned over and kissed me on the lips. He lingered there, and I felt my blood surge.

The bed squeaked as Jon sat down. I opened my eyes slowly and watched him take off his shirt and climb under the covers. Derek's kiss lingered on my lips, and guilt swept through me as I looked at my husband's back. How could I tell Jon about this? Would he forgive me?

Slowly, I began to realize it was all a dream. I *had* done the right thing. I'd given Derek the brush-off, and he wouldn't end up at my door. But I couldn't wash the guilt from my mind.

I sat up and looked at the clock. It was eleven. Jon rolled on his back and looked up at me.

"Did I wake you?"

"Yes. But that's okay. I was having a terrible dream." I brushed thoughts of Derek aside. Guilt lingered in my mind like the taste of onions after dinner. I hoped I couldn't be held accountable for my dreams.

"I'm sorry. Are you okay?"

"I'm fine." I lay back down on my side, still facing him.

"How was Emily's first day of school?" He yawned and rubbed his eyes.

"She was so cute. You should have seen her. Some of the kids were all scared and clinging to their moms. But not Emily. She charged right in there, raring to go. You give her a new box of crayons and she can handle anything."

"Yup. She's a determined soul, just like her mom."

"Am I like that?"

Jon chuckled. "Most definitely."

"How? I mean, give me an example."

"Well, everything you want you get. Look at how you romanced me. I never would have approached you. I was a scared English geek, a wiz with literature, but completely illiterate with real women. It didn't take you any time at all to completely change your life so you could pursue me. I think that makes you a determined soul. And it makes me a lucky man."

"Okay, I see that. But give me a current example. I know what I used to be like, but now . . ." I pictured Miss Wiggle flirting with Jon at school. Not only did I do nothing about it, I stood there like an intimidated child. "Any abilities I used to have are gone. That girl in your class, she's after you. Just like I used to be."

"What? Which girl are you talking about?"

"The beautiful redhead. She was flirting with you like crazy."

"You're imagining things. If she was flirting with me, I didn't notice."

"How could you not notice a girl like that? I mean, come on. Admit it, you think she's pretty."

"Pretty? Well yeah, I guess so, now that you mention it."

Right, pin it on me. The conversation wasn't going the way I'd hoped it would.

"But she's more smart than she is pretty," he continued. "Every semester there's a student who really gets it. Well, this semester it's Ashley. They held auditions tonight, but Ashley's had the part of Beatrice ever since Dr. Stratford decided to do *Much Ado,* so it was more of a formality for her, and she nailed her character. She's the ultimate Beatrice. I'll never read *Much Ado* again without seeing her face."

Great, something to immortalize her. I sat there quietly, thinking about Jon thinking about Ashley.

After a moment, he broke the silence. "What were we talking about?"

"*Me* being a determined soul," I said with a grimace.

"Oh yeah, and you wanted a current example."

"Please."

He thought for a minute then started rubbing his eyes.

"I'm too tired to think right now. Maybe you should ask me tomorrow."

I slapped the mattress with my hand. "See, you can't think of anything. But I can think of a few examples of me being inept."

"Inept? Come on."

"No, listen. There's the Monday fiasco where I waited around for you all afternoon just so my enchiladas could burn."

"That was my fault. You can't blame yourself for things that aren't your fault."

"And today, the picnic was a joke. We hardly had time to eat together, let alone talk."

"We're talking now." He yawned.

I rolled onto my back. "Yeah, but you don't want to."

Jon turned to his side and put his arm around me.

"I'm sorry things haven't worked out the way you planned them lately, and I take full responsibility for both cases. I've just been busy with this book and my classes. I don't want to miss Christmas break because I'm putting in the finishing touches like I did with the last book."

He'd missed Christmas break for the past several years because he was off working on one thing or another. And even though he said he didn't want to miss it this year, I doubted I would see him much during the month of December. It had been years since we spent two days in a row together without some kind of interruption.

I lay on my back and stared at the dark ceiling. "Do you ever want things to be the way they were? Especially before the kids?"

"You mean between us?"

"Yeah."

"No. I think things are better now. Our kids are fantastic. We've got our own home. I've got the career I've always dreamed of. We're stable enough that you can stay home with the kids. Look at what we've built together, sweetie. Life is great now. Why look back?"

It surprised me that he felt so good about things while I felt so unsettled.

"I love you, Lia. Quit worrying so much and get some sleep." He yawned and rolled his back to me.

Soon he drifted in deep sleep, with an expression so content you'd think all was well with the world. I tossed half the night, dreaming of new crayons.

The Call

Mom was right about one thing: life is full of choices. Little, meaningless ones like, "Do I have cereal for breakfast, or do I have time to fry an egg?" And bigger ones that could change your life like, "The caller ID says it's the executive secretary on the phone. Should I answer it?"

I worked with the young women for five years and loved it. When I got pregnant with Katie, they asked me if I wanted to be released. I said, "Are you kidding? I'll get a lot more help from the young women than from the Relief Society. They love changing diapers and rocking a baby. The old ladies have had their fill."

When they finally did release me, I begged them not to. The bishop said I was needed elsewhere for a while, and I should pray about my release until the Spirit testified it was the Lord's will. How do you contradict that?

I prayed like the bishop asked me to, and the Spirit told me he was ordained of God. To me, that meant if the bishop extended a new calling I couldn't say no to him. Dang it.

Maybe it was for Jon.

"Hello?"

"Hello, Sister Tucker?"

"Yes."

"This is Brother Allen."

"Yes."

"I was wondering if you could meet with the bishop sometime this evening?"

Ouch. It was for me.

"Of course. What time?"

"How about eight-thirty? Is that too late?"

Hopefully, Jon would be home by then.

"No, that's not too late."

"That's fine. He'll see you then."

"All right."

I hung up the phone, wondering what the Lord had in mind for me and why. I just hoped he didn't want me to teach the Marriage and Family course. I felt a little unqualified for that calling.

As I looked around at my cluttered house, I felt unqualified for a lot of callings. Even "Homemaker." But it was useless to follow the kids around the house, cleaning up after them.

Besides, they needed something to keep them busy while I made dinner. And since Jon wasn't home as early as he used to be, I had to cook while kids tugged at my pant leg, whining about one thing or another.

Poor Emily took the brunt of it all, which only deepened my guilt. She sat with Katie in the middle of the entryway playing with dolls when Jon pulled up.

"Honey, move away from the door so that Daddy can come in. He'll probably have his arms full."

"Okay, Mommy."

I tasted the bubbling spaghetti sauce and decided to add more salt.

I heard the door open, then a squeak from an abandoned toy, a scream from little Katie, and a huge thud that shook the house.

"Unbelievable!"

I left the kitchen to find Jon sprawled on his stomach and papers floating to the floor around him. Katie sat in front of the door, holding her leg tightly and wailing, her little face turning a deep magenta. I stepped over Jon and scooped Katie into my arms.

"Lia, can't you keep these kids away from the door when you know I'm on my way home? It'll take hours for me to organize these notes again."

Jon's face changed color too.

Katie covered a raw, rosy patch of skin on her leg with her sticky hands. Tears clumped her eyelashes together and wet her cheeks and my T-shirt.

"Emily," I said in as calm a tone as I could muster, "be a good girl and help your Daddy pick up the papers."

"No!" Jon shouted as he pulled himself up to his knees. "Let me do it. Some of them might still be in order. Don't touch a thing!"

Emily backed away from her dad, bowed her head, and sat down on the floor as she started to cry too.

"Lia, can you take care of her, please?"

He said "please," but his jaw clenched and rippled under his stubble.

"Emily, come here, honey. Don't step on Daddy's papers."

Emily tiptoed through the scattered notes and threw her arms around my waist. Katie wailed and hit her sore spot as if hitting it would make the pain go away. I pulled both the girls up to the bathroom and away from Jon, who knelt, muttering, in the middle of his scattered notes.

Emily sat on the closed toilet lid and wiped her nose while I pulled a clean washcloth from the linen closet.

"I'm sorry Daddy yelled at you, honey," I said.

"I was trying to help. I tried to be good," Emily sniffed and wiped her nose on her sleeve.

"I know, baby."

I pressed the wet washcloth to Katie's skin. She screamed and tried to push my hands away.

"Get that first-aid kit for Mommy, would you?"

Emily stood on her toes and reached for our first-aid kit, then set it on the counter next to Katie.

"We have to be patient with Daddy and forgive him for losing his temper. He's a little stressed right now. Maybe he had a bad day."

Emily's little chin shook and tears flooded her eyes again. "I had a bad day too."

I spread antibacterial gel on Katie's leg, bandaged it, and knelt down to hug Emily.

"I know. I'm sorry."

Jon stomped upstairs and slammed the bedroom door.

"Come on, let's go set the table."

We went in the kitchen, and the spaghetti sauce had boiled over, making a three-inch ring around the pot.

"Jacob, come and help your sister set the table."

I took the saucepan off of the unit, began wiping up the mess, and did some muttering of my own.

With the table set and the kids waiting in their seats, I went upstairs to get Jon. I had a few choice words in store for him.

I opened the door quickly, ready to yell. But I choked on my harsh words when I found him kneeling there at the side of the bed, his hands clasped together and his head resting on them.

He looked up at me and then bowed his head again and whispered the Lord's name in closing his prayer.

I couldn't yell at him after that.

"I'm sorry, Lia, it's just been a hard day. I know I shouldn't take it out on the kids."

"Well, why don't you go tell them that?"

"Is Katie really hurt?"

"She's got a two-inch sore on her shin."

Jon winced.

"I was hard on you too," Jon said.

"Yes, you were." I couldn't yell at him, but I needed him to know how I felt. "You're not the only one who has hard days, you know. You think I like being at home all day, trying to control three little kids and keep my sanity? I look forward to you coming home so I can have some adult conversation, and the first thing you do is yell at us."

"I'm sorry." Jon stood and pulled me to him. I returned his hug halfheartedly.

"Well, I expect you to watch the kids tonight," I said. "I've got an appointment with the bishop."

"Oh? Okay. I guess I'll just stay up late to reorganize." He sighed.

Mention of the bishop calmed me down and filled me with guilt for bawling Jon out even though I knew he was sorry. At least I didn't yell at him like I'd set out to.

"I wonder what he'll ask me to do," I said in a much calmer voice.

"Whatever it is, I'm sure you'll be great."

"Do you think there's some obscure calling in the Church they don't talk about much, where you go to an all-day spa and get pampered once a month? I'd be really good at that calling."

"I think I'd be good at that too."

"Yeah," I sighed.

Jon followed me to the dinner table and picked Emily up to give her a hug and a kiss. Fresh tears slipped down her cheeks, but this time her dad wiped them and tickled them away. He kissed Katie's bandaged leg and Jacob's head. Then we sat and had a quiet family dinner.

Jon encouraged me to go to the church early so I could have some quiet time before my appointment. I got the kids night-dressed before I left, hoping Jon would get the hint and have them in bed by the time I got home.

All the lights were on at the church, and I heard some people playing basketball in the cultural hall.

As I sat on the couch in the foyer I wiped my burgundy leather scriptures with a tissue until the gold engraving glowed "Liahona Powell."

There was a time when the name bothered me. I wasn't named after a person, I was named after a thing. It had its advantages, I learned, because my parents couldn't yell at me using my full name. My father picked it and never let me forget why. The Liahona was a gift from God to His people in the wilderness. For years, Mom and Dad tried to have a child, but nothing they did worked. Finally they got me, and even then Mom spent several months in bed making sure she could carry me to term.

But that wasn't the only reason they named me Liahona. Dad had a tradition of giving me a father's blessing at the beginning of each new school year. I loved it and looked forward to that blessing almost as much as I looked forward to seeing my friends at school. Every year, in every blessing, Dad reminded me that the Liahona couldn't function without faith. He never elaborated on that statement, but he never needed to.

As I ran my fingers over the engraved name, I remembered when Dad gave me the scriptures after seminary graduation.

"Wear them out," he said. "In these books you'll find the answer to every question, because in these books you'll find the Lord."

And I did wear them out, until the kids came. I used a different color highlighter for each time through the books until some of the Book of Mormon pages turned to rainbows. Especially Mosiah 18, Alma 42, and of course 3 Nephi 12. Those were my favorite chapters in the whole book, and I read them over and over, learning something new each time. I turned to Alma 42 and read over the highlighted verses about the Atonement. They embraced my mind like old friends.

A couple of girls burst from the cultural hall, laughing and breathing hard. One of them was Missy Wilson, her hair pulled back in a swaying ponytail, wisps of it curling and wet at the nape of her neck. The girls didn't notice me sitting on the couch, and they made their way to the drinking fountain.

"My heart's pounding. I need to sit down," Missy said as she bowed her head to drink.

"Are you still feeling sick? You should go to the doctor, Missy. You've been sick a long time."

The other girl was named Tonya. She'd moved in just before I was released, and Missy befriended her immediately. Since then, they'd been inseparable.

Missy drank steadily from the fountain then let the cool water course over her fingers so she could sprinkle her face. "No, I'm fine. I just need to sit down for a while."

"Yeah, right. I've never seen anyone so stubborn. You'd say everything was just fine if the world was burning down around you."

I looked up from my scriptures to see Tonya touch Missy on the arm and look her in the eye.

"I know something's wrong, Missy. You may as well tell me what it is. Is something going on with you and Sean?"

Missy stared back at Tonya with a lost, confused look in her green eyes.

She jumped when the bishop opened the door behind her, and a young man who was preparing to go on his mission stepped out. Missy moved away from the door, avoiding the bishop's glance.

"Let's go play. They'll be wondering about us," Missy said.

"Don't you need to sit down?"

"No, I'll be fine." Missy wiped the sweat from her forehead on the back of her arm and pulled Tonya back to the cultural hall.

Something was definitely wrong with Missy. First, the tearful talk on temple marriage, now a worried friend. And she avoided the bishop. But Missy was a good girl, with a strong testimony. She couldn't be in any big trouble.

When I sat across from Bishop Ames in the silence of his office, I wondered if I should bring up my concern for Missy.

Bishop Ames looked down at his watch and sighed. His eyes looked bloodshot and weary behind his bifocals, and his hair seemed whiter than usual.

"Are you all right, Bishop?"

"Yes, I'm fine." He took off his glasses and rubbed the red indentations at the bridge of his nose. "How are you?"

"I'm fine," I said as I leaned back in my chair. Maybe I'd talk to Missy before bringing up anything with him. He looked too tired to deal with mere possibilities.

"How is your husband, your children?"

"Well, Jon's really busy. I don't see him much. But nothing's new about that." I hugged my scriptures to my chest. "And the kids are great. They keep me busy and tired, but I love them and they're growing up too fast."

"Do you get time for yourself? That's important, you know."

I tried hard to think of the last time I did something just for me, without dragging at least one kid behind me, and shrugged my shoulders.

"Does your husband support you in your visiting teaching? Did he support you when you worked in the Young Women?"

The mention of Young Women lifted my spirits. Maybe he'd put me in with the Laurels, and I could keep an eye on Missy.

"Oh, yes. He's very supportive of my callings. In fact, he pushes me to 'magnify' them every chance he gets."

"Well, then I think it would be appropriate to extend the calling of compassionate service leader to you. Would you be willing to accept the call?"

I deflated like a week-old balloon.

"Well, what would it entail?"

"You would organize service for families in the ward who need special attention. Births, funerals, and the like. It's a calling that puts you on the front lines. You get to keep your baptismal covenants by comforting those who mourn. I've prayed about where to put you right now, and I believe this is the place."

"It sounds like a challenge."

"We all need a challenge occasionally. They wake us up."

"I didn't know I was asleep."

The bishop smiled with the kind, patient look a father gives his child. "I know it's challenging enough to raise three children. But there is something wonderful about being able to serve your fellowman. Sometimes lifting someone else's burden helps you carry your own."

I nodded. Part of me wanted to say no, but I didn't have the heart to. "Of course I accept, Bishop."

"Wonderful. We'll set you apart on Sunday."

The following Sunday, Jon wrestled with the kids in the foyer after church while the bishopric laid their hands on my head. The bishop said the blessing. He told me to use faith and prayer as I served the sisters in the ward.

After the blessing was done and I stood to shake the bishop's hand, he smiled at me like he knew more about my calling than he was letting on.

"You're named after the Liahona," he said. "Think about that name. The Liahona stopped working when Lehi and his family stopped obeying the Lord, and they were left not knowing where to go. If you want to function, if you want to succeed, you have to have faith. You have to obey." He smiled and nodded. "Your parents were very wise to give you your name."

I walked away from the bishop's office feeling overwhelmed. First, he talked about how I needed a challenge. I figured finishing the day with a clean house and clean, well-fed children was challenge enough. Then, he told me I would cease to function without faith. Yeah, no pressure. It wasn't that I didn't know how to live by faith or use prayer to help me make my decisions. But that was usually to bless my own life. It was easy to seek help for myself.

My mom always said that a new calling was like a new adventure, designed to teach you something you never knew before. I suddenly felt afraid of what the Lord had called me to learn.

Vulnerable

———— ❧ ————

The last day in September started with a knock on my door. Anna, the Relief Society president, stood there with a small binder stuffed to overflowing with papers.

"Hi, Lia. Here's your handbook." She pushed the binder into my arms. "Are you ready to get started?"

"I guess so."

"Great. We're so happy to have you on the Relief Society board. It's been such a busy year, and we need your help."

She came in and sat on the couch as she pulled another overstuffed binder from her bag.

"Can I get you something to drink?" I offered.

"Sure. Water would be great," she replied.

I went to the kitchen and got her a glass of ice water. I took a deep breath before taking the glass to Anna.

"Oh, thank you so much," she said as she took the glass. "I know it's only ten, but I've been running for a couple of hours already and I'm tired."

She took a long draw on the glass until the ice cubes slipped and hit her lip. She set the glass down at her feet and wiped the corners of her mouth with her finger.

"Okay, let's get down to business." She flipped open her binder, and I sat next to her on the couch to do likewise.

The paper on the top listed twenty women.

"This is the list of sisters in the ward who currently need special help. Sister Perkins just had her knees replaced. She's having a terrible time with pain right now, and she's asked if we could bring meals for a couple of days. You've got a list of the visiting teachers in the binder there. Just give her teachers a call and have them organize dinners for the next four days. That should be good enough for now. Do you have a pen?"

She looked up at me as I sat there, fighting to get my bearings with the information she threw at me.

"I'm sorry. Am I going too fast? I forget you've only been in Relief Society for a couple of months."

"Yeah. I'm looking at this list, and I don't know most of these sisters."

"Well, working with the young women for so long, you wouldn't know them. Some have been on this list for months. Bless their hearts, they can't seem to get well. Sister Shultz, for example—I don't think she'll be with us much longer." Anna sighed.

"Um, let me get a pen." I went back into the kitchen and fished in the utility drawer. I took another deep breath before I went back in the front room.

"Oh good, you found one. Are you ready?"

"As ready as I'm going to get," I croaked.

"Okay. I just got a call from Alexis Smith. Her husband got in a car accident last night, and his leg was crushed. He's going to have at least three surgeries and physical therapy and everything. They're likely to have financial difficulties too. The problem is that her visiting teachers aren't very consistent. You may have to make arrangements to visit her yourself. I planned to go today and assess the situation, but Sister Anderson's husband had a stroke two months ago, and she needs a ride to the nursing home to visit him. I planned with her last week that we'd go today."

I knew Alexis Smith. She was the serious woman who taught the Relief Society lesson the day I met Jane. It figured that the only woman on the list whom I knew was one I didn't like very much.

"Anyway, I'm sorry to dump this on you, but I'm running late. I'll call you tonight and you can fill me in on Alexis. I've got to go to work right after my visit, but I should be home by seven or so. I'll fill you in on the other sisters then, okay?"

"Sure." I tried to sound confident.

Then, as quickly as she blew in with her papers and her assignments, she blew out the door and tore down the street in her Jetta.

That meant I needed to call Alexis before seven. I sighed heavily. I may as well get it over with.

"Hello, Alexis?" I asked.

"Yes." She spoke dully.

"This is Lia Tucker. I'm the new compassionate service leader. Anna tells me your husband was in a car accident."

"Yes, he was." Her voice was hollow and monotone like she was distracted, or like talking to me was a hassle. I felt like a telemarketer.

"I'm so sorry. I'm calling to see if there's anything I can do for you."

"No. We'll be just fine," she said in a clipped voice.

"Oh, okay. You're sure you don't need anything?" I tried again.

Alexis sighed and talked to one of her daughters for a minute. "No, sweetheart. Mommy's on the phone right now. Go ask Grandma."

She spoke into the phone again, even more irritated than before. "I'm okay. My mother is here right now, helping with the kids. If I need anything, I'll contact Anna."

"All right. Um, Anna's a busy lady, so you can always call me if you need anything. I'm here all the time." I couldn't explain it, but I knew Alexis needed more help than she was letting on.

"I seriously doubt we'll need any help." She almost growled as she spoke.

"Okay," I conceded.

She hung up the phone without so much as a *good-bye.*

I remembered the prayer the bishop had said as he set me apart, and I knew I should have prayed before I called Alexis.

But obviously she didn't want my help. I would tell Anna that night when she called that Alexis wouldn't even talk to me. Anna would take care of it.

Since the worst part of my day was over, I looked out the window at the trees lining the street. I loved early autumn. I loved the way the leaves began to blush and droop, and that the days were warm but the evenings settled in a slight chill. After Emily got home from school, I put sweatshirts on all the kids and we went for a walk. Soon the sidewalks would be buried in snow, so I took advantage of them while I could.

As I rounded the corner, I noticed Missy on the Wilsons' front lawn. She sat in front of the small garden that traced the outside of the house, pulling out dead leaves and flowers.

"Hey, you. How's it going?" I greeted her cheerfully.

She looked up at me, tears leaving dirty streaks down her face.

"Is everything okay?"

She laughed and looked back at her work. "No. At this point, I'd say nothing is okay."

"Here, you guys run around for a minute. Emily, keep an eye on Katie."

Emily grabbed the handles of the stroller and started pushing Katie back and forth on the sidewalk in front of the Wilsons' as I sat next to Missy. Jacob ran ahead of the stroller.

"Talk to me."

She wiped her face with the back of her dirty hand and brushed a strand of blond hair away from her green eyes. No matter how much our bodies change as we age, our eyes seem to stay the same, I thought.

"You know that guy I was dating?" she sniffed. "I don't think you ever met him, but I thought he was really cool. I thought I loved him, and I was pretty sure we'd get married after school."

Tears collected in her eyes and dripped quickly down her face again.

After a moment, she tried to speak through her emotion. "He broke up with me today."

"Oh, Missy. I'm so sorry." I put my arms around her and let her cry on my shoulder until she broke our embrace.

"I told him all my secrets, really opened myself up to him, you know, and I guess he didn't like what I had to say." She shrugged her shoulders and sighed.

"What a jerk," I said.

"Yeah." Missy sniffed, raised her eyebrows, and nodded her head.

She returned to her work, clearing dead flowers out of the garden. Her fingernails filled with dirt as the pile next to her grew. I helped her pull at the dried stems and crumpled leaves.

"I hate the fall. This garden used to be so pretty. Now everything's dead and brown and headed for the garbage can." She threw a handful of leaves on the growing pile.

"You hate fall? It's my favorite season," I said. "Plants have to die so they can bloom again in the spring. Besides, not everything dies. Trees just sleep."

"Well, they look dead." She inspected the pile before her. Her eyelashes were clumped and wet.

"Maybe, but they're really not." I spoke gently, trying to comfort her.

"I really thought I loved him," she burst out. "And I thought he loved me. I gave him everything, Lia." She looked me in the eye. "I gave him everything I had."

My heart sank with what her words might imply. I hoped I was wrong.

She wiped her face again and took a deep breath. Spots of mud dotted her teary face. "I gave him everything." She raised her eyebrows, and I knew by her expression I was right.

Missy must have seen the disappointment in my face, because she looked away and dug in the dirt again, tears dripping from her chin.

"That's why you had such a hard time giving your talk," I whispered.

She nodded. "I don't deserve a temple marriage. I'll probably never have one."

"Now, don't say that. The Lord forgives us of our sins, Missy. If He didn't, why would He tell us to repent all the time? Have you talked to the bishop?"

"No. I haven't told anyone except you."

"What about this boy? What is he doing about it?" I asked, my voice tense with irritation.

She scoffed. "Nothing. I told him I wanted to stop. He thinks it's too late for that. He really doesn't have much of a testimony anyway, and I don't think he wants to go to church anymore whether he dates me or not. He says if I don't want to be with him, then he'll find another girl who does. I don't think that will be hard. He's probably got a date tonight."

I shook my head with frustration. Missy was growing up too fast, dealing with things no young woman should have to deal with. I felt a little nauseated.

"It's my own fault. I shouldn't have let my guard down. I shouldn't have hooked up with him. I should have listened to all the advice everyone has been giving me all my life." Missy looked away as despair settled in.

"Advice is hard to listen to sometimes," I admitted.

"I'll never forget the lesson you gave in Beehives about getting married in the temple. You said that you broke up with a guy because he didn't want to go to the temple, and even though you loved him, you loved the gospel more. I really felt the Spirit that day, but I *still* didn't do what I was supposed to." She looked toward the sky as she tried to understand herself.

Tears blurred her eyes again, and she shook her head.

"What's wrong with me?" she cried. "Why can't I just do what I know is right? Why can't I just be perfect and never even be tempted by things that are wrong?"

I put my arm around Missy and let her lean against me.

"I've wondered that about myself sometimes. I'm sorry, Missy. I wish things had been easier for you." I hugged her and kissed her forehead.

"Yeah. Me too."

We sat there and watched Emily and Jacob run back and forth with Katie in the stroller. I wished they could stay little forever.

"Have you told your mom?" I asked gingerly.

"No. She would die if she knew. And my dad would ground me for life. But even worse, they'd be disappointed in me. Mom's always talking about how great I am. I hate to prove her wrong. And then there's my perfect brother on his mission. And my perfect sister at BYU. I can't compare to them," Missy reasoned.

"You're still a great girl, Missy. You just made a really bad choice. I think you should go to the bishop and put it behind you. Start over. It's probably good he broke up with you. It will be easier to start over without him." I squeezed her shoulders as I tried to encourage her.

"What if I get disfellowshipped, or excommunicated? I don't want anyone to know. I'd rather die. I'm embarrassed that I told you, but the guilt is killing me and I knew you'd help me." She looked up at me as she spoke, her eyes pleading for direction.

"If you really want my help, then listen to this advice. If the bishop decides to do something like that, it will be because the Lord tells him to. And the Lord loves you. He wants you to have that temple marriage too, so He'll tell the bishop what's best for you."

"You think so?" She looked scared but hopeful.

"I do," I said, knowing I was right. The Lord did love her. If Missy was willing to do her part, everything would be fine.

Missy's tears stopped, but she looked terrified.

"Gather your courage and go to the bishop." I squeezed her shoulders and smiled.

She hesitated for a moment. Then she smiled weakly and nodded.

"Call me if you need anything, okay, Missy?"

"Well, I'll have my weekends open if you ever want me to watch your kids," she chuckled sarcastically.

"Hey, I might take you up on that, if you're serious. Jon and I need a date really bad."

She wiped the tears from her face and looked at me with puffy but dry eyes. "How about tomorrow, or Saturday?"

"Tomorrow would be good, I think. Jon has the priesthood session on Saturday, so yeah, tomorrow's good."

Missy gave me the first genuine smile since we started talking. It was tired, but it was still a smile. "Okay."

"You'll be okay, won't you?" I smoothed a lock of hair behind her ear.

She took a deep breath. "Yeah. Thanks so much for listening."

"That's what ears are for. And I have two of them."

She smiled again, looking at least a little relieved.

As I walked home with the kids, I ached for Missy. I could only imagine what she was feeling, a kind of pain I had never experienced. No wonder she was afraid to tell anyone. I hoped that her choice to tell me wouldn't make her think that I looked at her any different because of what I knew. If anything, I felt more love and concern for her than I had when I taught her.

"Mommy, who's that man looking in our house?" Emily pointed at a man pressing his face against the outside of our window with a clear view of the front room.

"I don't know, baby. But let's go find out."

My stomach tightened as I reached for my keys. Hopefully I could stab him with the Civic key if I needed to.

"Excuse me, but what are you doing?" I asked the man deliberately.

He wore a baseball cap low over his eyes, and he had a red goatee and a red ponytail sticking out the back of the hat. I glanced over his pale, freckled face for scars or anything I could tell the police about.

"Hello, Mrs. Jones. I'm here about the house." He extended his hand.

"I'm not Mrs. Jones." I left his hand hanging in the air, untouched.

"Oh, I'm sorry. So this isn't your house then?" he asked.

"This is my house. Who are you?" I questioned again.

"This house isn't for sale?" His eyebrows furrowed with confusion.

"No. Please tell me who you are," I demanded.

"I'm sorry. I must have made a mistake. Maybe I switched the numbers around. I'll check with the realtor. I hope I didn't bother you."

"You are bothering me," I said with irritation. "Please tell me who you are and why you were looking in my front window."

"I'm looking to buy a home in this neighborhood, and I thought I saw this house on the Internet. I guess I made a mistake," he explained.

"Well, you definitely made a mistake," I said emphatically.

"I see that. I'm sorry, ma'am." His apology wasn't very convincing, and he had a strange smirk on his face like he was trying not to laugh.

He nodded his head and crossed the street to climb in a green Buick that looked strangely familiar. Another man in a baseball cap ducked when I looked in his direction. I knew the man with the goatee was lying to me, and his partner didn't want me to see him.

He climbed in his car and drove away, his tires burning black skid marks on the pavement. There was no license plate hanging on the back of the car.

I couldn't think of any Joneses in the area or any houses for sale in at least a two-block radius.

I hurried the kids into the house and called Jon's office. It shouldn't have surprised me that he wasn't there, but I felt a heavy disappointment when he didn't answer.

Instead of going to bed early, I waited up for Jon that night. I kept my keys in my pocket, and my phone at my side, locked all the doors and windows and shut all the blinds. The man couldn't have been telling the truth, and I wondered all evening what he was doing at my home, and who was waiting in his car. We didn't have anything terribly valuable in the house besides the people who lived there. I couldn't chase thoughts from my mind about evil men staking out the house, planning their deeds with sketches of my house spread out before them. Strangers knew the details of the inside of my home, and it left me feeling far too vulnerable for comfort.

Jon pulled up around eleven, and I met him at the door.

"Hi, hon. Is everything okay?" he asked.

"No! There are a couple of guys stalking us," I exclaimed.

"Stalking us? What do you mean?" he queried.

I told him about the man with the goatee and the partner ducking in the green Buick.

"And," I said, "I think I've seen his car before. This whole thing is freaking me out."

"Do you think he knows someone who lives in the neighborhood?" he asked.

"I haven't seen his car that often. I've just seen it before." I hugged myself as I caught a chill.

"It's okay, sweetheart. We'll keep our eyes open, but don't worry yourself sick about it." Jon held me in his arms and gently rubbed my back.

I knew worrying wouldn't do any good, and I probably was overreacting. But I ran up the stairs ahead of Jon to get ready for bed. I didn't feel so vulnerable when he turned out the lights after I was tucked in.

A Night Out

The next morning dawned cloudy, and a steady rain pattered on the roof. The temperature was unseasonably cold, so I pulled on a pair of sweats and went downstairs to make breakfast. Jon didn't teach any early classes on Fridays, so he took his time and perused the paper while he ate.

"I talked to Missy yesterday on our walk," I said as I cleaned Katie up after her breakfast. She'd spread wet, soggy cereal all over the tray on her high chair, and then stuck her arms in it. "She said she'd watch the kids for us tonight. But I'm not sure I want to leave the house with those guys running around."

"I doubt he's a stalker. It was probably an honest mistake." Jon slurped another spoonful of cereal and scanned the movies section of the paper.

"Well, it didn't feel like an honest mistake. It felt like he was watching me and the kids, like he had some ulterior motive. He was creepy. And what about the other guy who ducked when I looked at him?"

"If they were watching you and the kids, then why was the goatee guy looking in our empty house? It doesn't make sense," he reasoned.

"Well, then he's watching our house."

"Well he'll be sorely disappointed when he breaks in and finds nothing of value to steal," Jon said with a smirk.

"Yeah, unless we're home at the time," I reminded him.

He brought his empty bowl to the sink and kissed my forehead like I was a scared little child.

"We should go out tonight and let Missy watch the kids," Jon said. "She's a responsible girl, and she'll take good care of them. Everything will be fine."

"I don't know. We can go out after we know who he was and why he was here."

"Tell you what. Do you remember Bob, the guy who works for the highway patrol?" Jon asked. "I'll ask him what he thinks. Maybe he can drive by the house a couple of times to check on things."

"Well . . ." I gave him my best look of concern.

"We don't get to go out very often, you know. When was the last time we were alone for more than two hours?"

"Probably when we saw *Hamlet*."

"See, and that was a good year ago," he reminded me.

"More than a year. Missy watched our kids then, too."

"It's not good for a married couple to spend most of their time apart. I've missed you. I've gotten a lot of work done, but that doesn't make up for the lost time with you."

He put his arms around my waist and kissed me softly.

"Come on, Lia. Please go out with me," Jon begged. His lip stuck out as he blinked and sniffed.

I rolled my eyes.

"Okay. We can go out if Bob will drive by and check on the house," I conceded.

"Deal. I'll talk to him today." Jon grinned like he was looking forward to a night alone with me. It eased my apprehension a little.

I made arrangements for Missy to come watch our kids at six-thirty, and amazingly enough, Jon got home in time. Bob met us at the door before we left, and we introduced him to Missy.

"Do you guys have a cell phone?" Bob asked.

"No. Once I get one, I'll never be able to get rid of it," Jon said. "I don't think we really need one anyway."

"Well, it would sure come in handy tonight. Okay, here's what we'll do. I'll drive by the house in an hour or so, and then again around ten-thirty, when I start my shift. Just call my cell phone and check in with me. Good?"

"Good. We'll be going to that little Italian restaurant down the street, just in case. But you probably couldn't call us during a movie."

Bob wrote his cell number on the back of a business card and handed it to me. "Just use that if you get worried."

When we were satisfied that everyone knew what was going on and whom to call if they needed help, Bob hopped in his car and took off, and we left for our date.

"Okay, Jon, here's the rules for the night."

"There's going to be rules?" He groaned in mock disappointment.

"No Shakespeare talk, okay? Unless you're quoting simple love poems to me—about me. Got it?"

"Okay, no Shakespeare. But if we're going to enforce that rule, here's rule number two. No kid talk. Don't tell me about how much the kids fought today or about how much PBS you watched. Deal?"

"Deal."

We rode the rest of the way to the restaurant in silence. Everything I could think of to say had something to do with the kids.

After we sat in the restaurant and ordered our big plates of pasta, Jon took my hand in his and looked me in the eye.

> *"Let me not to the marriage of true minds*
> *Admit impediments. Love is not love*
> *Which alters when it alteration finds,*
> *Or bends with the remover to remove:*
> *O, no! it is an ever-fixed mark,*
> *That looks on tempests, and is never shaken;*
> *It is the star to every wandering bark,*
> *Whose worth's unknown, although his height be taken.*
> *Love's not Time's fool, though rosy lips and cheeks*
> *Within his bending sickle's compass come;*
> *Love alters not with his brief hours and weeks,*
> *But bears it out even to the edge of doom.*
> *If this be error and upon me proved*
> *I never writ, nor no man ever loved."*

He smiled and kissed my hand.

"Okay," I giggled and shook my head.

"You said I could quote a sonnet," he teased.

"But now you have to explain it."

"It's about love and how constant it is. It's about marriage. It's about traveling through life together, knowing that we can count on each other no matter what."

He kissed my hand again, then let go and sipped from his water glass.

"It's about you," he smiled and winked.

The waiter brought our steaming food and placed it in front of us. I nodded my thank-you and spun my fork in the pasta.

"I've been thinking a lot about love lately." Jon winked at me as he spoke. "See, I gave an assignment to my Shakespeare class. I wanted them to write about love and what it is, how you fall in love, how you stay in love. They really wrote some interesting essays."

"Especially Ashley?" I said. But Jon didn't pick up on my sarcasm.

"Yeah. Especially Ashley. That girl's got a good head on her shoulders," he said with admiration.

My heart sank. I didn't want to talk about Ashley. Jon was breaking the rules. But . . . at least he was talking.

"What did she write?" I asked, just to carry on the conversation and avoid what I really wanted to say.

"She wrote about how much people need each other. We need people to help us figure ourselves out. And love is something we feel and show long before we recognize it. Sometimes others have to point out the obvious because we're so involved in our own problems and concerns that we can't see what's really going on. It was an interesting essay. Of course, she backed up every theory with quotes from *Much Ado*. She was very thorough."

"I'm sure she was," I murmured.

He tilted his head and raised one eyebrow as he looked at me. "You don't like Ashley very much, do you?"

I set my fork down. And though I didn't want to have that discussion in public, I felt a wave of relief fill me to my toes. No more skirting the issue.

Then our waiter came to the table. "Excuse me, are you Jon Tucker?"

"Yes, that's me."

"You've got a call at the reception desk."

Jon looked at me with wide eyes. Panic rose in my throat, and I suddenly felt nauseated.

We both got up and followed the waiter to the front desk, and Jon picked up the phone.

"This is Jon." He paused and stared straight ahead as he listened on the phone.

"Really? So what do you think we should do?" he continued.

I wished people would stop clinking dishes and glasses for just a moment. Maybe I could hear more than one side of the conversation.

"Okay. How are Missy and the kids?" Jon asked.

I held my breath.

"Well, that's good," he replied with relief.

I let my breath out.

"I'll see what Lia thinks and we'll get back to you. I really appreciate it, Bob. Thanks so much."

Jon hung up the phone.

"Well, what's going on?" I prodded.

"Your green Buick showed up. Bob decided to pass by after he got dinner for his family, and he saw the guy pull away. Our Buick friend left a rose on the front porch. Missy called the cops when she saw the car, just like you told her to, but Bob was there at the house when the cops got there, and he handled the whole thing—gave a description of the car and where it was headed when it took off," Jon explained.

"He left a rose on the front porch?" I asked trying to piece together the clues the mystery man had left behind.

"Yup. They're trying to see if the car or the rose fit any crime profiles. I think you're right, Lia. This guy is a creep," Jon said, his eyebrows furrowed with concern.

"So what should we do?"

"Well, Bob is in the house with the kids and Missy, and he said he'd stay there until we get home. He's armed. I think the kids will be safe if we stay out and go to the movie, but they might be a little scared."

"Then let's go home."

When we got to the house, the kids were a bit frantic. Especially Emily. She wrapped her arms around Jon and wouldn't let go until she fell into a fitful sleep. Bob requested that a couple of officers drive by the house occasionally during the night until they spotted the Buick, and they promised to call us if they thought we were in danger.

By the time Missy left and Bob had climbed back into his Lexus, the sky had grown dark and we were both exhausted. We laid out sleeping bags on our bedroom floor and all of us slept fitfully. The phone lay at my side of the bed, and a baseball bat lay on the floor next to Jon.

"How was that for a night out?" I whispered in the dark.

"Well," Jon whispered back, "I think I'll be content if we stay in for a while."

Perfect Eggs and a Non-Stick Surface

I jumped when the phone rang, then picked up the receiver with a clumsy hand. Little Katie stirred in the bed between Jon and me, her blond curls tangled at the back of her neck.

"Hello?" I cleared my throat and breathlessly hoped for an officer to tell me they'd caught our stalker.

"Lia, did I wake you?" Anna asked.

I let my breath out slowly. Jon looked up at me through half-closed eyelids.

"It's Anna. Go back to sleep," I whispered.

Jon rolled over and slept again.

"I did wake you. I'm sorry. I figured you'd be watching television. Conference starts in ten minutes."

"We didn't sleep well last night," I explained.

"I'm sorry. Everything's okay?" Anna asked hopefully.

Jacob stirred on the floor next to me, so I carefully climbed out of bed and stepped over him, taking the cordless phone with me. If I couldn't sleep, my family should still be able to.

When I had left the bedroom, I answered Anna's question. "I guess everything's okay, besides the fact that someone's stalking us."

I stepped gingerly into the hall. The other bedroom doors were still closed, and sunlight flooded up the stairs from the large windows in the entryway. Flecks of dust caught the sunlight and drifted aimlessly in small drafts of cool morning air.

"What did you say?" Anna asked with a squeak in her voice.

I related the story of the night before as the steps creaked under my weight. The front door didn't look forced open. The windows over the entryway and the large window in the front room were all intact.

"I bet my phone call scared you to death," Anna realized.

"Well, it certainly woke me up."

"Is Jon home today, or does he have to work?"

"He's always home for conference."

"Oh, that's good. Still, I'd be in a hotel if I were you."

I'd thought about it. It would be nice to get out of the house and not have to worry about the goateed man or his green Buick, but part of me didn't want to let him chase me out of my house.

"The police say it isn't necessary yet. There really hasn't been an 'overt threat.'" I caught a chill and wished I had wrapped my robe around me.

"When will it be necessary? After this guy breaks in and hurts somebody? Heaven forbid."

"Heaven forbid," I said as I checked the kitchen and the sliding glass doors to the backyard. Everything looked fine.

"I must admit," I said, as I headed toward the front porch to get the newspaper, "I can't stand another night like last night."

"Did you get hold of Alexis?" Anna finally reached the point of her call.

"I called her, but she wouldn't talk to me." The paper sat on the welcome mat, and as I picked it up, I noticed another flattened red rose lying beneath it. I picked up the rose, leaving bruised petals on the mat. Apparently our stalker had passed by again between patrol cars and the paperboy.

"She wouldn't talk to you?" Anna sounded confused. "Was she busy or something?"

"No, she just wouldn't talk to me. She only wants to talk to you."

"Well, maybe there's more going on there, and she wants to talk to the Relief Society president about it, you know, something she needs official Church help with."

"Maybe. Or maybe she just doesn't like me," I offered with a snicker. I believed it more than I wanted to let on.

"I doubt that. Well, don't worry about it anyway. It sounds like you've got enough to worry about right now."

"Yeah." I set the smashed rose on the kitchen table to give to the police later. I'd certainly see an officer sometime that day.

"Call me if you need *anything* at all," Anna said.

"I will." I hung up the phone and collapsed on the couch. It was too much.

As I wiped sleep from my eyes, I noticed the dust floating in the sunlight—random flecks of matter colliding in space. There was nothing random about this stalker. This was personal, but which member of our family were the roses intended for? I always kept my children close to me. I drove Emily to school every day, and picked her up too. There was never an opportunity for someone to eye her without Emily's teacher or me noticing. Jacob and Katie never left my side. Besides, the roses couldn't be for the children. They were oblivious to the significance of them. The roses were a message for Jon or for me.

The whole thing seemed strange. If the stalker had wanted to do something sinister, why had he only left roses on the doorstep? He knew I'd seen his face and could identify him in a lineup if it came to that. Something about it didn't make sense. I closed my eyes in an attempt to picture where I'd seen the car.

The fateful Monday evening when I'd gone to Jon's office and heard Ashley giggle behind his office door, I'd rushed the kids back to the car and into their seats. As we headed home, I cut someone off just outside the parking lot near the English offices. I remembered seeing a flash of red hair when the driver honked at me. The green Buick was at the university at the same time as Ashley, and our stalker was a redhead. Could Ashley's brother have left the roses on our porch, using a car that he and Ashley shared? If that were true then the roses were for Jon from Ashley, and she really was pursuing him. I wasn't imagining things.

Jon's alarm clock buzzed at ten. Conference was starting, and soon Jon would come downstairs. I stood and went to the kitchen. I needed more time to think, and spending the morning sequestered in the kitchen making enough food to feed a pioneer family would give me just enough time to plan something to prove my theory. Something had to be done before Jon fell for the determined girl who would send roses to her married teacher's home.

John turned the television on during the opening prayer, then he came into the kitchen, stood behind me, and folded his arms around me. When the prayer finished, he whispered, "Amen," and kissed the back of my head.

"Did you sleep okay, under the circumstances?"

"I guess so." I whisked half a dozen eggs, then added some grated cheese and minced onion.

"Oh, you're making a big breakfast? I thought we'd spend the day with your parents and get us all out of the house."

"I think we'll be fine."

"Really? Last night you were almost as scared as Emily."

I turned my back to the eggs and looked up at him. His face was so full of love, and if Ashley was sending Jon roses, it wasn't his fault. I couldn't suggest anything until I had more proof than a flash of red hair in a green car at the U of U. He already thought I was letting my imagination run wild, and if I were wrong, he'd have proof. I forced myself to smile.

"I think we should hang around the house just in case this creep comes back. I mean if he's been stalking us for a while, and I think he has—at least since the beginning of the semester—he would have been violent already if that was his intent. Don't you think?"

"I guess that makes sense."

"Besides, what could we accuse him of anyway? Trespassing? I guess we could call him a Peeping Tom, except no one was even home when he looked through our windows."

"What changed your mind? Yesterday you were scared to death of this guy, and today he's just a pest."

"I had a night to think about it, is all."

I ran cold water over my fingers and flicked the water on the heating skillet. The water sizzled and evaporated. Since the skillet was hot enough, I poured the eggs and scrambled them with the whisk.

"Well, for safety's sake, I want to take you to your parents' house during the priesthood session tonight. Okay?"

"Sure."

Jon went into the front room as the Tabernacle Choir sang another hymn. The eggs coagulated in the heat. I always cooked perfect eggs. The trick was planning—mixing them enough and making sure the skillet was the right temperature before pouring them. When things were just right, Jon would realize Ashley was after him. Maybe he could make arrangements to have Ashley move to a different class, and maybe he had enough research about the production of *Much Ado* to stop attending rehearsals three times a week.

I dumped the perfect eggs into a serving bowl. They slid off the skillet's surface. I hoped Jon would let go of his star pupil just as easily.

In conference, they talked a lot about marriage and the importance of loving, respecting, and trusting each other. One of the talks was so moving I cried and had to hold a box of tissue in my lap until the talk was done. The Apostle mentioned his own wife and how special she was to him. He stopped talking while tears flooded his eyes, and when he could speak again, his voice was scratchy and he kept clearing his throat.

I wished that Jon felt that way about me. When I looked at him, hoping for some hint that he empathized with the Apostle, I saw his head nod with sleep. A pit of disappointment formed in my stomach, and I hoped he would feel the Spirit just as I had when he read the talk in the *Ensign*.

When the doorbell rang between sessions, I shot from the couch, hoping to find our stalker standing behind the door. But when the door was open, Bob stood there instead.

"Hi, Lia. Is Jon here?" Bob asked.

"Yeah. I'll get him."

I walked to the lounge chair and shook Jon awake.

"Bob is here." I nodded toward the door and raised my eyebrows.

Jon sprang from his chair and hurried to the door. "Hey, Bob. Did you find anything out?"

"Yeah. They pulled the guy over for speeding in Parley's Canyon about seven o'clock this morning. His name is Gary Simms. Ring a bell?"

Jon wrinkled his brow as he tried to place the name. I hoped the last name would jar his memory.

"Nope, I don't recognize the name. Do you, Lia?" Jon asked as he turned to me.

"No." My heart sank, and fear crept up in its place. I hadn't solved the mystery, which meant there was still a faceless someone behind the whole thing.

"We've booked him for trespassing. And his car wasn't licensed," Bob continued.

"What's the punishment for that?" Jon asked.

"Not much, since he doesn't have a record. They found out he's a contractor, so maybe he was just admiring your house and lied to you when you caught him because he was nervous," Bob reasoned. "He didn't try anything, did he?" Bob looked at me and waited for an answer.

"No," I said as I recalled the incident. I looked down at my folded arms.

"Well shoot, Lia, don't sound so disappointed," Jon laughed and put his arm around my waist, squeezing me.

"Yeah, there's nothing to be disappointed about." Bob smiled right along with Jon. "He'll leave you alone now, because he knows that if he leaves anything here again, you'll tell us and they'll know just where to find him. Then he'd really have a problem on his hands."

"So no more stalker?" Jon extended his hand to Bob.

"No more stalker." Bob cranked Jon's hand and went back to his car.

"Isn't that great, sweetheart!" Jon said as he squeezed me.

"Yeah. I still want to know why though." I tried to formulate another explanation, but I kept coming back to the car at the university.

"Well, me too," Jon said. "Maybe he did have the wrong house after all."

"Then why did he drop off roses?" I questioned Jon's reasoning. "If he'd been going to the wrong house, he would have figured it out after he saw me."

Jon sat back down in the lounge chair and sighed. "I don't know. I'm just trying to help."

I'd hoped for a confrontation with the stalker, a confirmation that my suspicions were correct, but Bob hadn't offered us that.

"Are you sure you don't recognize the name?" I asked, grasping at strings. "Do you know anyone else with that name? Anyone with red hair?"

Jon looked at me from the corner of his eye, then turned to me with a disbelieving grin.

"You think Ashley was behind this, don't you?"

I shrugged my shoulders. "It's possible."

"Well, Ashley's last name is Bills, okay? So you have nothing to worry about." He shook his head and looked back at the television.

I stood in the middle of the room, looking at Jon. He ignored me, pulled the paper from the floor to his lap and studied the front-page story.

With a nod of my head I went into the kitchen to wash dishes.

Knowing our stalker had been warned eased my mind for a while, but every day that week I checked the front porch for a rose. I knew Ashley had something to do with it, and my failed attempt to prove it to Jon strained our marriage like the way a heavy dumbbell strains weak muscle. He hardly spoke to me that week, and when he did speak, it was the type of small talk necessary to run our home.

I'd hoped on conference morning as I fixed breakfast for my family that Jon would let go of Ashley, and she would slip into his past like eggs from a non-stick surface. Instead, Jon was slipping from me. In fact he was far away, light years away, like a bright star that shone as a pinprick in the velvet sky—too far to reach in a lifetime.

A True Brush-off

For ten years, our ward had hosted the best Super Saturday in the valley the week after October general conference. We prided ourselves on this monumental occasion, and it would probably be an annual event until the Second Coming. It was the only Relief Society event that sisters in the Primary and the Young Women all went out of their way to attend.

I wasn't exactly a crafter, but attending the event was worth it because it gave me a break from my kids as well as an opportunity to visit with every sister I knew in the ward. Usually Jon was able to stay home with the kids, but this year he wanted to do some editing. So I dropped them off at the nursery.

The Enrichment committee arranged five areas where we could spend our time: scrapbooking, tole painting, cooking, quilting, and service. Each area had a sign above it and a member of the Enrichment committee stood below the sign to instruct and supervise.

The tole painting station was a standard at every crafty Enrichment function. I attempted it several times, but I always ended up attacking my project with sandpaper and giving it to someone who could actually make it presentable.

Mary sat at the tole painting table. She held a wooden doll about an inch from her face, dabbing bits of navy blue with a thin-tipped brush.

"Mary! How are you today?" I walked over to her with a smile on my face. Truth be told, the best part of a Relief Society function really was visiting with the other sisters in the ward.

"Great! I've finished three projects already, and I've only been here an hour. It's amazing how much you accomplish when you can concentrate on one thing at a time. I'll probably warm this seat all day long."

"How is everything at home?"

"Oh, okay, I guess. Jimmy's still really sick. He says his companion is tired of staying in the apartment and studying all the time. They're giving him huge shots every day. He won't tell me any details, he just assures me that he's fine. But judging by the last pictures he sent, he's lost at least twenty pounds. Trisha loves BYU. I never hear from her, and I have to take that as a good sign. I'm sure she'd call if something went wrong."

Mary set down her brush and rubbed her eyes. "I have to get me one of those magnifying glasses for crafters. Have you seen those things?"

Being creatively challenged, I had no idea what she was talking about. I shook my head.

Mary rinsed the brush in a cup of murky water and dipped it in black paint. With a steady hand, she painted dainty eyelashes on the doll. "Missy is giving me a heart attack."

I thought of the conversation Missy and I had on her front lawn and wondered if Mary finally knew. "How come?"

"Her boyfriend broke up with her and she's been taking it kind of hard. She's sick all the time lately, stomach cramps, vomiting, horrible headaches." Mary's face twisted with concern. Then she pulled herself from her own worries and looked up at me. "But you probably knew about the breakup because she watched your kids last week. Did they catch that guy?"

"Yeah, they caught him."

"Oh, good." Mary looked genuinely relieved. "I thought I had problems. At least no one's stalking us."

I hugged Mary. "I'll pray for you. Everything will be all right."

"I know everything will be fine. Thanks for reminding me." Mary flashed a wan smile.

I walked to the service area and picked up a list of instructions. Some sisters were sewing together little bags with a drawstring at the top. The instructions listed items that needed to be put in the bags: pencils, a notebook, a small chalkboard, chalk. Sisters had donated the items throughout the previous year. These were school bags that would go to children all over the world.

The designated leader came up to me with about ten bags in her hand. "Would you like to stuff or sew?"

"Stuff, please."

She pushed the bags at me. "I see you've got a list. Let me know if you need anything."

I worked my way down the table, stuffing the items in my bag one at a time. As I neared the end of the table, I noticed Alexis walking toward the service area. She didn't see me. I couldn't figure out why she'd been so cold when I called her. I hadn't done anything to warrant such treatment. Maybe Anna was right, that there was some need there that only the Relief Society president or the bishop could help with. But even if that was the problem, there was no reason for her to treat me so rudely. Maybe she was just having a bad day.

She was talking to the service area leader, choosing between "stuff or sew." I set down my half-full bag and walked over to her.

"Hi, Alexis. It's good to see you here today. I wasn't sure I would."

She nodded at me coolly, but avoided eye contact.

"How is your husband?" I asked in an attempt to break the ice.

"He had surgery this morning. He's miserable," she snapped.

"Oh, I'm sorry to hear that." I *was* sorry too. I would have touched Alexis in a compassionate effort, but she wouldn't even look at me.

"Well, is there anything I can do?" I pressed.

"You can mind your own business." Her gold eyes pierced me as she pushed past and started stuffing bags.

I stood there, stunned. She definitely had something against me, that much was clear. But I had no idea why.

"What was that all about?" Jane asked as she walked to my side.

"Let's just say she's not willing to accept my help," I replied.

"Oh," Jane said with a quizzical look at Alexis.

The service leader didn't even ask Jane what she wanted to do. She just shoved a handful of bags at her with a pleading smile.

Jane smiled back and took the bags.

"So, how is everything with you, Jane?" I asked, relieved to speak to someone friendly.

"Pretty good. Things are going well." She grinned.

"Yeah?" I asked, trying to get her to elaborate.

"Yeah." She nodded her head and smiled like she held a sweet secret in her heart and she wasn't about to tell me.

Just then, a chair crashed to the floor on the other side of the room.

Mary stood, completely unaware of the chair crashed to the floor behind her. Hyrum, Mary's husband, spoke in earnest, low tones while he and Mary haphazardly filled a box with her paints and projects.

"Jane, something's wrong," I said. Then Jane and I rushed over to Mary.

"Mary, is everything okay?" Jane asked. I picked up the chair and pulled it out of Mary's way.

"Missy's ill. We're taking her to the hospital. She didn't want to go without me." Mary's round face flushed, her forehead creased with lines of worry. "Tell Anna, will you? We may need some help here."

Mary and her husband left the cultural hall as quickly as they could, dodging sisters, tables, and chairs.

Anna ran to our sides. "Is everything okay?"

"No. She said we should warn you that they might need some help. They're taking Missy to the hospital," I explained.

Anna looked around in dismay at the biggest Relief Society function of the year.

"We'll go to the hospital with them," I offered. "I'll call Jon's office and ask him to come get the kids."

Anna sighed with gratitude. "Thanks, Lia."

Jane and I made our way out of the church and to Jane's car. The pieces were fitting together by then. Missy's confession, the symptoms Mary had listed only moments before. Why else would Missy demand they stop to get her mother on the way to the hospital? Why else would an irresponsible boy, who was getting everything he wanted out of his relationship, be so quick to give his girlfriend the brush-off?

The truth was there, though unspoken. I felt the situation coming to a head. Soon the truth would shout so loudly that no one could ignore it. Not even Missy.

Secrets

———————⌘———————

I spoke to Jon on Jane's cell phone as we navigated the winding streets to Primary Children's Hospital. Mary and her husband, Hyrum, drove not three car lengths in front of us. Mary sat in the backseat with Missy's head in her lap. Occasionally, Mary looked back at us.

"I left the kids at the church, Jon. They're in the nursery. They don't even know I left, so you might want to hurry." I ended the call. "He'll get the kids."

"I hope everything is okay. I wonder if it's her appendix, with the way she's curled up like that." Jane pulled into a parking space while Hyrum drove to the emergency entrance.

"Well, this is the best place to take her. They'll figure everything out. She'll be okay," I said, trying to convince myself.

Jane and I speed-walked to the emergency room. Hyrum sat filling out paperwork while Mary paced the waiting area. Tears flowed free down her face. She let them drip off her chin. When she saw Jane and me, she nodded and sat next to Hyrum, trying to look calm. I saw a box of tissue and brought it to her.

"They took her right away. Hyrum carried her in here." Mary pulled out a tissue and kept the box on her lap.

"Have you made arrangements to give her a blessing?" Jane asked.

Mary looked at Hyrum, and he looked back at her.

"I suppose we could call President Davis, see if he's available."

"Yes, or Bishop Ames."

"I'll call President Davis." Hyrum pulled his cell phone from his pocket and headed for the exit so he could place the call.

I sat next to Mary and held her hand. She whispered, "Thank you," and wiped the moisture from her face.

After a few minutes, Hyrum came back and sat next to Mary. "President Davis is on his way. We caught him just in time. He was on his way to a meeting. But he said the meeting could wait."

"Dean Davis lives on their street. He's in the stake presidency," I explained to Jane.

"He's a good man," Hyrum said. "We've been very blessed to have him as a neighbor."

College football played on the TV. Mary watched the game with a blank stare, occasionally glancing back at the double doors they'd rolled Missy through minutes before. Notre Dame scored, and one man in the room cheered.

A mother came in carrying a little boy who had obviously broken his arm. He cradled the injured limb close to his body and leaned his head against his mother's shoulder. His little pale face peeked out from the hood of his jacket, and he caught me staring at him. He stared back, expressionless, for a moment, then he looked up at his mother and closed his eyes.

"It's all right, sweetheart. Momma's here. Everything will be okay." She kissed his forehead through his hood. "Momma's here."

We heard the clock tick behind us. I wished I had brought a book.

"Did Dean mention when he would get here?" Mary asked Hyrum.

"He just said he was on his way."

I thought of Missy and our discussion as we worked in her garden and wondered if she'd only told me half her secret. It seemed so obvious—her shame at speaking about temple marriage, her conversation with her friend by the bishop's door, the way she avoided looking the bishop in the eye, her constant illness. Why hadn't I seen it before?

Just then, Dean Davis walked through the door. Hyrum stood and President Davis hurried over to us, taking the hand that Hyrum extended. "Hyrum, sisters." He nodded to each of us. "How is she?"

"We haven't heard yet, Dean. We're still waiting."

"Ah, that's the hard part. No worse feeling than helplessness." Dean took Mary's hand in his and looked her in the eye. "And how are you holding up, Mother?"

Mary nodded and ignored the tears that streaked her face again. "I'm hanging in there."

"Maybe we should give you a blessing too, huh?" He held her hand in both of his, looking at her with soft brown eyes and all the love of a father.

Notre Dame scored again. The man cheered again. Mary glanced back at the double doors. I stared at Mary, debating on whether to break the news to her before someone else did.

"So tell me what happened." Dean sat in a chair across a small table from Hyrum.

"She complained of nausea this morning and wouldn't eat breakfast at all. Then, around ten-thirty, she came in the front room doubled over. I asked her what was wrong, and she said that I needed to take her to the hospital, and she wanted her mother. She said she wouldn't go without her mother."

"Did she have any fever?" Jane asked.

"No, she felt fine to me. I practically carried her out to the car. She cried the whole time."

"If there was no fever, it probably wasn't her appendix." Jane's face twisted quizzically. I looked at Jane. She wouldn't be happy to learn about the secret either.

I leaned over to Jane and whispered, "You know, Jane. Maybe we should go and come back later."

The double doors opened and a young man came out. Probably an intern.

"Mr. and Mrs. Wilson?" the intern asked.

Hyrum and Mary stood.

"Melissa and the baby are both doing fine now." He smiled calmly, oblivious to the fact that his mood was inappropriate under the circumstances.

I closed my eyes and sighed. There it was, shouted from the rooftops. Before the announcement it was just a suspicion. While the words hung in the air, reality settled. I watched Mary's countenance blanch.

"Her blood pressure was 175 over 110. That's quite a bit higher than we like to see it, so we would like to keep her overnight for observation. And we would like to recommend bed rest . . ." He looked up at Hyrum and saw the look of shock on his face. Then he turned to the rest of us and found similar expressions.

"Did you say 'baby'?" Hyrum asked.

My heart plummeted.

"You didn't know your daughter was pregnant?" The intern's face blushed with embarrassment. "I'm sorry, I just assumed. She's at twenty-four weeks gestation." Mary sat down hard. Her teary eyes dried and took on a shocked stupor.

"The baby is fine. Preeclampsia is more dangerous for the mother than for the baby, at least at first," he said.

I hoped silently for a miraculous gain in bedside manner.

"Baby," Mary said, staring into space.

"I could tell you the baby's sex if you'd like." The intern smiled with his weak attempt at cheering everyone up.

I gave him a dirty look.

"Yeah." He backed away, turning his head to speak to us over his shoulder. "We're moving her to room 312 soon. You're welcome to go there and wait for her." He turned and walked away before he could do any more damage.

Dean reached for Mary's hand and helped her up. "Come, let's go where there's more privacy." He patted Hyrum on the back. I gathered up Mary's coat and purse. Jane and I quietly followed the rest toward the elevator.

An empty bed sat in the small, dimly lit room. Three chairs lined the wall to our left. Hyrum guided Mary to the chairs and helped her sit. Mary leaned her head back until it bumped the wall. Hyrum sat and put his face in his hands, resting his elbows on his knees. Dean sat in the remaining seat and pulled a small vial of consecrated oil from his jacket pocket.

"Should I turn on a light?" I asked.

Dean nodded up at me. I did as I was told.

Obviously President Davis had everything under control. The thought of witnessing Missy's confession filled me with dread and a sudden need to leave. I put Mary's coat and purse in a closet near the door.

"Listen, we're going to take off now. Call me or Jane if you need anything." I glanced at Jane and backed out of the room. Jane's eyes glazed over, and she seemed barely aware of her surroundings. An angry scowl creased her forehead.

As we strode down the hall, Jane walked faster until I had to hurry to keep up. Jane slapped the elevator button with the palm of her hand and pulled her keys out of her pocket as we waited, evidently preparing for a getaway.

"Uh, Jane. Are you all right?" I asked.

"No," she snapped.

The elevator beeped and we walked in.

A nurse dressed in blue scrubs stood behind a wheelchair with a young girl sitting in it. A woman stood beside the wheelchair and held the girl's frail hand in hers. I nodded at the nurse and looked down at the child. She clutched a doll wearing a tiny hospital gown with stitches drawn on the doll's head. The girl looked up at me, and I noticed a large bald spot just over her right ear with stitches in the middle of it. Thin, tangled blond hair covered the rest of her scalp. The girl was pale, and dark circles rimmed her eyes. But she smiled at me with her narrow, chapped lips.

I smiled back.

The nurse, the woman, and the young girl in the wheelchair followed us out of the elevator.

"Here, baby. Let's pull this blanket up over you so you don't get cold."

"I'm okay, Mom. I can't wait to go outside. I forgot what grass looks like."

Jane hurried out of the hospital. I speed-walked in silence about two feet behind her all the way back to the car. She unlocked my door first. I got in while she unlocked her door. The car rocked as she jumped in and crammed the key in the ignition.

"Okay, Jane. Spill it."

Permission was all she needed to open the floodgates. "This is the kind of stuff that made me quit working the neonatal unit. These teenagers go out and get pregnant, without trying, might I add, and they don't even tell their families. They don't get prenatal care. Half the time, the baby has birth defects because of it. And I bet Missy's got preeclampsia, with her blood pressure that high." She revved the engine and threw it in reverse.

I didn't know what preeclampsia was, but as Jane tore around the corner and onto the road, I figured I would wait for another opportunity to ask her.

She threw the car in drive and her tires squealed.

"You saw that little girl in the elevator, and how good her mom was with her. You never know what kind of trials your children are going to go through, and as a parent, you have to be able to support your kids no matter what. Do you think some teenager could handle a child with a brain tumor?" Jane's blood was boiling and she'd begun to vent.

I couldn't help but think that Missy probably could handle a child with a brain tumor if she had to. But judging by the look on Jane's face, that wouldn't be the best thing to mention.

"Some irresponsible punk easily gets what I've wanted and worked for the past ten years. She's not grateful. She doesn't even care enough to see a doctor. And what kind of life is she going to give that baby, huh? A horrible life. No child should grow up feeling like he's a burden. But that's what this baby will be to his mother. I see it all the time."

Sweet, spiritual Jane was on a rampage. And she drove like a maniac. I fastened my seat belt even though we were halfway home.

"Missy's child will probably end up being Mary's responsibility, even though she's ready to move to another season of her life. Or he'll become a ward of the state. I see it all the time. Occasionally the mothers are smart enough to consider adoption, but most of the time they're too selfish to do anything about it. Which really shouldn't surprise anyone—it was selfishness that got them in that position in the first place."

Jane slammed on her brakes in front of my house. I pried my fingers from the door handle.

"Jane, don't you think you're being a tad judgmental?" I ventured.

"I've tried for ten years to get pregnant, Lia. Ten years of figuring out when I would ovulate. Ten years of hormone therapy of one kind or another. That's the only reason we're at the U instead of back home in Iowa. One more treatment, one more try, one more in vitro. Then it's over. I'm done trying." Jane burst into tears. Her shoulders shook and her nose ran. "I'm tired of trying."

Jon came out of the house and headed toward the car. I motioned to him to wait for a minute.

"I'm sorry, Jane. I'm sure it's been horrible." I put my hand on Jane's shoulder and she melted immediately into my arms and wet my shoulder with her tears.

"I can't visit Mary for a while, Lia. I hope you understand, but you'll have to go it alone until I come to terms with this." Jane pulled away from my embrace and wiped smears of mascara from her cheeks.

"That's fine. I can visit alone for a while. Take all the time you need."

"I'm sorry. You hardly know me and I've dumped on you," Jane said.

"Well, I asked you to tell me what was wrong. It's okay that you told me."

I glanced out my window and saw Jon standing there, waiting for me with his arms folded over his chest. "Listen, Jane, it looks like Jon needs me for something, so I've got to go. Just do me a favor, okay? Don't say any of that stuff to Mary or Missy."

Jane sniffed and wiped her nose with the back of her hand. "Oh, I'm embarrassed I said it to you. Don't worry. I'll keep my mouth shut."

I hugged her again and got out of the car, smiling at Jon.

He didn't smile back. "You got something today that I found rather interesting."

"Oh?" I couldn't imagine what.

I followed Jon into the kitchen. In the middle of the table sat a single long-stemmed rose in a frosted glass vase with a delicate neck. I thought for a moment that our stalker was back, but that wouldn't explain the vase. Then I hoped Jon's stern expression was a ruse, and I smiled at him. Jon never gave me flowers. What a welcome surprise. He handed me a small card. His expression didn't change.

I opened the card, and as I read the words, I understood.

> *I'm sorry if Simms scared you last week. Obviously he did because I had to bail him out of jail and get his car out of impound. The roses were from me. When we came by and Simms looked in your window, I was waiting in the car. You looked upset, and the roses were supposed to cheer you up. Bad idea I guess. Anyway, I'm sorry.*
>
> *Love, D.*

The roses were for me. And they were from Derek. I'd kept quiet about Derek's letter, but as I looked in Jon's angry face I waited for the trumpets to blow, announcing my secrets as they joined Missy's and Jane's—out in the open at last.

Arguments

———— ⌘ ————

"Am I to assume that 'D' is Derek, your old boyfriend?" Jon leaned against the counter and looked at me, his face calm, but his eyes burning.

"Yes. But you can't possibly think I knew I was going to get this? I thought he didn't know I was married, let alone what my married name is, or where I live. I haven't talked to him since we broke up."

"Then how did he find you?"

"I don't know. It's not like I've moved all over the country since then. I mean I still live in the same valley. He's a wealthy man. He probably has connections."

"You don't think your mother would say anything?" Jon wondered aloud.

"Of course not," I retorted.

I looked at the ground. I'd never told Jon about the letter or the ring. I figured sending them back would end our correspondence anyway.

"What? What are you thinking about?" Jon asked, his eyes searching my face.

"It's not a big deal, Jon. So don't make a big deal out of it."

"What's not a big deal? The rose from your *ex-boyfriend?*"

I folded my arms and took a small step back from Jon. "Well, I said I hadn't talked to him since we broke up, but he sent a letter to my parents' house a few weeks ago."

"What kind of letter?" Jon's face flushed, but he kept his voice low.

"He apologized for leaving the Church, and he said he hoped I was happy. Mom sent it back without a reply. It's not a big deal."

"Not a big deal? You were engaged to him, Lia. You loved him. And all of a sudden he's coming back. He sends you flowers and I'm supposed to ignore it! No wonder you weren't so worried about it during conference. You figured it out. And then you blamed Ashley!"

"Don't yell at me in front of the kids," I whispered, even though they were in the next room. "Besides, who are you to talk?" I felt defensive by then, backed into a corner. So I came out fighting.

"What?"

"Ashley, that's what. You practically can't stop talking about her and you see her every weekday. I'll probably never see Derek again, no matter what that stupid card said."

"Ashley is my student."

"Oh come on, Jon. I saw you watch her walk away that day I went to your office. I know how a man looks when he wants a woman. You had that look on your face. And the other day, when I brought that picnic, she was talking during class and you were looking at her like you had a deep connection with her. Then she asked you to lunch!"

"You're imagining things," Jon said, brushing it off like it was a silly idea from a fevered, female mind.

"Am I? You're an intelligent man, Jon. Can you honestly tell me she isn't throwing herself at you? And can you tell me you don't like it? Come on, you have experience falling for your students."

Jon looked at me like I'd stabbed him. His eyebrows dipped toward his nose as he squinted at me. He covered his mouth with his right hand then rubbed his fingers down along his stubbled face.

"The only student I ever fell for was you, and if you recall, you weren't my student at the time. And, I wasn't married either."

I didn't have a comeback to that one.

"Besides, you are the only woman I've ever been committed to. I can't believe you'd question that. I thought you knew me better." His words sounded like a challenge, but he looked genuinely hurt. His eyes grew moist and he looked away from me.

I did know him better. But I felt unsure, like I was trying ice skates for the first time.

"People change, Jon. How can I be sure you won't change?"

"Well, I guess you can't." Jon sat at the kitchen table, a lost look on his face. I sat across from him. The rose stood on the table between us. "The only thing I can tell you, Lia, is that I made promises to God long before I made any promises to you. And I will keep those promises, come what may." He tried to look at me across the table, but the rose blocked half of his face. He looked away.

We sat there in silence for a moment. Jacob and Emily played together in the front room. They laughed.

Jon stood and walked toward the back door. "Can you say the same, Lia? Will you keep your promises?"

"Of course I will." I tried to look him in the eye, but he avoided me.

"I hope so." He grabbed his keys from the key rack and left.

I put the kids to bed at eight-thirty and called my mom. Jon still hadn't come home. I picked up the phone several times to call his office, but I couldn't bring myself to dial. Even though I participated in the argument, I still wasn't sure what really happened. The only thing I knew was that my marriage had been damaged, maybe beyond repair.

"I've had a wild day, Mom. You wouldn't believe it. First, I found out that Missy, one of my old Beehives, is pregnant."

"Oh no. I guess she's not married," Mom said.

"No. And her mother looked particularly devastated. I haven't called her to talk about it yet. She's probably still at the hospital anyway."

"Everything's all right, I hope."

"As good as it can be, I guess. But my visiting teaching companion isn't handling it too well. She's been trying to get pregnant for a while, and as far as I know nothing has worked. Now this."

"The poor thing. That's a hard position to be in. I remember," Mom said, her voice thick with empathy.

"And Derek sent me a rose, Mom. Jon was the one who signed for it this time."

"What is Derek trying to do to you?"

"If he's trying to mess up my life, he's doing a good job. And all the old feelings I had for him are washing up in my dreams. I dreamed he asked me to go away with him. He said it would take courage, but it would be worth it." I felt anxious as I remembered the dream, like I was on the verge of a dangerous discovery.

"Well, it was just a dream you know," Mom reminded me.

"Yeah, but I don't think I would have dreamed it if part of me wasn't at least curious about . . . changing my life." I hesitated as I spoke. I didn't want to think along those lines anymore, but I couldn't seem to stop.

"You can't be serious, Lia."

"Well, I'm not that serious. I wonder what my life would have been like if I had stuck with Derek. I'm curious, that's all."

"What makes you think life with Derek would have been any better than life with Jon is? You've got it pretty good, Lia." Mom tried to stay patient, but I could tell by the rising tension in her voice she didn't want me thinking about it anymore either.

"I know that. At least my mind does. I don't know what my heart knows right now."

"You can't even allow for the possibility, Lia. You can't open the door to temptation and not expect it to come waltzing in." Mom tried to stay calm, but her voice tensed as she spoke, nearly begging me to drop the subject. "If Derek found your married name and your address," she continued, "how long before he shows up at your door? Don't allow the question, Lia. You're asking for trouble."

"But Derek was my first love, Mom. What if I was supposed to stick with Derek and just be patient? I haven't been really happy for a long time, but the more I think about it the more I wonder how happy Jon is with me. It's like he avoids me half the time. I just wonder if we all would have been happier if I'd stayed with Derek."

Something pushed me on toward honesty. I did have doubts. And I needed to express them. The dreadful, ultimate question hung bitterly in my mouth. I had to ask it, let it out into the open and acknowledge my greatest fear.

"Mom, what if marrying Jon was a mistake?" I whispered the question, even though I knew the kids were asleep and Jon wasn't home.

"You ask that question, and you're really asking for trouble. I'm telling you, get the thought from your head. The answer doesn't matter anyway, because you're committed to Jon *now*. You're *sealed* to Jon. God led you to Jon, and you know it."

I did know it. Everything she said was true, but images filled my mind of Derek helping me into his private jet and flying me to Europe. We'd see the world together. I'd be a prominent scientist, a cultured member of New York high society who really made a difference in her community, a gleaming gem on Derek's arm with his ring on my finger.

"But, Mom," I said. Then I clenched my jaw. I couldn't say what was in my mind because I was afraid of it, and I couldn't find the words. Where something had pushed me forward along my path of thought, suddenly something held me back.

"Lia, call me back when you can get control of yourself and be logical."

She hung up the phone. My mother had never hung up on me before.

I'd been in far too many arguments that day.

I flopped to the couch and turned on the TV, but I didn't really watch the images flickering on the screen. I was tired. Tired of worrying about everything. Tired of thinking and paying attention to my second guesses. The TV lulled me into a stupor. It was one-thirty in the morning when I looked at the clock then slipped into the darkness of sleep.

Hour of Prayer

Sunlight filtered through the closed drapes in our front room. Sleeping on the arm of the couch kinked my neck, and needles of pain coursed through my shoulder. I groaned and tried to stretch the pain away. The TV was off, and the remote lay on the floor in front of me. I didn't remember turning it off during the night, so Jon must have done it when he got home.

I stood and rubbed my neck as I peeked out the front window. Jon's Chevette sat parked in the driveway.

As I made my way up the stairs, I heard the shower running in our bathroom.

Slowly it dawned on me it was fast Sunday, and we would have to put on a happy face for the ward. The last thing I needed was everyone at church speculating that Jon and I were unhappy.

I peeked at my children still sleeping in their beds. They looked so peaceful there, sleeping soundly, without a care in the world.

Jon toweled his hair as I entered the bedroom. He pulled a white dress shirt from the closet and slipped it on.

"I remember you," I said.

"Hi." His response was clipped and cold, not his usual "I remember you too." It broke my heart.

"Did you sleep well?" I asked, fighting tears as I steadied my voice.

"Nope."

I pulled clean clothes from my drawers and prepared to take a shower too. Suddenly, the thought of going to church was very unappealing. I just wanted to curl up in my bed and sleep. But I knew I needed church that day, even if I wasn't looking forward to it.

With a sigh, I asked, "What should we fast for today?"

"I started my fast last night," he said.

"Oh." Every month since we'd married, minus when I was pregnant or nursing, we had fasted together for the same thing. I hadn't been on my own in a long time.

"Did you bathe the kids last night so they can get up and get dressed?" Jon asked as he twisted his tie into a knot.

"Yeah, they're clean."

"Okay." He straightened his tie and left the room without even looking at me. I heard him cooing at Emily in the next room as he woke her.

"What do you want to wear today, beautiful?" Jon asked.

"The pink dress. The one with the flowers," Emily's sweet voice replied.

A hanger clinked as he took the dress from the closet.

"This one?"

"Yeah. I love that dress. It spins really good."

"It does, huh?" Jon laughed.

I could picture the smile on his face as he spoke so tenderly to our firstborn.

"Let's go down and get you some breakfast, and I'll iron it for you, okay?" he said.

He opened Jacob's door and began a similar, sweet conversation with him. I shut the bathroom door and took off my clothes. The mirror over the sink taunted me as I climbed in the shower. The water ran hot until my skin turned pink.

"Father," I said aloud, my voice lost in the sound of the water hitting the tile. I wondered if my prayer would bounce around in the shower too, or if it would reach the heavens. "I am fasting this day for my marriage. Help me to know Thy will. Help me to strengthen my marriage and save my family."

A wave of humility overwhelmed me, and I realized I had caused the argument. If I'd told Jon about the letter the day he came back from the festival, we would have been saved so much grief over the past week. Together we might have guessed that the roses left on the porch were somehow connected to Derek, and we might not have spent a night in fear. Also, the rose that Jon signed for would not have surprised him, and he would only have been mad at Derek, not at me. And if that wasn't enough, I accused Jon of having a relationship with Ashley, something I knew in my heart he wouldn't do. My legs melted beneath me and the water beat on my head and ran in rivulets down my face. My tears washed down the drain with the water.

When I came downstairs, everyone was ready to go. The kids were all clean and shiny, and though Emily's ponytail was a bit off center, she still looked beautiful in her neatly pressed dress. Jon held his scriptures in one hand and Katie's little hand in the other.

"Lia, will you do me one favor as soon as possible?" Jon asked.

I looked at him, hoping the redness in my eyes had gone away. "Anything."

"Will you throw that away?" Jon nodded at the rose still sitting on the kitchen table. I'd forgotten about it during the night.

His eyes penetrated me, pleading. Throwing the rose away was symbolic of repentance to him, and I knew it by the way he looked at me. If I threw the rose away, it would be as if yesterday's fight never happened. He asked one simple act of me, like Moses asking his people to look to the rod and live.

I picked up the vase and threw the whole thing in the trash.

My neck ached as I sat down on the back row in the Relief Society room. I leaned my head back against the wall and rubbed my sorest shoulder.

Anna stood at the front of the room and looked at her announcements. "I'd like to ask you to include a few of the sisters in your prayers today. Mary Wilson is having some difficulties in her family right now. Also, Alexis Smith is struggling."

I noticed Alexis wasn't there that day, which was very unusual for her. Mary was probably still in the hospital with Missy.

Jane sat next to me with a white handkerchief in her lap. Her eyes were red and puffed, as if she'd been crying all morning.

I don't remember what the lesson was about. I sat there and thought of Derek, Jon, Missy, and Mary. What a roller coaster the past week had been. The ride left me nauseated, dizzy, and frantic to find sure footing again. To my left sat Derek, a rose in hand and all the riches of the world behind him. To my right sat my sweet husband, confused and lost. In front of me sat Missy, holding a baby she wasn't ready for. Mary sobbed at her side. Jane stood with her back to Missy, looking at me with pleading eyes. Alexis turned her back to me every time I looked her way. All of them swirled around me in a blur of color and the smells of rich cedar, sweet red roses, salty blood and tears.

I sat up with a start as Jane tapped my shoulder. "Relief Society is over. You slept through it."

"Oh. Sorry. I hope I didn't snore." I picked up my scriptures and struggled to stand.

"You didn't. No sleep last night, huh?"

"No." I rubbed my neck.

"Me either. Listen, I'm really embarrassed about blowing up like that. I'm just having a hard time with this."

"It's understandable, given your circumstances. Please don't worry about it," I said.

"Well, I do worry about it. My circumstances are no excuse. Have you talked to Mary to find out how everything is going?"

"No. I honestly haven't had a chance since yesterday," I confessed. "Things are a bit crazy at my house."

I was able to focus a little better during Sunday School, but all I really got out of it was the idea that wives should submit to their husbands as long as their husbands were living God's law. That was about the last topic I wanted to discuss that day.

Tired and aching, in sacrament meeting I leaned forward on the empty bench in front of us in the chapel. Sleep sounded wonderful—light and liberating. But sleeping in that position would likely make my neck worse. I sat up and concentrated the best I could on the opening announcements and hymns. The only way to stay focused during the sacrament was to pull out the hymn book and glance through the lyrics.

I came across "Where Can I Turn for Peace?" and I could see why Jon loved the hymn so much. It seemed so simple, and yet so poignant. It fit Jon like his own skin.

After the bishop bore his testimony and turned the meeting over to the congregation, Jon tapped me on the shoulder and set Katie on my lap. Then, he walked to the pulpit.

"Brothers and sisters. I am very humbled this morning, and my thoughts are on Enos, who wrestled through the night in prayer. I have found that there are two places to turn when we struggle. We can turn to the world for answers, or we can turn to God.

"You all know that I teach for a living. And I'm working on a book right now about dramatic interpretation of Shakespeare. Through this endeavor, I've spent a great deal of time with wonderful people whom I've come to trust and care about."

Jon looked at me, and I met his gaze.

"Unfortunately, I have not spent as much time with the people I love the most in this world."

The tears flowed freely down my face, collected under my chin, and dripped to my lap.

"I have been having difficulties lately, and last night I almost turned to one of my professional associates for answers to some of my questions. But I felt the need to turn to God instead.

"What could have happened if I had turned to the world for my answers? I might not be standing in front of you today. I might not be able to tell my wife that I love her. I might not tell my children today that I know this gospel is true, I know Jesus is the Christ. When the Spirit speaks, my brothers and sisters, we must listen. We must listen or we'll miss the blessings He has in store for us.

"There is so much more to our existence than we can understand at once; that is why we learn a little at a time and are judged according to our knowledge. I have learned a little today, but I will have to keep listening if I am to learn more tomorrow."

He didn't take his eyes off of me as he closed his testimony and came back to sit beside me and lift Katie to his lap. He wiped my tears as his eyes glistened.

The rest of the day floated by. All was well in Zion. Jon treated me with extra kindness. He did the dishes after dinner and let me rest alone behind the closed door of our bedroom.

After the kids were in bed, Jon and I read our scriptures together for the first time in weeks. We discussed our impressions as we read. We prayed and cried together that night, and our prayer kindled sweet, long-absent feelings. I felt closer to him than I had in months. His image lingered in my mind and heart as I drifted off to sleep.

But crayons popped up in my dreams. Curvy girls with red hair and blond boys holding roses paced in front of our house, calling my name. When I awoke and Jon had left for work, the spirit of the day before dissipated with dawn, like autumn fog.

Skeletons

———————

The trees lining the street blushed and drooped until leaves covered the sidewalk and the autumn breeze carried them through the neighborhood. A hint of the coming winter whispered across the Salt Lake Valley and frosted the mountains. Emily and Jacob couldn't stop talking about Halloween and how terrible it was that they had to wait a week before they could parade through the school in their costumes. Our elementary school allowed preschoolers to parade with their older siblings, so it was as big a day for Jacob as it was for Emily.

"I want to be a skeleton for Halloween." Jacob pointed at a costume in one of the local ads. The little boy's face was painted white where his bones were, and a black hood covered his head. He held his arms out to his sides and let his hands dangle.

"Why a skeleton?" I asked.

"'Cause they're gross." Jacob smiled and wriggled his fingers at me as if they were covered with goo.

"I don't want to be anything gross, Momma. I want to be a princess." Emily spun around, pretending a flowing gown billowed out around her.

"That doesn't surprise me much," I said.

Emily continued. "I want to be a purple princess, and I want my hair curly with lots of sparkles in it."

"What should Katie be for Halloween?" I asked.

"She could be a skeleton too," Jacob said as he let his hands dangle like the boy in the ad.

"No. Only boys are skeletons." Emily shook her head like Jacob had made a silly suggestion.

"Actually, Emily, everyone has a skeleton," I said.

Jacob laughed right in Emily's face.

"I don't." Emily stuck her tongue out at Jacob.

"If you didn't have a skeleton, you'd have a hard time standing," I pointed out.

Emily thought about that for a minute. "Well, my skeleton isn't gross."

"Hey, Momma, somebody's here." Jacob swung his hand up and pointed out the front window with his 'bony' finger.

Leaves swirled around the black BMW parked in the driveway. The driver's side door opened and a long, khaki-covered leg stepped out of the car. The tall man stood and took off the dark glasses that covered his eyes. The October breeze ran its fingers through his blond hair and pressed the silk of a hunter-green shirt against his chest. A goatee covered his prominent chin. He belonged on a magazine cover, not on my doorstep.

Derek looked up and saw me staring at him through the window. He waved and gave me a crooked grin. My heart fluttered like his hair.

Everything grew hazy and gray around me, and my stomach flipped like it did when he came to pick me up for dates years ago. I hadn't felt that girlish flutter in a long time. I focused on Derek's face, the face of my first love, and moved in slow motion as I reached for the door handle.

You can't open the door to temptation and not expect it to come waltzing in. My mother's voice echoed in my mind. But it was Derek. Years of laughing together, hiking, stargazing, studying, all the joyous freedoms of youth flashed through my mind. I'd spent so many moments with him. I missed him and the times we spent together. How could I turn away such a dear, old friend? I needed to talk to him first, tell him to stop his foolish behavior. But we could be friends.

I gripped the doorknob, put a surprised smile on my face, and opened the door.

"Hi, gorgeous," he said, and gave me that crooked smile.

I cleared my throat and somehow found my voice, then batted the compliment away with my hand. "Quit talking to yourself. People will think you're nuts."

He entered the house, walking past me. The smell of musk and spice lingered behind him. He turned and held out a single-stemmed rose.

"Oh, Derek. You really shouldn't have." I remembered the rose and delicate vase in the garbage can, and with that memory came the guilt I felt over my fight with Jon.

"I had to," he said. "For old times' sake."

I never thought I would hear his voice again. It almost brought tears to my eyes. "Yeah. Old times," I echoed.

"I see you still have the Civic," Derek said, pointing over his shoulder at my car in the driveway. "I figured that thing would be junked by now."

"It's amazing how long old things can last." As the words left my mouth, I wished I could suck them back in. I dreaded the way he could interpret those words. He flashed his crooked smile again.

I slipped into hostess mode and offered him the sofa. He sat down and rested his right ankle on his left knee. Slowly, he looked around the room, taking in the pictures of the children, a large picture of Jon and me next to the eastern temple doors, a large picture of the Savior watching over Jerusalem.

"Can I get you something to drink?" I asked.

"Water's fine."

I went to the kitchen to get his glass of ice water. My hand shook slightly as I pressed the glass against the ice dispenser in the fridge.

"Who's that man, Mommy?" Emily asked.

"Um, he's just a man that I went to school with a long time ago," I whispered.

"You went to school?" Emily was incredulous.

"Yes. That's where I learned about skeletons." I smiled at her and went back to the living room.

Emily took the Halloween ad from Jacob and he chased her up to her bedroom.

"Emily, don't tease your brother," I called after her.

"Wow, you're a mom," Derek mused.

"Yep. I've got three," I admitted.

"Well, you look great," he said, glancing at my jeans and slightly stained T-shirt. I felt uncomfortable seeing him look at me. "And I like your house." He looked around. "It's just the way I imagined it would be."

"Really?" I sat in the lounge chair across the room from him.

"Yeah. You used to carry a picture of Jesus in your wallet. Remember?"

I'd forgotten, but his words brought the memory back. "Yeah. I can't believe you remember that though."

"I remember everything." His voice was so tender, but he looked around the room again to avoid my eyes. He folded his arms in front of him. The Derek I knew only did that when he was nervous.

"So, what are you doing here anyway? I mean, all these years without a word, and suddenly you're sending me a two-karat diamond ring and roses, and now you're visiting my home."

"It's your ring." He smiled, his teeth gleaming.

"*Was*. It *was* my ring. If you recall, I gave it back to you. You've really messed things up you know. My husband and I had the worst fight of our marriage because of you."

Derek looked at me with a dreadfully straight face. "Usually when you fight with someone, it's because you've been holding back your pain for a long time. I know you. If you fought with your husband, it's because you wanted to. I was just a catalyst." His words rang uncomfortably close to true. Panic rose in my throat. He leaned forward as if shortening the distance between us by a couple of inches would make me believe him better. "I know you. I can tell you haven't changed."

How could he know me? He'd been absent from my life for too long. Derek had nothing to do with the children I bore, the poverty Jon and I endured while he finished his doctorate, the sick children, the car problems, or the moments of bliss. Could he know me because he loved the awkward teenager I once was?

"So why are you fighting?" he asked.

"I'm not sure I'm comfortable talking about this, Derek. I mean, you're not a marriage counselor."

"No, but I've been to a few of them." He cleared his throat.

"Really? You were married?"

"Twice."

The news surprised me. Apparently he'd done some living that had nothing to do with me too. "Twice? But you're not married now."

"No. I haven't been married for five years."

"But you were married twice?" I tried to do the math in my head.

"After you broke up with me, I went to New York and married a girl I'd known for a month. It lasted about six months then I married someone else. She left me because I was a drunk," he admitted.

"A drunk? You?" Derek never touched liquor in high school. I couldn't imagine him with a drinking problem.

"Then I went into rehab. While I was there, I rediscovered my passion." He grinned and fixed his eyes on me.

I wondered if he was referring to me and I squirmed in my seat.

"Remember how much I loved architecture? I doodled pictures of houses and made up basic blueprints and stuff like that. Well, I decided to become an architect."

"You're kidding! Good for you!" I smiled, mostly out of relief that his passion involved something other than me.

"Yeah. Remember the plans we made for our dream house?" he asked.

I gasped as the memory flashed in my mind. "The one with the sky roof?"

"And the balcony." He smiled and nodded. "I'm still finishing my degree, but I wanted it to be my first project, so I hired someone licensed to help me build it."

"You built our dream house?" I felt a sense of envy creep through me for whoever got to live in that home. I also felt a deep longing to see it.

"I did. Simms is my contractor, and my friend," he explained.

"Simms is the guy with the goatee?"

"The one you got arrested, yeah."

"He's known as 'the stalker' around here. Why was he snooping around my house?" I asked.

"He was trying to get me to talk to you. I told him about the house and why I wanted to build it so badly. Simms thinks I should show you our dream, now that it's real. To be honest, I was too embarrassed to even contact you after you sent your ring back. I thought you didn't want to have anything to do with me."

His eyes looked so tender and vulnerable that I couldn't admit that he was right. When I sent the ring back, part of me hoped to never hear from him again. But he sat there in front of me, warm, tender, and complimentary. He'd built our dream house. After all those years, he'd remembered.

"It's good to see you again, Derek." I flashed a soft smile at him.

"It's good to see you too." His eyes sparkled. They were the same eyes I'd looked into for hours on end. The same eyes that made my knees weak when I was young.

"So why aren't you married now?" I asked, trying to shake the misty sense of reverie.

"Well, after I got out of rehab I dated a girl pretty seriously for a while. She wasn't a member of the Church, and didn't have any religious tendencies. I guess I was looking for something more than she had to offer me, something I'd want forever. Something like what you've got." He pointed at the wedding picture hanging on the wall.

I nodded. A mixture of regret and relief came over me. I still cared for Derek, and knowing that he had found his way back to the gospel eased my mind far more than I expected it to. Simultaneously, the question I'd voiced to my mother haunted me. What would have happened if I'd stuck with Derek?

"So, would you like to see the house?" Derek asked.

"I would love to," I answered before I thought about what he was asking.

He beamed. "Really? Well, let's go. Can you go now?"

"Oh, I can't go now. Emily has kindergarten in about an hour."

Derek nodded. "Well, maybe another time."

He looked at me like he was memorizing my face. I smiled and felt my cheeks warm.

"I'll let you take care of your family." He stood and set his full glass of ice water on the coffee table.

"Here, I'll walk you to the door." I walked a step behind him until he turned around. We stood a foot apart. I could smell his musky cologne.

"It's so good to see you, Lia. Here's my card." He pulled a business card from his shirt pocket and handed it to me. "That address is to the dream house. I'm living there right now. And that phone number is for my cell. Call me anytime you want to talk, even if it's just to hear another adult's voice."

I took the card and slipped it in the back pocket of my jeans. I had no intention of ever calling his number. I knew that would be inappropriate. But it would be unkind to reject the card.

With a swift step forward, Derek put his arms around my waist and held me close. I gingerly returned his embrace and realized his rose was still clasped in my fingers.

Just as swiftly, he pulled away and opened the door. When he was out on the porch, he turned to look at me and smiled again.

As I walked to the kitchen, I pressed the soft rose petals to my nose and breathed their sweet scent. The delicate vase sat in the garbage can. I lifted the vase and threw the wilted rose away, replacing it with the new, just-blooming one.

The rose stood on our kitchen table, fresh and fragrant. I remembered the look on Jon's face the day we argued, the way he tried to look at me around the rose. As I stared at it there on the table, anxiety crept into my heart. Was there any truth to what Derek said? Did I want to fight with Jon? There was still the issue of Ashley. I shook away the question. It probably was all in my imagination. If I wanted to fight with Jon, Ashley was just another way for my mind to provide an excuse.

Katie tugged at my pant leg and reached for me. I picked her up and held her, let her little head rest on my shoulder. In minutes she slept soundly. I set my hand on her back and felt her slow, steady breath.

Feeling my baby in my arms was like touching reality. With each breath Katie drew, I became less aware of the lingering scent of Derek's cologne. Eventually, I pried my thoughts from the mansion we'd designed together and the coordinates for that mansion burning a hole in my back pocket. I focused on the task at hand. Emily had a half hour before we had to leave for school.

The phone rang, and startled me. I wondered for a moment if it was Derek. Jon's voice thrilled me and filled me with guilt. He never called during the day.

"Hey, you. How's everything with my little family?"

"Oh, we're fine." I knew I had to tell Jon about Derek's visit. I'd learned my lesson about keeping secrets from Jon when I confessed my news about Derek's letter. Of course, he still didn't know about the ring. I shook my head. Telling him such things over the phone while he was at work would be brutal.

"Well, I was wondering if you might be able to find someone to watch the kids tonight, and you could come to the rehearsal with me," Jon inquired.

"Who could I ask? It's family night, so I can't ask anyone from the ward," I thought out loud.

"Would your mom be too put out? She could have a family night with her grandkids," Jon suggested.

"That's a good idea. I'll check with her."

"Cool. I hope you can come with me. I want you to see how I'm spending all my time." I could tell by the sound of his voice that he was smiling in that soft, romantic way of his.

I loved that he wanted me with him. I loved that he was smiling.

"I'll call Mom right now."

As I hung up the phone, I saw the rose blooming on the table. It was beautiful, but I didn't need it. I also didn't have the heart to throw it away. Jon thought it was all in the garbage. I was certain he wouldn't mind if I took the vase out and gave it and the new rose to someone else. Missy would appreciate it, I knew. And I needed to visit her anyway. I'd take the rose to Missy and tell Jon everything that night.

I called Mom and made the babysitting arrangements. She was happy to have a family home evening with little kids again. Then we piled in the car to take Emily to school.

Sins and Satellites

———————❧———————

Missy sat in her hospital bed with a magazine lying open on her lap, but she wasn't reading. She stared into the silence of the dim room. I hated hospitals. And from the look on Missy's face, she wasn't too happy there either.

"Hey, you."

Missy looked at me with a start, then a weak smile.

"I thought you'd be out of here by now. Your mom said they're keeping you at least another night."

Missy sighed and rubbed her belly. Now that I knew she was pregnant, I could see how much rounder she was. She really couldn't hide it anymore.

"Maybe longer. They say I've got preeclampsia or toxemia. Really high blood pressure. Lots of vomiting. Swelling." She held her hand out in front of her and looked at her swollen fingers.

"They say it's really dangerous for me and the baby. I have to stay in bed."

She leaned her head back on the pillow.

"Well, staying in bed isn't all bad. I'd like to stay in bed for a while." I sat in one of the chairs against the wall. Derek's rose in its delicate vase rested in my hand.

"It's not fun when you have so much to think about." Her eyes teared.

"Well, here's something to cheer you up. Isn't it pretty?" I set the frosted vase on the table in front of Missy, next to her tray full of untouched food.

"It is pretty. Thank you." Missy wrapped shaking fingers around the vase and lifted the flower to her nose briefly.

I sat back in my chair and watched Missy reach for a tissue and dab at her bloodshot eyes.

"I'm sorry. I can't quit crying." She blew her nose.

"It's understandable, Missy. I'd probably be crying too."

"My doctor is trying to be really open with me, and he's scaring me to death. He says my son will have low birth weight and his lungs won't be fully developed. They've got me on steroids to help his lungs, because they don't think I'll carry him long enough. He could have all kinds of problems, even retardation. And we'd both be in better shape if I'd come in for prenatal care. He's really making me feel guilty for that. Like I don't have enough to feel guilty about."

Missy was no longer my little Beehive. She'd grown up. Too fast. I felt helpless, and watching her there, so deep in her sorrow, all I could do was cry with her.

"My mom and dad are so shocked, they don't know what to say around me anymore. They come to visit, and the first thing they do is turn on the TV. But I'm not interested in TV. Most of the time, I just sit here and think." She looked out the window at the cloudy sky.

I took a deep breath. I had to ask. "What about the father, Missy? Does he know?"

"Oh, he knows. I told him I was pregnant the day he broke up with me. That's why he broke up with me. He asked not to be on the birth certificate. He wants nothing to do with me or the baby. He's going to school in California, and he's completely written me off."

"I hope you got that in writing. I think you need his permission to put the baby up for adoption, don't you?" I asked.

Missy's eyes moistened and she looked at me with her mouth dropped open in shock. She rubbed her swollen belly and looked away.

"The Church supports adoption, Missy. You know that, don't you?"

Missy nodded but didn't look at me. "I can't think about that yet. I just want to have this baby. And I want him to live." Her green eyes, swollen and red from crying, looked so sad, so lost. I'd never seen eyes so sad in my life.

"The bishopric stopped by for a while last night," she said thoughtfully.

"Really?" I looked down at Missy's hand in mine and felt her shake as a fresh wave of emotion moved her.

"Yeah. Bishop Ames was so nice to me. He gave me a blessing and told me that the Lord can turn our greatest sins into His greatest miracles if we're willing to work with Him and forsake our sin."

For the first time since I entered the room, I saw a glimmer of the Missy I knew. Her lips twitched into a small, but promising smile as she asked, "Do you believe that?"

"Yes, I do." I squeezed her hand.

"I do too." She nodded and sighed. "So even though I don't know what I'm going to do, I know I'm going to do the right thing. I'm going to pray. I'm going to listen to everyone's advice. And with the Lord's help, everything will be all right." She smiled weakly and turned her face toward the window.

"Missy," I said quietly, trying to be as gentle as I could, "this baby needs a daddy. You know that, right? Giving him a mom and a dad is the right thing."

"Bishop Ames wants me to talk to someone from LDS Social Services in a couple of days." Missy shook her head and closed her eyes as tight as she could. "Part of me doesn't want to give my baby up. I may not have planned on him, but he's a part of me. I've got my parents and some good friends. I think I could raise him on my own."

I sat back in my chair. The thought of giving up one of my children was unbearable. But I was blessed with a husband who loved my children as much as I did. My thoughts flashed to Jane and every other parent like her. No wonder Jane was having a hard time with Missy's pregnancy.

I didn't quite know what to say. I knew what the right choice for Missy and her baby was, but in the end it was Missy's decision. All I could do was make my suggestions and support her. So instead of speaking, I watched Missy get control of her emotions.

She eventually pried open her eyes and pinched the bridge of her nose. "Man, I've got a headache."

"You look tired too. I'm gonna go now." I stood up, still holding her hand.

"Are you sure? You can stay longer if you want to." She looked up with weary eyes.

"I have to go. I'm going to one of Jon's rehearsals tonight. It starts soon."

"Okay," Missy said. She looked grateful for my visit, but equally grateful that I was leaving. "Thanks so much for coming. It was good to talk to you."

"Anytime, Missy. You've got my number, right?" I asked.

"Yeah, I do. And thanks for the rose."

"No problem. I'm glad you like it, and I hope it makes you feel better."

Missy lifted the rose and smelled it again, smiling softly as she waved good-bye. I found comfort knowing that Derek's gift brought someone happiness instead of wasting away in my garbage can.

The rehearsals for *Much Ado* were held in the Babcock, a small theater in the basement of Pioneer Memorial Theater. As I slipped in the back of the room, I saw Jon sitting near the front, talking to a thin man with long blond hair. They each bit into a burger as they reached a lull in their conversation, and Jon looked up at me. I was so relieved to see him talking with someone other than Ashley.

"Lia! I was beginning to wonder if you were coming." Jon stood and smiled as I walked down the aisle toward him.

"Sorry. I decided to stop by the hospital and see Missy on my way." I sat in the row behind the thin, long-haired man and Jon so that I could see between their shoulders.

"Oh, how is she?" Jon picked a bag of fast food off the floor and handed it to me as he spoke.

"She's not great. But she's hopeful. That's good."

"I hope your burger isn't cold. We decided not to wait for you. We like to be finished with our food by the time the students get here. It's hard to direct while your mouth is full," Jon said with a smirk.

The thin man nodded his head as he wiped his face with a paper napkin.

"Oh, I'm sure it's fine," I said, as I pulled the burger from the bag. It was a little cold.

"Oh, forgive me. Lia, this is Mark Stratford. Mark, this is my wife, Lia."

"Pleased to meet you." He extended his hand and I took it. He shook it warmly and smiled. A bit of lettuce covered one of his teeth.

We finished our food and a few students slipped into the theater. They read their lines in different areas of the stage, lifting their voices in that almost foreign language that my husband spoke fluently. I sat there, just behind Jon, separate from their language and their experience. Jon laughed and joked with them easily.

Then I noticed I was the only woman in the room. There was a time in my life when such an experience would have been fun, a chance to flirt ruthlessly with everyone. But any of my social gifts left me with the birth of my children. I longed for a little child on my lap. At least then I would know where to direct my attention. And I knew I would get some attention in return.

Mark stood to begin the rehearsal. He introduced me, and I felt my face flush as all the boys looked at me. Then he began the rehearsal. "Gentlemen, let's begin with Benedick's soliloquy."

A handsome young man with shoulder-length blond hair and deep brown eyes leaned back in a chair and began.

"I do much wonder that one man, seeing how much another man is a fool when he dedicates his behaviors to love, will, after he hath laughed at such shallow follies in others, become the argument of his own scorn by falling in love; and such a man is Claudio."

I was already lost. I'd expected to see Ashley there, either on the stage or flirting with Jon. I leaned forward and tapped Jon on the shoulder. He leaned his head back but didn't take his eyes off of the young man, who continued speaking about a "fife" and a "tabor."

"Where's Ashley?" I whispered with an edge of sarcasm, like a sister teasing her brother about his crush.

"She's not in this scene, so she didn't have to come tonight," he whispered back. He'd been happy before, but as he responded, he got a hurt look on his face that I hadn't seen since our argument, and I regretted mentioning her name. I slumped back in my seat.

I was ready to tell Ashley what I thought of her, or at least drape my arms around Jon as often as possible just to stake my claim with her as a witness. Her absence disappointed me more than I thought possible. Then I wondered if Jon had asked me to come to the rehearsal that night because he knew Ashley wouldn't be there. Either he didn't want me to confront her, or he didn't want me to see them together. Somehow, that idea cheapened the evening. I felt like a stand-in for Ashley.

"Very good, Neil." Mark clapped a couple of times then coaxed the other boys onto the stage. "Okay, now let's get on with the scene here. Just to set up your motivation, this is an afternoon with the guys. They're together, laughing over a couple of drinks. And Tim here is singing the song about how women should lighten up and just let men be men, and not get so emotional about everything."

A couple of the guys on stage chuckled.

Mark turned back and looked at me. "No offense, of course."

"Of course," I said. But I was already irritated. At that point, I really wondered why Jon had invited me.

> *"Sigh no more, ladies, sigh no more!*
> *Men were deceivers ever,*
> *One foot in sea, and one on shore;*
> *To one thing constant never.*
> *Then sigh not so,*
> *But let them go,*
> *And be you blithe and bonny,*
> *Converting all your sounds of woe*
> *Into Hey nonny, nonny."*

The boy Mark had called Tim sang the simple tune with a sweet, tenor voice. I loved his voice, but I hated the song.

> *"Sing no more ditties, sing no more,*
> *Of dumps so dull and heavy!*
> *The fraud of men was ever so,*
> *Since summer first was leavy,*
> *Then sigh not so,*
> *But let them go,*
> *And be you blithe and bonny,*
> *Converting all your sounds of woe*
> *Into Hey nonny, nonny."*

The fraud of men. I remembered the feelings I had when I first caught Jon looking at Ashley. I couldn't forget Missy's pain with a boyfriend who broke up with her because he got her pregnant and couldn't stand the responsibility. And Shakespeare wrote a song about the fraud of men and how women should just sit back and let them be jerks. I didn't want to hear it anymore. I felt a surge of anger toward the male gender at that moment and was keenly aware I was surrounded by the enemy.

"Jon, where's a rest room?" I leaned forward and whispered in his ear as sweetly as I could, trying to hide my feelings.

"You go in the main hall just out this door and turn left. I think the ladies' rest room is in a little hall to your left." Jon took notes about the song the curly-headed boy sang, and he didn't look up at me or even lift his pencil from his notepad as he answered my question.

I found the rest room and splashed water on my face. I was being irrational. What did some silly song in a silly play matter?

And yet, I knew it mattered. It mattered because Jon loved those silly plays, and he thought about them so often. More often than he thought about me.

As I headed back to the theater, determined to keep cool and not let things bother me so much, I heard that giggle. The laugh I'd heard from the other side of my husband's closed office door.

The door was open, and Ashley had taken my seat behind my husband. She leaned forward and looked over his shoulder at the young men as they ran through their lines. Their faces glowed and twisted with the words, especially Neil's, the blond boy with brown eyes. He reacted to everything the other boys said and sent Ashley into fits of laughter.

"Isn't he just great?" She put her hand on Jon's shoulder and laughed.

The blond boy hammed it up even more, competing for her attention. The other three boys left the stage area, and the blond boy spoke alone again: "But doth not the appetite alter? A man loves the meat in his youth that he cannot endure in his age. Shall quips and sentences and these paper bullets of the brain awe a man from the career of his humor? No, the world must be peopled. When I said I would die a bachelor, I did not think I should live till I were married."

Ashley laughed again at Neil's expression. Her soft curls slipped across her shoulders and down her back toward her thin waist as she turned her head, revealing her perfect profile. She clapped her hands and the blond boy bowed. All of the male eyes in the room were on her. They gravitated to her, like satellites tied by an invisible string to a celestial body.

Jon looked at her too, but he eventually glanced over her shoulder and saw me standing in the doorway. He looked down at his notebook.

Mark stood and made his way to the stage area, applauding as he walked. "Very good, all of you. See how much it helps to have an audience?"

I wasn't sure whether Mark referred to me or to Ashley, who leaned back in her seat and twisted a strand of hair.

"What did you think, Lia? Aren't they great?" Jon asked, looking back at me again.

They all looked back at me, including Ashley. The courage I'd built up as I thought of telling Ashley off melted in the public eye.

"Oh, yeah. They're great. But I have to leave. No offense or anything."

"Where do you have to go?" Jon's eyebrows furrowed as he looked at me. He knew I didn't have anywhere to go but home. And he knew my mother had the kids.

"Well, Katie seems to be getting a cold. And she was really grumpy when I left her with the sitter." I exaggerated a little. Katie did have the sniffles, and she was grumpy when I left.

I slunk into the room, hoping everyone would stop watching me, and I picked my purse up from the floor at Ashley's feet. Her long legs were bare and smooth sticking out from beneath a short denim skirt.

"Good to see you again." She smiled down at me.

My expression must have shown how angry I felt, and Jon must have seen it, because he stood quickly and took me by the arm.

"I'll be right back, Mark. I'll just walk my wife to her car."

He escorted me from the room, never loosening his grip.

As soon as we left the building, Jon let go.

"You were going to pick a fight with her. Right there in front of the students and Mark. My word, Lia, are you in the fourth grade again? You've been acting so crazy lately, I don't know what to think," Jon stammered.

I watched him pace the sidewalk. The light of the streetlamps glinted off of his gray-streaked hair. He pinched the bridge of his nose, and his eyebrows twitched.

Gently, I put my hands on his face and rubbed his eyebrows with my thumbs.

"She intimidates me, Jon," I said honestly.

He grabbed my wrists and held my hands near his chest. "Why? Why on earth does she intimidate you?"

"She's beautiful. She has more in common with you than I do. You find her attractive, along with every male ever born, evidently."

"Does it matter that every male ever born finds her attractive? Does it really matter? There are men around that you find attractive, and you don't see me throwing a fit over that," he reminded me.

I remembered the thrill I felt when I saw Derek on my doorstep, his green silk shirt rippling in the breeze. His eyes penetrating mine. That grin.

My hands flattened against Jon's chest and I rested my forehead on them. He wrapped his arms around me and kissed the top of my head.

"And you have more in common with me than anyone else ever will. We have children together, remember? What's more important than that?" Jon squeezed me. "You have absolutely nothing to worry about. There is no chance you could ever lose me to anyone."

I looked up at his blue eyes. I'd forgotten how blue they were. I could drown in such pacific eyes.

"Well, at least you're admitting you think she's attractive. I guess that's a start." I smoothed his cream shirt against his chest.

"So what happens when I admit I'm attracted to you? And I don't just mean I think you're pretty. I mean I'm *attracted* to you. Like a magnet." He pulled me close to him and I rested my cheek against his chest.

"Oh, you're not attracted to me anymore," I sighed as I squeezed him. "I'm just your wife. I'm not a tall, thin, redheaded tease."

He stepped back and tilted my head up so I could look him in the eye. His face was smooth and serious. "Well, I want my wife, not a tall, thin, redheaded tease."

I smiled. "Good. That's as it should be. You remember that."

"Lia, I remember you. I always remember you."

He kissed me there in the light of the streetlamp. Kissed me like he was attracted to me, like we were two college students deep in infatuation. And as he pulled away, I giggled. I hadn't giggled like that in a long time.

"I remember you too," I said.

We stood there for a moment, holding each other in the cool air. He spoke after a while, quiet and hopeful so he wouldn't ruin the mood. "I have to go back in, Lia. Are you coming with me?"

"Oh, no. I'd be too embarrassed, what with my grand exit and all," I confessed.

"We'll sit in the back of the room. And if anyone asks, we'll say we called to check on Katie and everything's fine. Of course, I'm assuming Katie isn't really sick." Jon raised one eyebrow.

"She's fine," I admitted. "I just didn't want to watch that girl flirt with you anymore."

"She's not flirting with me. Not as bad as you seem to think she is."

"I'm a girl. I know when a girl is flirting."

"Well, I'm a guy. I know when it works."

He took my hand in his, and we walked in the building. We slipped into the back of the theater and quietly took two seats near the door. Jon walked past Ashley and picked up his notebook, then brought it to our new seats.

Ashley watched him walk in front of her, then looked at me with a smile. I searched her face in the darkness for a hint of derision, challenge, or jealousy. But it was just a cordial smile. She turned her face toward the stage as the boys started the scene again, this time implementing the directions Mark had given them. Jon put his arm around me and we sat back to watch the rehearsal together.

When the rehearsal ended, Jon and I walked to my car. The air chilled and I pulled my jacket around me. With Jon by my side, I almost understood what was going on during the rehearsal, though I would have to look up some words in the dictionary when we got home.

"Why don't we meet at home, and we can go together to pick up the kids?" Jon suggested.

"That sounds good."

He kissed me and opened my door for me. After my seat belt was done and my door closed and locked, Jon turned and walked briskly toward his car.

I needed to tell him about Derek's visit, but I didn't want to. The pain of our argument was still just under the surface, and our time together that evening had been so wonderful after I got over my tantrum.

As the blocks flew past between the university and our home, I tried to think of a tactful way to bring it up. But one thing was certain—I wasn't going to keep it secret.

Jon pulled into the driveway next to me. He looked up and smiled. I took a deep breath and got out of the car.

When Jon sat in the driver's seat and I sat next to him, we backed out and headed for my parents' house.

"So how do you like Shakespeare now?" he queried.

"Well, I liked *Much Ado*. I can see why you like it. It's like a little puzzle for you to figure out, and I think you get a kick out of that."

"Yeah, that's part of it."

I folded my arms across my chest and looked out the window. I knew Jon would be upset, and I felt an unexplained need to protect Derek from Jon's temper.

"I got a visit from an old friend today," I started, then held my breath.

"Really? Who?" He kept his eyes on the road. The lights of oncoming traffic flickered across his face.

"Derek." I choked on his name, but managed to squeak it out.

The muscles in Jon's jaw flexed and his eyes hardened as he focused on the road. "He came during the day, when he knew I'd be working?" Jon's lips twitched with anger.

"He came this morning, right before you called," I confessed.

"Before I called? How come you didn't tell me then?"

"I wanted to figure out how to tell you because I knew you'd be upset." I watched his jaw clench and knew I'd been right.

"Of course I'm upset. This guy is a coward. He won't come around when I'm home because he can't stand to look me in the eye. Instead he has to work behind my back when you're vulnerable."

"I'm not exactly vulnerable. I can handle it." I looked out the window again. Jon was treating me like a child and it chafed me.

Jon sighed heavily. "Why did he come visit you, Lia? What did he say?"

"He apologized for the stalker. He's living in town now and the contractor who built Derek's house talked him into contacting me."

"I'm sure he had a terrible time," Jon said, his voice thick with sarcasm. "Derek just needed an excuse to get his foot in my door."

"He's had a hard life, Jon. I think we need to cut him some slack." I looked at Jon. "Since I broke up with him," I added, "he's had two failed marriages, and he had to go into rehab because he had a drinking problem."

His eyes softened.

"He said he wants something like what we have."

It was the wrong thing to say. Jon's expression hardened again and he flashed a bitter look at me.

"You mean he wants something like what *I* have," he retorted.

"He doesn't *want* me, Jon. He *needs* a friend," I said, trying to convince myself while I convinced Jon.

Jon's glare softened this time.

I rested my hand on his knee and smiled as sweetly as I could. "I love you, Jon. You have nothing to worry about."

He squeezed my hand. "Just be careful, okay? I don't like the way he's handled this situation. I don't like that he's done this behind my back, like he wants you to keep it all a secret."

"That's why I told you, Jon. I don't want to keep secrets from you." As I spoke, I remembered the ring.

"Speaking of not keeping secrets, there's one more thing." I held my breath as Jon glanced at me.

"When he sent the letter a while ago," I continued, "he sent my engagement ring with it. But I sent it back, and when he came to visit me I told him I was upset about the whole thing."

Jon shook his head and let go of my hand. "I don't like this, Lia. I don't like it a bit."

I folded my arms. The air hung heavy with tension and the window to my side fogged. I needed to draw the line, to tell Jon exactly how I would handle the situation so he wouldn't worry.

"I'm not going to call Derek even though he left me his number and told me to call him. But if he asks for my help, I think we should give it because it's the right thing to do." I counted on Jon's compassion. He'd never turned down someone who asked for help in his life, and neither had I.

"How about you tell him to find another friend, someone he doesn't have a history with? Everyone needs help occasionally, and I think everyone should get the help they need, but does he have to turn to you?"

No, I thought. *He doesn't.*

"And I really don't like him coming to the house when I'm not there. Don't let him in if he comes by again. You may have known this guy once, but you don't know him anymore. A lot can change in eight years."

I nodded. Jon was right. "I promise I won't let him in the house again."

Jon seemed to relax after that.

"Hey, if I can trust you with Miss Wiggle," I teased, "you can trust me with a recovering alcoholic." I slapped his leg playfully.

"A *rich* recovering alcoholic," he reminded me.

"He's too tall," I joked.

"He probably has a huge satellite dish in his yard, and nice, thick hair," he said with a smile as he picked up on my banter.

"Yeah, but it's not gray enough for my taste." I smiled and Jon smiled back.

"Seriously, Lia. Be careful." He looked me in the eye as we came to a stoplight, his forehead creased with worry.

"I will." I returned his steady gaze as I spoke. "I promise."

Anomalies

———◆———

The following Saturday morning I gathered the laundry to wash. I couldn't believe how much laundry we gathered with my husband and our three little kids. I emptied pants pockets and made a little pile of receipts on the dryer. On top of the little pile sat Derek's business card. I couldn't help but wonder what the house looked like, but I'd promised Jon I wouldn't contact Derek at all. I crumpled the card and tossed it in the trash.

The phone rang as I started the load.

"Hello?" I answered.

"I'm going to visit Alexis today. Do you want to come with me?" Anna spoke quickly, as usual, and papers shuffled in the background.

"I don't think she'd like that." I shook my head. "She's got something against me, and I can't figure it out."

"All the more reason to serve her. If she's got something against you, it's because she doesn't know you well enough." She sighed heavily. "We can see Missy too. I called Mary early this morning, and I guess things have gotten worse."

"Really?" I asked. "I was there a couple of days ago, and I thought she was doing better."

"I guess it's pretty serious. I don't know much about what's wrong, but they're not letting her out of the hospital until she has the baby," Anna's voice slowed with concern.

Missy would have plenty of time to think. I wondered if she knew, or if the doctors were keeping the news from her.

"Well, I'd love to see Missy," I said.

"Okay. I'll come get you at say, one? Kim can watch your kids."

"That would be great, thanks. See you at one."

I hung up the phone thinking about Missy, Alexis, and Anna's husband, Kim. Kim was from China with an accent so heavy I could hardly tell he spoke English. But when he arrived, the kind wisp of a man smiled wide at my children, nodded, and held them with gentle hands. Emily's radar detected a man she could speak to unceasingly, and she was quite content to have him stay.

Alexis lived in one of the apartments in the ward, at the opposite end of the complex from Jane. We climbed two flights of stairs to number 31, where two identical jack-o'-lanterns adorned the door, with the names "Evelyn" and "Jaqueline" perfectly penned beneath them. Anna rang the doorbell, and I stood behind her, wishing I could wait in the car.

When Alexis opened the door, I could hardly tell it was her. Without makeup, her face looked sallow and old. Her hair hung in a limp ponytail down her back, and her faded red T-shirt had a gray stain on its shoulder.

"Hi, Anna." Alexis hugged Anna, then looked up and saw me.

I cranked out a weak smile.

"Lia." She nodded her head and brushed stray strands of hair from her eyes.

"Please, come in." She backed out of the way and we entered her apartment. It surprised me how cluttered it was. I expected perfect Alexis to have a perfect home, everything in its proper place at all times, but empty Chinese-food cartons littered the kitchen table, books were scattered across the floor, and at least two weeks' worth of newspapers filled the corner of the room, still rolled up and bound with rubber bands.

"Where are your twins?" I asked.

"They're with my mother for the weekend. I needed a break." As she spoke, Alexis dropped in a recliner and offered us a seat on a worn, flowered couch.

"So, how is Isaac?" Anna started in.

I crossed my legs and planned to sit back and let the two of them talk. Alexis didn't want me there anyway, so I'd just pretend to be part of the couch.

"He's progressing well enough. They say he'll be able to come home next week, but he'll still have physical therapy sessions to go to and lots of meds to take. I'll pretty much be his nurse."

"I'm so sorry to hear that." Anna's face creased with concern.

Alexis nodded and glanced at me. I cranked out another smile.

"So, what can we do to help?" Anna asked.

Alexis looked straight at me. "Nothing."

I squirmed under her gaze.

"Come on, I know there's something we can do. How about we help you straighten up?" Anna stood and picked up a few books, then set them on the bookshelf.

"That's not necessary, Anna," Alexis said stubbornly. "I can manage."

"It's not a big deal, Alexis. It's what we're here for." She slid more books on the shelf, then stacked some magazines and placed them on the coffee table.

I lifted a few magazines from the floor near me.

"That's not necessary." Alexis grabbed the magazines from me and threw them on the coffee table.

"I'm sorry," I said, a little irritated.

"I don't need your help." Alexis pointed right at me.

"What have you got against me, Alexis?" I felt sincere, and did my best to show it in my voice. "Did I do something to offend you? Because I certainly didn't mean to if I did." I spoke meekly, trying to apologize.

"Did you offend me? Well, you're sarcastic. You make fun of me during my lessons. And then they call you as compassionate service leader! That's a joke. You don't even know how to think about someone besides yourself. You came here because Anna forced you to, I'm sure, and you sit there all smug like I'm just a waste of your time. What do you know about me anyway?" Alexis had counted my faults on her fingers, then tossed them at me with her accusatory question.

"Nothing, Alexis," I answered honestly. "I don't know anything about you because every time I've tried to learn anything you push me away."

"You're one of *those*, Lia." She ignored the answer to her question and continued to chastise me. "You're one of those people who has everything handed to them, and you can't see what you've got. You're selfish and blind, and yet you have everything that anyone could possibly want."

My patience ran thin, like watered-down paint. I'd tried to be kind to her. I'd tried to mend the fence. But she returned insults for my kindness.

"What makes you think that? Who do you think you are?" I kept my tone controlled though I leaned toward her, my hands clenching into fists at my side.

Anna grabbed my arm firmly. My heart thumped in my chest and I felt its beat in my head.

"And your daughter is just as spoiled as you are. Do you know how badly she teases my girls? She pulls their hair and runs away from them on the playground at school. She sits on the opposite side of the room from them when they go into Primary. I can see where she gets her arrogance," Alexis taunted, almost as if she were begging me to lose my temper.

No one in my life had ever talked to me that way. And try as I might, I couldn't imagine Emily acting that way toward anyone. Mention of my daughter hurt. She could offend me all she liked, but speaking poorly of Emily was a low blow.

"Are you sure you're talking about my Emily?"

"Oh yes, I'm sure," Alexis said as she picked up another stack of books and slammed them on the bookcase. "Obviously you don't even know your own child. Yet another thing you've been given that you don't appreciate."

I watched her, dumbfounded and growing angrier by the minute.

"I can clean up my own mess, thank you very much." Alexis stormed over to her kitchen table and stacked the food cartons, then slammed them into the garbage.

Tears collected, hot in my eyes, and I couldn't calm my heart. I tried to take deep breaths. Anna sat down on the couch, and pulled me down to sit next to her.

"Why do you feel this way about Lia? Come on, Alexis, let's get it all out in the open. You'll both feel better."

Alexis wiped the table off with a paper towel, then tossed it in the garbage. She turned to me with tears in her eyes.

"You don't even remember me, do you?"

I searched my memory for her face, her name, then I shook my head.

"I'm the forgotten. The nameless anomaly."

"What?" I vaguely remembered calling someone from Stargazers Club an anomaly.

"I went to high school with you. It really wasn't that long ago, about nine years, right? I remember, you dated Derek Sullivan."

"Yes," I admitted. I remembered him all too well.

"I'm still amazed you didn't marry him," Alexis scoffed.

"Well, our lives went in different paths." I still couldn't remember Alexis in high school. And her mention of Derek struck a tender nerve. I wished I hadn't set foot in her apartment.

"I asked Derek out once. I sent him a singing telegram during lunch. But you came to the table right after she started singing. Everyone looked at you like you were the most beautiful thing in the world. Derek went to that dance with me because I asked him first, which actually was nicer than what a lot of boys did to me, but he flirted with you the whole night when he thought I wasn't looking."

Suddenly I saw the face of the awkward young woman with braces and hardly any figure. She was the only other girl in the Stargazers Club, but she didn't have any friends. Not even me.

That night, at the dance, Derek looked at me over her shoulder. He couldn't take his eyes off of me, like I was an award he'd longed for, worked for, and finally earned; all he needed to do was claim me. The tears slipped, and the pounding in my chest turned to an ache for the young woman in my memory, for the worn but beautiful woman sitting before me.

"You got along with all the guys. You made the geeks feel like they were popular because they looked at the stars with you. You made the popular guys feel like you were out of their league. You dated the nicest, richest guy in school. And you were smart. You had it all.

"I must admit, I felt some satisfaction when I found out Derek went to New York without you. But somehow, you still did okay. You married an established, good man, who worships the ground you walk on. You had three kids who adore you and bend over backwards to please you. You didn't have to declare bankruptcy and live with your mother for three years, or go through two miscarriages and infertility treatments and finally give birth to twins, only to have your husband cheat on you, get in a car accident, and then end up an invalid," Alexis said with a heavy heart.

The silence of the room ate at me. Part of me wanted to leave the discomfort. Another part wanted to embrace Alexis and let her tears wet my shoulder. The lines on her face were lines of sorrow, pain, and endurance. In the weeks previous, I had imagined the pain of betrayal, seen the pain of infertility in Jane, seen the pain of sin in Missy. I didn't really know what any of these women felt. My life had been relatively painless. But at that moment I saw the burden that Alexis carried, and knew with a stab of guilt that I put part of that burden on her.

I walked to the recliner where Alexis stood. She stepped back and braced herself for an attack, but I embraced her.

"I'm so sorry, Alexis. I was stupid. I didn't know."

She put her hands on my shoulders and pushed me away.

"I think you should leave now. I need to be alone. I need to rest." She wouldn't look at me, and I headed for the door. Anna followed me, hugging Alexis as she passed her. Alexis returned her embrace.

"Call if you need anything," Anna said.

"Thanks, Anna. I will."

Somehow I made it downstairs to the car. And when I finally sat down and clicked my seat belt on, I looked out the window at Alexis's apartment.

"I'm sorry about that. I had no idea she felt that way about you," Anna said, as she sat in the car.

"I had no idea she had reason to feel that way about me," I said thoughtfully.

Anna started the engine. Then she asked quietly, "What's an anomaly anyway?"

"It's something strange, different—weird." I looked away from Anna, out my window. "It's also an astronomical term. That's why we thought it fit her so well."

Anna didn't reply. But what could she say?

Anna backed the car from its parking space and we left the apartment complex. We reached a stop sign where the road home and the road to the hospital went in opposite directions.

"You still up to visiting Missy?" Anna asked.

"Sure," I said with a sigh. "Missy will be a relief after that."

Touchdowns and Cheerleaders

We weaved through the hospital to Missy's room. Alexis's voice rang in my ears, sharp and condemning. Occasionally, Anna glanced at me, but I ignored her. I was embarrassed about my adolescent behavior, and knowing that the Relief Society president witnessed my guilty discovery certainly didn't help.

Mary walked down the hall toward us, carrying a can of pop in one hand and a cup of ice in the other. She came to meet us before we reached Missy's room.

"Hi, Mary. How is everything?" Anna asked.

"Not so great. She's really swollen now. They've got her on a magnesium drip to keep her from having seizures, and it makes her even more nauseated than she already was. They've also got her on steroids to help develop the baby's lungs. She's in a very bad mood, and wants terribly to have the baby and just get the whole thing over with."

"Should we leave?" Anna was concerned at our timing.

"Oh no. I think it will do her good to see you. Just be aware, she's not her usual lovely self."

Mary's hair was unkempt, and she looked as if she had slept in her clothes.

"How are you, Mary? Are you holding up okay?" I asked. Looking at her, it was hard to believe this was the same jovial woman who wrapped her big arms around Jane and tossed one-liners. The bags under her eyes were more obvious. The gray in her hair progressed from a flash near her forehead to salt and pepper streaks everywhere. In one month's time she had aged five years.

"I just never expected this kind of trial, you know?" Her eyes blurred.

"Has Missy said anything about adoption yet?" I asked.

Mary drew a deep breath. "Not really. She's avoiding the discussion. But I think, judging by her actions, she wants me to raise him."

I searched Mary's face for a sign of how she felt about raising the baby, but she just looked bewildered.

"Can you do that?" Anna asked.

Mary shook her head. "I don't think I can. I'm ready to be a grandmother, not to start all over with diapers and no sleep, potty training—the whole thing. I'm not patient enough anymore. I don't have the energy. I can't be the kind of *mother* this baby needs."

Anna put her arm around Mary. "We're all praying for you."

"I know." Mary nodded and wiped her cheeks.

"God doesn't give us more than we can handle," Anna said as she pulled Mary to her.

"Yes, but He expects us to help each other. Thanks for helping me," Mary said as she returned Anna's embrace.

Missy's face was so swollen, I hardly recognized her. Her hands and feet were swollen too. She looked as if she had gained twenty pounds in one week.

Missy couldn't meet our eyes when we came in the room. Instead, she looked up at a BYU football game on the TV.

"We're about to score a touchdown," Missy said in a monotone voice. "That is, if our quarterback can get his act together."

Mary poured the pop in the cup of ice, and Missy took the cold cup and held it against her forehead.

"Is it warm in here?" Missy asked with irritation.

"No, sweetheart. It's just you." Mary folded the cover down and revealed Missy's hospital gown, which was stretched tightly over her belly, and her red, swollen legs.

"Figures," she replied.

"Hi, Missy. How are you holding up?" I sat in the chair next to her. She looked up, and her expression softened for a minute.

"I'm fat. I'm grouchy. All I want to do is sleep, but I can't get comfortable." She adjusted herself in the bed. "Plus, whatever it is they're giving me makes me sick. I wish this baby would just come out, and I could at least feel good again."

"They say that every day increases the baby's chance of survival by about four percent," Mary said, "so we've got to hold on as long as we can."

"We? I'm the one who's swollen, hot, and miserable!" Missy snapped.

Mary took a towel and tenderly wiped some sweat from Missy's forehead.

Missy looked up at her mother's face and gave her a weak smile.

"Hey, you want to see something gross?" Missy asked. Then she held her arm out in front of me and pressed her forefinger into her flesh. The pressure of her touch left an indentation in her skin.

"It'll take about thirty seconds for the dent to go away. Gross, huh?" Missy snorted.

BYU scored their touchdown and the crowd on the television cheered.

"You're lucky BYU isn't playing against the U today. I'd have to root for the U," I said.

"Oh," Missy gasped. "Traitor." Her eyes grew large, then she smiled.

"Well, kid, at least you've still got your sense of humor. A sarcastic one, but a sense of humor." I put my hand on hers and patted it gently.

"A little laughter goes a long way," Mary said.

BYU scored their extra point and we all cheered. Missy smiled as tears gathered and pinched out of the corners of her eyes.

"I'm glad you came," Missy whispered, her chin quivering.

"I'll cheer with you any day," I said.

"The counselors from LDS Social Services came yesterday." Missy spoke quietly. I had to lean in to hear her over the game.

"What did they say?" I asked.

"They talked about the Proclamation on the Family, and how the best situation for a child to grow up in is with a mother and a father. They encouraged me to put my baby up for adoption."

"And how do you feel about that?" I asked, hoping for a positive response.

Missy looked at Mary, who smiled softly and opened a can of pop for herself.

"I don't know how I feel about anything right now. I told them to go away and let me think."

Tears pooled in Missy's eyes. "I have a wonderful family. It's weird right now because I've messed everything up, but I know my mom and dad will be there for me, and my baby will be loved in our home."

Mary let tears fall freely down her round face.

"How can I let my baby go?" Missy rubbed her belly absentmindedly. "How can I go through all of this and go home without a baby?"

She leaned her head back in her pillow and covered her face with her hands. Mary turned her back to us and sniffled quietly. I pulled tissues from the nearest dispenser for myself and for Anna.

"I feel him move inside of me, and I know he's part of me. I know he's mine. What if I gave him away and he grew up thinking I didn't love him? What if . . ."

Her voice trailed off as sobs shook her body. Mary turned back to Missy. Her face was red and wet. She leaned down and hugged Missy, kissing her forehead softly. Missy put her arms around her mother until her body stopped shaking.

I wiped tears from my face. It made me ache to watch the scene. Mother, daughter, and the small grandchild still wrapped in his mother's womb. I could only imagine the painful decision that lay before Missy.

"Missy, if you gave him up to a couple who wanted a baby more than anything else, they'd teach him that you gave him up because you loved him, because you wanted him to have a mom and a dad, the kind of family you were blessed enough to grow up in. What better gift can you give him? What better way can you prove that you love him?" I spoke gently, but I told the truth, knowing that Missy could accept or reject my words with a torrent of emotion.

Missy curled away from me, toward her mother. She cried again, deeply. Mary stroked her arm with a light touch and let her cry.

After the tears subsided, Missy slept. Occasionally, a small sob stirred her, but exhaustion kept her asleep.

Mary looked at me and whispered, "Thank you for saying that. You couldn't have put it more beautifully."

I nodded. "I hope it helps."

We watched the remaining few minutes of the football game. Missy slept as BYU scored their winning touchdown and the crowd cheered.

Pursuit of Perfection

"Missy's going through quite the trial, isn't she?" I commented to Anna after we'd started on our way home.

"She sure is. I wouldn't wish it on anyone. I guess that's why we keep telling these kids to do what's right. Imagine having to make such a decision."

I couldn't imagine it, not without getting closer to tears than I wanted to be. My arms ached to hold my children until I finally had to fold my arms across my chest, gripping my forearms with my cool fingers.

"I didn't mean to leave my kids for so long," I said as we rounded the corner onto my street.

Anna winked at me. "Don't worry about Kim. It's good for him."

We parked in front of my house after three hours of visiting with Alexis and Missy, and I was sure my kids were getting hungry. And when kids get hungry, they get grumpy.

Kim looked very glad to see us. He held the front door open as we walked up the porch steps, and I noticed a fruit punch stain on the front of his white T-shirt. I looked at Anna.

"You let him wear a white shirt when you knew he was going to babysit?" I teased Anna.

"Well, I don't have kids. I don't think about things like that," she explained.

"Were they good for you, Kim?" I asked hopefully.

"Ah, yes. Very good."

Toys cluttered the floor, and Jacob stood in the kitchen, turning the light on and off repeatedly. I got the feeling Kim was being generous in his assessment of their behavior.

Katie ran to me with her arms stretched wide. Jacob soon followed her. I kissed their sweet heads and held them close.

Anna and Kim left the house, and Emily waved at Kim from the open front door. As I watched Emily wave, I remembered everything that Alexis had said.

"Emily, sweetheart, let's talk." I sat on the couch and coaxed Emily to me.

"Okay, Mommy." Emily skipped over and sat up on my lap.

"Do you remember Evelyn and Jaqueline from church and from school?"

"Yes," she said.

"Well, why don't we have them over to play for a while soon? What do you say?"

"Okay."

"It's very important to be nice to them, because their daddy got hurt really bad."

"Okay."

She twisted her doll's hair and played with the eyes that opened and closed. I felt like she wasn't listening to me.

"And their momma went to school with me a long time ago, just like the man in the green shirt who came to our house the other day. Remember him?" I didn't mean to change the subject. Derek popped into my mind and I mentioned him without thinking about it.

"Yes. I didn't like him, Mommy."

"You didn't?" I asked in surprise.

"No." She shook her little head emphatically.

"Why?"

Emily shrugged her shoulders and wiggled to get off my lap.

Derek hadn't done anything that I could think of to make Emily not like him. I wondered why she would have a strong visceral reaction to him.

Thinking of the past made me want to look at my old yearbook. It had been a long time since I had seen the pictures and read the messages from the people I spent my youth with.

I pulled the blue book from the bookcase's bottom shelf and let it drop open to the page with Derek's message on it. I'd read it so many times after we broke up that the book naturally opened there. I skimmed through the words.

> *You are the most wonderful woman in the world. I can't wait to make you mine forever, to watch our children grow, and to watch our grandchildren. We graduate tomorrow, and leave behind us a life we have shared to begin a better life. A life where we will never be separated. I will always love you and care for you, my rose. See you tomorrow.*
>
> *Love, D.*

It only took a few months after he wrote that message for him to change so much that I hardly recognized him. My mother always said that Derek would have changed anyway, and it was better he did it before I made a huge mistake and married him. I shook my head and turned the page.

Our Stargazers Club picture had us lined up in front of a map of the night sky during the winter. Orion was just over Alexis's head. She smiled weakly at the camera, covering her braces as much as possible without wearing a glum expression. Her hair was frizzy and unruly. I remembered teasing her once or twice about her hair too.

I glanced through the list of names, and there she was, on the third row, left side. Alexis Woods. I was on the other side of the picture, on the front row, sitting on some boy's lap. I didn't even remember the boy.

I looked long and hard at my face, cheek to cheek with the unknown boy. My clothes were stylish, for the time. My hair lay just where I wanted it to lay. As I looked at myself, I knew that Alexis was right. I did get everything I wanted. All my life. As an only child, I never even had to share my parents. They doted on me and probably spoiled me. I dated every boy I was ever attracted to. Eventually, I married the English teacher I had a crush on.

The boy who held me on his lap looked at me with his eyebrows cocked and a sly, crooked grin on his face. I got that look a lot back then. It was the same look Ashley got from every boy at the rehearsal.

Ashley. Remembering her filled me with dread and anger. Almost hate. Why did I hate her so much? I thought of her flirting with all the guys at the rehearsal, then looked at the picture of me in the Stargazers Club.

She was me. I was Ashley. And Ashley gets everything she wants, just like I did.

The front door opened, and Jon walked in.

He startled me and I jumped, slamming the book shut.

"Strolling down memory lane?" he asked, looking away from me as he took his overcoat off and hung it on the coatrack near the door.

Tension hung in the air as if lightning had just struck. He must have thought I was thinking about Derek.

"Remember Alexis Smith from our ward? She has twins the same age as Emily."

He rubbed one of his eyebrows. "Oh, yeah. Is she Isaac's wife?"

"Yes," I replied.

Jon nodded. "Yeah, I remember them."

"Well, we went to high school together. I didn't even remember her, so I had to look her up."

He smiled with relief and compassion. "A lot of kids went to your high school. It's hard to remember them all."

"She was in Stargazers Club with me, Jon. I should have remembered her." I felt like crying long and hard until I couldn't cry anymore. But I didn't.

"We all forget things and people from our past. It takes energy to remember, and sometimes we just don't have the energy to remember everything. Don't beat yourself up over it."

"She sure remembers me. She hates me," I lamented.

Jon sat on the floor behind me and wrapped his arms around me.

"How could anyone hate you?" He kissed my cheek.

"I wasn't very good to her. Right now, I'm not very fond of me either."

"You're not? Well, I adore you."

"Why?"

"Because you're my wife." He kissed my neck.

"No, I'm serious." I turned to face him, and locked my eyes onto his. "Why do you love me? I'm nothing special."

Jon returned my steady gaze and brushed my hair behind my ears. "I love you because you're not perfect now, but you want to be."

The tears finally started to fall. I let them come. They splashed on my closed yearbook.

"I think you see more in me than is really there," I said without looking at him.

"Well, that's better than seeing less than is really there."

I looked up. He stared at the splash marks on the blue binding. His thinning hair was grayer than I remembered it. Dark rings shadowed his eyes, and small wrinkles formed along his forehead. My heart tightened in my chest, and I realized that I underestimated him. Even just the thought that he might desire Ashley, or do anything inappropriate with her, betrayed him. I knew Jon, and he wouldn't do anything like that because he wouldn't allow himself to do it. He would keep his covenants.

Jon wasn't perfect. But he definitely wanted to be. And he worked at it every day.

When Bishop Ames set me apart as compassionate service leader, he counseled me to turn to the Lord and use faith in everything I did. But over the past weeks, my prayers had been trite, repetitive, hollow. I wasn't perfect. I wanted to be. But I wasn't doing anything about it. If there was any failure in my marriage, it was my failure. If there was failure in my calling, it was my fault.

"How did I get so lucky to have you?" I put my arms around his neck and cried on his shoulder. He rose to his knees, pulling me up with him, and held me close. It was as if he knew what was going on in my mind. He held me so tightly, I couldn't tell where I ended and he began. My body quivered as I cried.

"Shh. It's okay. Everything's okay."

"I feel so guilty, Jon."

"Why? Don't feel guilty," he said gently.

"I underestimate everyone. Even you. I'm sorry."

He looked at me, wiping the tears from my cheek.

"I forgive you." He smiled, even though his eyes blurred with tears. Then he kissed me. He radiated love, like a white-hot star radiates light. And I soaked it in, bathed in it until I was clean.

Katie wiggled her way between us and broke our embrace. We laughed and picked her up together, Jon kissing one cheek, and me the other. I felt so blessed as I held them that I called for Emily and Jacob to join us in a family hug. It amazed me that I could pursue perfection with such wonderful people. It amazed me and left me feeling very unworthy.

Scars and Tassels

At eight o'clock the next morning, the phone rang. I watched through weary eyes as Jon groaned and rolled over, slapping the phone as if it were the alarm clock. When it kept ringing, he finally picked it up.

"Hello?" he croaked.

He rubbed his eyes and nodded, looking at me.

"Yeah. I'll tell her. Yeah. She'll be there soon."

He hung up the phone and sat up, brushing his hair back with his fingers.

"Missy had her baby by C-section at two o'clock this morning. She's asking for you."

"Oh. Okay." I climbed out of bed and got dressed.

"It's Saturday, right?" Jon asked. "You go do what you need to do, and I'll take the kids to your mom's if I need to get some work done."

"Thanks, sweetie." I bent over and kissed him, pulled my hair back into a ponytail, then headed for the door.

As I slammed the car door shut and started the engine, I remembered that I hadn't said my prayers that morning. With thoughts of Jon and our conversation the night before, I knew that I needed to pray before I left for the hospital. Missy needed all the help she could get, and the Lord needed me to provide some of that help.

"Dear Heavenly Father," I started. I sat in the car with my arms folded. But that didn't feel like enough. I needed to kneel.

I got out of the car and went back into the house. Everyone still slept in their beds, and the house was quiet and inviting. I knelt next to the couch in the front room and tried again.

"Dear Heavenly Father," I started. It had been a while since I'd knelt in prayer alone. Jon and I said our personal prayers silently, together in the same room. This complete solitude was personal and warm, like prayer in a sunlit garden.

"I thank Thee, Father, for my many blessings. For Thy gospel, for Jon, and our children."

Images of all my blessings flashed in my mind. Alexis was right, I did have everything I ever really wanted. Sure, there were a few things missing here or there, material things. But I had all the things that made a difference.

"I don't know why Thou hast blessed me so much, but I thank Thee. For everything."

I thought of Missy, sitting there in the hospital, and then I thought of Jane. Though I hadn't seen or heard from her since the day after we found out Missy was pregnant, I knew she needed to visit Missy with me that day.

I rose from my knees and picked up the phone. Jane answered with a scratchy voice.

"Hi, Jane, it's Lia."

"Oh, hi. Is everything okay?"

"Well, Missy had her baby early this morning, and I'm on my way to visit her. I wondered if you wanted to come."

She hesitated, and silence hung on the phone line.

"I think Missy needs our help," I prompted.

"She's really early, isn't she?" Jane asked.

"Yes. She wasn't due until December. I think she's about ten weeks early."

Jane sighed. "I'll meet you there. I need to get up."

"Okay." I smiled. "I'll see you there."

I hung up the phone and went back to my spot next to the couch.

"Thank you, Heavenly Father. Please bless Missy, her baby, and all of her family today. And soften Jane's heart." I smiled as I finished the prayer and rose from my knees.

Mary met me just outside Missy's room. She looked exhausted but relieved.

"Mary, how is everything?" I asked.

"Fine. Missy's sleeping now. She got really miserable during the night, and was going in and out of consciousness. But they say now that the baby's been born, Missy will be fine. It's been touch and go with the baby too, but they think the odds are good that he'll make it."

"Oh, Mary. That's wonderful," I said with relief.

"Would you like to see him? You have to look through the nursery window, and he's in a little neonatal intensive care unit, but you can see him."

"I'd love it."

Mary turned and we walked to the nursery together. I wondered if Jane would really show up.

"He weighs one pound, fifteen and a half ounces. And I should warn you, they've got him hooked up to all kinds of tubes and wires and stuff. But he's a fighter. We almost lost him during the night, but he rallied and now he's stable. There's something really special about this little guy."

We got to the nursery, and Mary went to the large window.

"There he is, in the far corner," she pointed.

I could barely see a baby among the monitors, the heat lamp, and the IVs. But he was there, a tiny but perfect baby with a little white knit cap on his head. He looked too small to be real. Katie had dolls bigger than him.

"How long will he have to stay in there?" I asked.

"It all depends on how he does. The doctor says a minimum of four weeks, but since they had such a hard time resuscitating him this morning, it might be longer."

"They had to resuscitate him?"

"Yeah. It was really scary. Missy's done a lot of crying in the past couple of days. Bless her heart."

I looked around to see if I could spot Jane anywhere close. I hoped she'd come. Then I looked back at the tiny baby.

"Did Missy get to hold him at all?"

"No. There were too many problems. He's only twenty-eight weeks gestation. Actually, he's pretty big for being so premature."

"I called Jane, and she said she would come. We should keep our eyes open for her," I said with a glance down the hall.

"Oh, good. I haven't seen her since that first day at the hospital. I've wondered about her." Mary's voice was tender and thoughtful.

"Well, she's had kind of a hard time with all of this, too. She might not want me to tell you this, but remember that medical condition she talked about?"

"Yes." A look of worry creased Mary's forehead.

"She's getting infertility treatments. She's trying for an in vitro. This has all been hard for her."

"Oh, I can see how it would be." Mary nodded and gazed at the little baby. We looked at him in silence and wonder as a nurse changed his diaper. "That's my first grandchild, you know? I may not like what brought him here, but isn't he beautiful?" She rested her hand against the glass.

"He is beautiful, Mary. I can't believe how tiny he is."

"I wish I could hold him," Mary whispered.

Mary leaned her head against the window and wiped tears from her cheeks. "Missy's decided to keep the baby."

"She has?" I understood Missy's desire to keep her baby, but the news tied my stomach in knots.

"I told her it's her decision and I'll support her. If she's determined to keep him, I'll help her. And I'll love him with all my heart. Even if I disagree with her decision."

"Does that mean you'll need help babysitting sometimes?" I asked. "If you do, I'm sure the compassionate service committee can help you out."

"We'll see. He'll be in the hospital for a while. We'll make the necessary adjustments when he comes home."

I put my arms around Mary's shoulders as tears slipped down her cheeks.

"Come on, let's go back to the room," I said. "You must be exhausted."

When we got back to Missy's room, we found Jane sitting there, in the dim light, watching Missy sleep. Jane's eyes were red and swollen. But she stood and went to Mary with a warm embrace.

Jane drew a deep breath and asked, "How are you doing, Mary?"

"I'm fine, dear. How are you?" Mary looked at Jane with such compassion. It amazed me that Mary could worry so much about Jane when her own life was heavy with so many burdens.

"Well, I've been better." Jane smiled weakly, and looked down at her hands. Then, she looked back up at Mary with tears in her eyes.

"Could I see the baby?" She seemed unsure of whether she really wanted to see him or not.

Mary nodded and put her arm around Jane's waist, then guided her out of the room.

"I'll just wait here," I said.

The door shut behind Mary and Jane, and Missy stirred. She pried her eyes open, and saw me standing next to her bed.

"Hi, Lia."

"Hi, Missy." I smiled and held her hand. It already felt less swollen.

"Did you see him?" Missy asked.

"Yes. He's so tiny. I've never seen a baby that small."

"Me either." Missy scratched her face, and tried to sit up, but winced in pain.

"Be careful there, young lady. You just gave birth. Don't sit up on my account."

"They had to take him by emergency C-section. Did Mom tell you?"

"Yes."

"I've got a scar across my stomach now." She smirked, like she may have felt a bit of resentment about the changes in her body.

"Yeah, but he's here and he's alive. And so are you."

"I guess we were both lucky." Missy scratched her face again. "They said the morphine might make me itch. They weren't kidding."

"Wow, it's weird to think of you as a mother," I said with a smile, trying to support her as well as Mary was trying to.

"Tell me about it. I don't feel like a mother. I feel like a kid."

I squeezed Missy's hand. "You are a kid."

"Where's my mom?" Missy asked.

"She took Jane to look at your baby."

"Jane is your visiting teaching companion, right? She was at my house after I gave my talk on temple marriage." She smirked again.

"That's her. It was hard for her to come today. She can't have children, and she's in Salt Lake to get infertility treatments."

"Really?" Missy's eyes opened a slit, and she looked at me under heavy eyelids.

"Yeah. I think it's been hard for her to see you get pregnant so easily when she's tried for years and been unsuccessful."

Missy nodded and turned her face away from me. "She must hate me."

"No," I said. "She doesn't hate you. But she might be a little jealous. I'm sorry. I probably shouldn't have said anything." And yet I knew somehow it needed to be said. "Don't worry about Jane," I continued. "She's a good woman and she'll work through her problems. You've got your own problems to worry about."

"Yeah, and I have the incision to prove it."

I pulled a chair closer to the bed so I could still hold Missy's hand while I sat down.

"Lia, how am I supposed to forgive myself and forget what I've done if I have a huge scar across my belly to remind me of it all? And I have a baby to remind me of it too. How can I move on when all I feel is guilt?"

"Well, I'm not sure you want to forget what you've done. At least, not totally."

"Oh, yes I do. I hate the memories of Sean that pop up in my head. I hate him, and I hate myself because of what I did with him. I hate closing my eyes at night, because I know what will be there in the back of my mind."

"You know what Jon told me about remembrance? Remembrance takes energy. It's a choice, really. I'm not talking about those thoughts that pop up into our minds. That's going to happen no matter what we do. But what do you do with those little thoughts? Do you dwell on them? Do you *choose* to spend time thinking about them? Because if you choose to think about something, it will affect everything you do. Dwelling on something from the past changes our present. See what I mean?" I knew what I was saying was true. And I also knew I needed to listen to my own advice.

"If you think about it, Missy, what we choose to remember shapes our lives. What do we promise when we take the sacrament?" I looked at Missy, waiting for an answer from her.

She thought for a moment then responded. "That we will always remember Jesus."

"That's right. There's a scripture somewhere about how He remembers us. Do you have a Book of Mormon?"

Missy pointed at the worn book just out of her reach. I opened it and leafed through the thin pages to 1 Nephi 21.

"Here it is, verse fifteen. 'For can a woman forget her sucking child, that she should not have compassion on the son of her womb? Yea, they may forget, yet will I not forget thee, O house of Israel.' And verse sixteen—this is important. 'Behold, I have graven thee upon the palms of my hands; thy walls are continually before me.'"

I looked up, and Missy's face was wet with sorrow.

"He always remembers us. And He has the scars to show it," I said.

"I don't want to feel this guilt for the rest of my life, Lia. I can't bear it." She covered her face with her hands and held her breath between sobs.

"I don't mean you should always remember the guilt. Just the opposite. Eventually, this scar will remind you of the wonderful way forgiveness feels. The scar should remind you of the Atonement and the Savior, just like His scars remind Him of you."

Her face relaxed, but the tears still coursed down her cheeks. I pulled a tissue from the box next to the bed and handed it to her. She wiped her nose and dabbed at her wet cheeks. "I've learned so much in the past few months it's not even funny."

"Like what?" I sat back in my chair. My heart was full and warm, and I couldn't get rid of the smile on my face, even though my eyes were wet.

"Like the gospel is true. Like there really is an Atonement, and I really can be forgiven of this if I repent." She smiled and leaned her head back on her pillow. "Like there's more to life than high school."

"Those are very good lessons to learn," I agreed.

"Yeah. But I'm tired of learning. I need a break." She closed her eyes and scratched her face.

"Should I go, and let you sleep a while?"

"I might sleep whether you go or not." Missy's eyes were still closed as she spoke.

I stood and bent over to kiss Missy's forehead.

"You're a wonderful girl, Missy, and your Heavenly Father loves you. Never forget that." I kept hold of her hand.

"I think I'll name him Ethan. It means 'strong'. Maybe he'll be stronger than I was."

She smiled weakly, and her breathing slowed.

The door opened, and Mary brought Jane in the room. They were both teary eyed.

"She's still sleeping, huh?" Mary said.

"She was awake for a while. She's pretty worn out," I explained.

"Well, a lot has happened to her in the last few months," Mary said as she sat next to the hospital bed. "It's changed her life forever."

"How could it not?" I asked.

"You'd be surprised how many girls don't let this kind of thing change their lives," Jane said. "But I think Missy's going to be okay. And so is this baby. After all, they've got Mary with them." Jane put her arm around Mary and looked at me.

I smiled and nodded.

On the way home from the hospital, I decided to stop by my parents' house and see if the kids were there. Since Jon's deadline was quickly approaching, I was sure he'd left the kids with Mom.

The high school graduation tassel hanging from my rearview mirror danced as I turned onto Mom's street. It didn't even have a color to it anymore, just an ugly gray. As I pulled into the driveway, I took the tassel from the mirror. What was the point of keeping such an ugly old thing in my car? Besides, it reminded me of things I didn't need to remember anymore. Seeing it hang there didn't cheer me or make me want to be a better person. I tossed it in the garbage can and floated in to pick up my kids.

Skeletons on Parade

"Jacob, you make a great skeleton," Jon said, as he put on his coat.

"Thanks, Daddy. Momma made it." Jacob held his hands out to his sides and showed off the bones we'd covered in glow-in-the-dark paint and pinned to his black sweat suit. His facial bones were outlined in paint too, so he would glow as he walked around the neighborhood.

"Yeah, but Jacob helped," I admitted. I had to give credit where it was due.

"Aren't I pretty, Daddy?" Emily spun around in her purple dress. Her hair was as curly and glittery as I could make it, and the smile on her face glowed brighter than the glitter.

"You are beautiful!" Jon picked her up and danced with her cheek to cheek. "The most beautiful Emily in the world!"

"Princess Emily, Daddy," she corrected him.

"Oh, forgive me, *Princess* Emily," he laughed.

"And here's our little ladybug." I handed Katie to Jon as I spoke. He kept hold of Emily and took Katie in his other arm, kissing each of Katie's eyes since they were the only part of her face not covered with makeup.

"Okay, let me take pictures of everyone," I said. They all gave me their best smiles.

Jon took the kids through the neighborhood while I handed out candy. Our neighborhood was full of small children, since most of the parents in the area were students, so Halloween ended up almost as expensive as Christmas. But we loved it. The kids loved dressing up, and I loved seeing all the other kids in the neighborhood. The older ones always made me guess who they were. I always guessed wrong, just to see them giggle.

Some of my old Beehives came by, and I thought of Missy in the hospital. She loved Halloween too.

Then I opened the door to Alexis Smith. Her twins stood before me with open pillowcases, chiming, "Trick or Treat" in chorus.

Alexis smiled weakly.

I smiled back, as warmly as I could. "Well, who are these beautiful angels?"

They said their names at the same time.

"You both look fantastic," I said. "Did your mom make those costumes?"

"I'm an angel, and I have wings," one of the girls said, turning around and showing her wings to me.

"I see that," I said. "And they're lovely wings too."

The girls giggled.

"So, are you having fun?" I looked at the girls as I put a handful of candy in each of their sacks, then I looked at Alexis.

"Yeah. Isaac usually does this, but I'm doing it this year. It's not too bad." She nodded at me and smiled again.

"I'm glad. How is Isaac anyway?"

"He's getting better. It's hard work, but he progresses a little every day."

One of the girls tugged at her mom's hand and started pulling her away.

"Say 'thank you,' girls," Alexis said as they pulled her out of the glow of my porch light.

Together they called, "Thank you."

Maybe Alexis was warming up to me. The thought cheered me so much that I couldn't stop grinning.

The next time I opened the door, a tall man stood there wearing a Phantom of the Opera mask, and a black cloak was pulled around his body. I couldn't tell who he was, and he didn't have any children with him.

"I'm glad to find you alone." The mask muffled Derek's familiar voice, which filled me with a rush of anger and relief.

"Derek, you scared me for a second there." I sighed and put my hand over my heart. "What are you doing here anyway?"

"I'm trick-or-treating. So, trick, or treat?" He took off his hat and held it in front of me.

I put a handful of candy in the hat.

"Have a nice night." I smiled and started to shut the door.

"Wait! Wait, Lia, that wasn't the treat I had in mind."

Then what do you have in mind? I thought. His eyes glazed over and he grabbed onto the doorjamb to keep from falling over.

"Derek, are you drunk?"

"Oh, maybe a little." He leaned his head against the doorjamb and a slow grin spread across his face.

"Derek!" I said, letting my disappointment flood my voice.

"I've been in so much pain since I saw you last, I had to do something. I feel great now!" he said with a grin.

"Yeah, but you won't in the morning," I scolded, a hint of disgust in my voice.

"I have to tell you the truth, and if I don't tell you now, I won't have the guts."

"How did you get here? Did you drive? With all these little kids walking around tonight?" I looked out the door for Derek's BMW. It was parked in front of the house at an angle, the tail of the car sticking out in the street.

Jon walked up the sidewalk and saw me standing in the doorway. I saw him hurry his steps as Derek tried to come in the house.

"I have to tell you the truth, even though it's probably a stupid thing to do. It's burning a hole in my heart and if I don't tell you what I'm feeling, I think it might kill me."

He tripped on the top step onto the porch and Jon caught him, turned him around, and held him away from the door.

"Excuse me, sir. Who are you?" Jon asked.

"Hey, Mr. Tucker? Aren't you the lucky man!" Derek pulled the mask from his face and put it on top of his head. "You got the most wonderful woman in the world to marry you. What'd you do? Read her poetry? That's something I never tried."

Jon's nose curled in distaste. "I thought you said he was sober."

"Apparently he isn't anymore," I whispered.

"I think it's time for you to go, Derek. You wait here and Lia will call a cab." He turned to me and whispered, "Or a cop!"

"I was hoping I could sleep it off here. I'd really like to talk to Lia if you don't mind. It's been ten days since I talked to her last, and I expected her to call me."

I shrugged my shoulders and went to call a cab for Derek. I listened to the conversation in the doorway while I looked through the phone book.

"I don't appreciate you courting my wife. You should stop contacting her."

"'Courting'? Man, you're older than I thought."

"Derek," I said, shaking my head. When I found the number, I dialed as quickly as I could and peeked at Jon's back. His legs were spread apart slightly in a defensive position. I hoped the conversation wouldn't escalate, but they were on a tender topic for both of them.

"And I don't think she appreciates it either," Jon continued. "She's been under a great deal of stress lately, and I'm sure it's largely due to your attention."

"Or maybe it's due to your lack of attention, Mr. Tucker." Derek finished his sentence with contempt, leaning in so close to Jon's face that some spit landed on Jon's cheek.

Jon wiped the spit from his face. "You call me Dr. Tucker."

"Come on, kids, let's go down to the family room and go through your candy." I ushered them downstairs with their bags full of sweets. "I'll be there in just a minute."

Derek stood a good inch taller than Jon as they squared off on my porch, their eyes burning into each other. I approached them with a smile.

"The cab's on its way," I said, hoping to get Derek to back down.

"What, is your degree supposed to scare me?" Derek's face was an inch from Jon's. Derek's upper lip snarled and I wondered if he was mean when drunk.

"Get off my property." Jon stared Derek down with more authority and power than I'd ever seen in his face.

"But I haven't done what I came here to do," Derek said, trying to push past Jon. He fixed his eyes on me.

But Jon steadied himself so he stood strong and solid, blocking the doorway.

"Get off my property," he growled.

I opened the screen door, stepped onto the porch, and put my arm around Jon.

"Let's not ruin a perfectly wholesome holiday with violence, okay? Derek, go home. And stay there."

I rubbed Jon's back to try and calm him.

"You're right, Lia. I knew this was a mistake." He turned and started to descend the front steps. Then he stopped and turned around. "Maybe I can make it up to you. Maybe we can go out to dinner. I know a couple of neat places that you've probably never been—judging by your income." He eyed our cozy house and our worn-out cars.

Jon tightened his muscles, ready to strike at any moment. I kept rubbing his back.

"You know, the house I built is our house, Lia. Our dream. Remember?" He looked in my eyes with longing and sorrow. I looked away.

Jon's muscles tightened, and his jaw worked as he bit his tongue. I squeezed Jon's waist.

I knew waiting for the cab together would be the longest moments of our lives. I opened the door and directed Jon into the house.

"Wait for your cab out here, Derek. And please don't get in your car."

"Oh, I almost forgot." Derek ran down the front steps, and picked up a rose from the shadows. He staggered back up the steps, extending the rose toward me.

"Get off of my property!" Jon shouted, and he squirmed past me with clenched fists. Determination and fury glowed in his face, and Derek backed away enough to tumble down the steps, landing hard on his back.

Derek groaned and staggered to his feet.

"Hey, man. It's all right. No need to get rough." Derek showed me the rose, still clasped in his hand. Then, looking me in the eye with that longing, loving gaze, he placed it on the bottom step. "I'll just leave it here."

I stepped in front of Jon and made eye contact with him.

"Let's go inside," I said, keeping my eyes locked on his. Jon nodded and went in the house.

"Good-bye, Derek." I looked at him over my shoulder as I followed my husband, willing Derek to leave before someone got hurt. I closed the door behind me and turned the dead bolt.

"What an unbelievably vile man. I can't believe you ever dated him." Jon pushed past me and made his way to the telephone.

"Well, he wasn't so vile when I dated him."

"He was drunk, Lia. I've never smelled anything so awful."

"I know. He told me he was sober, and I thought he was active in the Church again."

"Well, he lied. He probably just told you what he thought you wanted to hear."

I sat down hard on the couch. What was going on in Derek's head? And what would have happened if I had let him in the house? I really didn't want to know, and the thought fanned fear in my heart.

"Hello, Bob?" Jon held the phone to his ear and peeked out the front window at Derek. "Yeah, it's Jon. I'm sorry to bother you, but a guy is sitting on our front porch waiting for a cab. He's drunk. I wonder if you know how I could get his car off my property. I also want to get a restraining order against him."

I shook my head and glared at Jon. A restraining order seemed extreme.

He saw my expression and glared at me.

With a grimace I went downstairs to go through candy with the kids.

When the kids had eaten their quota and were tucked in their beds, I went up to our bedroom. Jon lay on his side, trying to read his scriptures.

"Don't you think a restraining order was excessive?" I asked quietly.

"Not given the fact that he was after something when he came here, and he's a drunk. No, I don't think it's excessive. I can't believe you do."

"We're talking about an old friend. If you were going through this with an old friend, I wouldn't jump to conclusions like this." I knew it was a stretch, but Jon's compassion was all I could appeal to.

"You wouldn't? Well then, you'd be wrong."

"Why?"

"Because for one thing, he's not just an old friend. He's after more than you can give him. Besides I know you wouldn't be this patient if it were an old friend of mine—look at how you've acted with Ashley."

"Ashley had nothing to do with you and everything to do with me," I admitted.

Jon looked up from his book.

"I used to be just like her. I was confident, pretty, the center of attention. I'm no psychologist, but I think I was so awful to Ashley because I miss what I used to be."

I sat on the bed with my back to Jon and took off my shoes. I felt Jon looking at me, but he didn't have any response to what I had said.

As I lay down next to Jon, he turned to me. "When did you discover this?" he asked.

"After I visited Alexis and spent a few minutes staring at my yearbook. I was a big flirt. I don't think Derek even knows how many guys I flirted with."

"Maybe that's why I'm so uncomfortable with Derek. He knows a side of you that I don't." Jon looked down, his expression thoughtful.

"Well, that side of me doesn't exist anymore. I don't remember how to flirt with anyone but you." Jon smiled tenderly and rubbed my shoulder. "We're being honest with each other, right?" I asked, mainly as a reminder to Jon of what I was trying to achieve.

"Always." Jon squeezed my shoulder and smiled, though his eyes looked worried, almost defensive.

"When Derek was here, the time he was sober, he said something else that I didn't mention to you because I wasn't sure how I felt about it yet."

"What's that?"

"I told him we fought because of the rose he sent, and he said that if we fought with each other it was because we wanted to. He said he was only a catalyst. He thinks I'm unhappy."

Jon snorted and rolled his eyes. Then, he saw the serious look on my face. "Was he right? Are you unhappy?"

My heart ached with the look on his face: concern, love, and guilt mixed in a heart-wrenching expression.

"Not *really* unhappy. You know me, I'm just a whiner."

"Why are you unhappy?"

His blue eyes looked like the ocean in all the pictures I'd seen of the earth from space. Clear, crisp, aching blue. As I looked at him, I thought about my answer. I wanted to be honest with him, and honest with myself.

"Because life at home with little kids gets dreary sometimes. I'm unhappy because I'm caught up in my own thoughts, like wondering what you're doing when you're not with me. That's mostly out of jealousy. I get jealous of your freedom, your ability to have a professional relationship with people. I'm unhappy because I'm selfish and bored and feeling a bit neglected."

Jon rolled onto his back and looked up at the dim ceiling for a moment, as if deep in thought. Then, he propped himself up on his elbow and looked me straight in the eye.

"If you're bored, I could give you some homework," he said.

I thought he might be kidding, but from the straight look on his face, I knew he was serious.

"I think you'd get Shakespeare if you tried to. Or maybe we could save up for a couple of months and buy you a telescope. When was the last time you looked at the stars?"

"It's been a while," I thought aloud.

"See, you need something to occupy your mind. Keep you busy. And this calling is great for you if you're feeling selfish. The best cure for selfishness is service."

"You're right." I smiled. Jon had developed a take-charge attitude in the face of our little crisis.

"And as far as the neglected thing goes, am I doing better with that one? I'm trying to be home earlier. I'll invite you to come to rehearsals with me anytime you want to." His voice was so hopeful and sincere it brought tears to my eyes.

"You know, I think I was so busy being selfish that I neglected myself. I mean, I stopped trying to make myself happy and just sat around waiting for someone else to do it," I observed.

Something clicked in my mind and I knew I'd just hit the heart of the matter. Jon had made some mistakes in our marriage, but I had too. I needed to fix myself and trust that Jon would do the same.

"Remember that sonnet I quoted to you the night Missy babysat?" Jon asked with excitement.

"Vaguely." I tried to remember.

> "Let me not to the marriage of true minds
> Admit impediments. Love is not love
> Which alters when it alteration finds,
> Or bends with the remover to remove . . ."

He nodded his head, waiting for me to recognize the poem.

"Oh yeah." I nodded, but I didn't understand much of what he'd said.

"Can I explain it to you? You're not going anywhere for a while, are you?"

"Explain away. I'm staying right here." I snuggled into him, and he explained the poem line by line.

Until that night, I had no idea Shakespeare wrote a poem about us.

It felt good to lie there next to Jon, more honest than I'd ever been with him before. I had no more secrets that I was aware of, no more skeletons to hide. My life felt clean and organized, like a closet in spring.

Remodeled

———⟡———

"So how was your Halloween?" Mom sat across her new oak kitchen table from me and handed sugar-free candy to my kids. Emily popped the candy in her mouth and ran to the backyard with Jacob close at her heels. She evidently couldn't tell the difference between the candy from Grandma and the sugary candy from me.

"Halloween was fun, terrifying, and incredibly romantic."

"Oh? Well, that's an interesting combination. Do tell," Mom insisted.

She sipped a cup of sugar-free hot chocolate, and looked at me over her cup.

"The kids brought home enough candy to last us until next Halloween. I learned a little about Shakespeare, and Derek went home with a bump on the back of his head after Jon spooked him down our front stairs."

"Derek was there?" She grimaced, anticipating a tense story.

"Yes. And he was drunk."

"He was? Are you sure?"

"Yep. He was so rude, Mom. He really insulted Jon. So, Jon let him have it." I laughed.

"Jon hit him?" Mom's eyes grew wide like she was hearing something scandalous.

"No, but he almost pushed him. Derek got spooked, and if it hadn't been for the railing by the stairs he would have fallen in my rosebush."

"So, what do you think about it all?" To Mom, everything had a moral.

"Well, I feel better now that I've really talked to Jon about it. But I'm a little scared actually. For all I know, Derek came to the house with some horrible things in mind. If Jon hadn't come home when he did, I don't know what would have happened."

"So, don't let Derek in the house if he comes by again," Mom counseled.

"I've already promised Jon I won't let Derek in. Besides, we've got a restraining order against Derek. He's not supposed to come within five hundred feet of the house. He really freaked Jon out. I've never seen him so angry. And he was really scared for me too."

"Can you blame him?" Mom asked, shaking her head. "Do you think Derek will try anything else?"

"I couldn't begin to predict Derek at this point. He's got me a little scared, I'll admit. I thought I knew him, you know? But now . . . well, I don't know him now."

"And how are things with Jon?"

"Better than ever. He's almost done with his book. Ahead of schedule, by the way. And the dress rehearsal is next week. They're all nervous about that, but I'm sure they'll do great."

"What about the student that's been flirting with Jon?"

"She's not an issue. Jon loves me," I said, the grin on my face growing to a bright smile.

Mom smiled back and sipped at her drink again. "Have you tasted this stuff? I know it's sugar-free, but I bet you'd like it."

She got up and pulled a mug from the cupboard, filling it with hot water and a scoop of hot chocolate mix. She dropped a spoon into the mug and placed it on the table in front of me.

I stirred the mix and sipped at the chocolate.

"Well, what do you think?"

"It's not too bad. Yeah, I could get used to this." I smiled. I was happy. I wanted the feeling and the moment burned into my memory, like a photograph.

"And I could get used to this new kitchen." Mom looked around at the freshly painted cream walls, oak trim, and oak cabinets.

Dad came in wearing paint-spackled clothes with an armful of supplies. "What do you think? All I've got to do now is put the finishing touches on the grout around the sink."

"Dad, you did a great job! It's gorgeous."

"I'm pretty proud of it myself," Dad said as he wiped sweat from his bald head. "It's a good remodel—a nice change, and long overdue."

Mom and I drank our chocolate together, and snowflakes fell outside. Emily and Jacob spun around in the light November snow with their mouths open toward the heavens, trying to catch a flake or two on their tongues.

Through a Closed Door

"Well, Mary, what do you think?" I held up the cookie jar lid I'd just covered in white paint.

Mary looked at it and smiled. "It's perfect, dear. Trust me, you can't mess this up. You're just putting on the base coat."

"I'm not so sure. I think I could mess up a base coat." I'd certainly messed up my hands; white splotches covered my fingers. I set down the wooden circle, and a small section of paint came off on my finger.

"See, I messed it up," I laughed.

A long paper-covered table filled Mary's living room, and sisters from the ward lined either side of the table, painting their hearts out. With all the days spent in the hospital, Mary fell behind the schedule she'd set for her annual craft boutique. The compassionate service committee got together to put her back on schedule, and four other sisters volunteered to help, including Jane. Mary worked alongside the other women, occasionally looking up at the faces of the sisters, dabbing at the corners of her eyes.

"The nice thing about doing this for you is that if we do a project we really like, we can actually buy it and take it home. My best projects are hanging in someone else's house," one sister said with a chuckle.

"Isn't that the truth!" Mary exclaimed.

"And it's the same with baked goods. Every time I bake something, my family darts in and out of the kitchen, waiting for me to tell them whether they can have a cookie or whether they're for my visiting teachers," I said.

Various sisters chimed in. "Or the sisters you visit teach."

"Or the home teachers."

"There's always someone else who needs things more than I do."

"Well, I certainly don't need these cookies." Mary patted her round stomach and set a plate of chocolate chunk cookies in the middle of the table. "Please, sisters, eat up."

"So, Mary, when does Missy get home?" Jane asked.

"Tomorrow afternoon."

"And she has to leave the baby there?" I asked.

"Oh yes. Ethan isn't ready to come home yet. Probably another ten days or so. But he's doing so well, and he's so beautiful. You should all see him."

"Is she nursing? How can they send her home without the baby?" one of the other women asked.

"She's not nursing. And even if she were, she'd have to pump her breast milk because he's just too tiny to latch on."

"That's too bad. I loved nursing," I said.

"Well, she doesn't want to nurse because, hopefully, she'll be able to graduate with her class. We've made arrangements with the principal, and she does have one class she needs to make up, but it should work out."

"Is she going back to classes at the high school?" I asked.

Mary nodded. "In January. She'll have the rest of this quarter to heal and get used to the idea of having a baby around. I guess we'll all have to get used to it."

"Are you going to watch the baby while she's at school? And while she studies?" another sister asked. Her voice had a sharp edge to it, like she didn't approve of Mary watching little Ethan. Jane looked at Mary, holding her breath.

"Well," I interrupted, "by how often she mentions how cute that baby is, I imagine that won't be too much of a sacrifice."

Mary just smiled.

We finished enough projects to make hundreds of dollars for the Wilson family Christmas. Mary cried when she saw the stacks of crafts.

"Now I can focus on helping Missy and Ethan and still have the boutique. And it will be a great Christmas."

"You deserve something great," I said as I put my arms around Mary.

"Thank you so much, Lia."

"It's what I'm here for. By the way, I'm thinking about a baby shower for Missy sometime in December. Not an official compassionate service deal, just a neighborhood thing. Missy could bring some of her friends. I figure if Missy's really going to keep this baby she'll need all the help she can get. Do you think that would be appropriate?"

"I really don't know yet. Why don't we put that on the back burner for a while?"

"Okay." I nodded. I wasn't too sure about the idea when I thought it up, but it didn't hurt to ask. "Can I help with anything else?"

"I think we're good. I'm sure Missy would like you to visit after she gets home."

"You can count on it."

Jane walked toward the door.

"And you too, Jane. Missy would like you to visit too."

"I will." Jane looked a little sad, but she smiled anyway.

"Listen, Mary." Jane leaned in close to Mary's face and lowered her voice. "I have a lot of experience with newborns. Especially ones with special needs like Ethan. I've learned a lot of things that can help with his development and with bonding and stuff like that. With him in the NICU, he hasn't had the bonding time that most babies have with their mothers. I can help Missy make up for lost time."

Mary's eyes glistened. So did Jane's.

"Would Missy object if I came by with some books and a little advice?" Jane asked.

"Like Lia said, we could use all the help we can get." Mary nodded and wrapped her arms around Jane. "You're a blessing to this family. Do you know that?"

Jane smiled and took a deep breath as she pulled away from Mary's embrace.

"I'm just trying to be the person God wants me to be." Jane smiled, her chin quivering.

"Well, you're succeeding. I'm sure it's very difficult for you to help us so much."

"Oh, but it's worth it." Jane smiled.

We left the house together and walked to Jane's car.

"You really are handling everything well," I said.

"Yeah. You don't see me go home and bawl my eyes out," Jane said.

"I don't need to." I squeezed Jane's arm.

"You know, the past few weeks have been so hard. I didn't tell you, but we tried the in vitro."

"Really?" I asked.

"Yes. It didn't take." She leaned against her car, with the keys in her hand, and took another deep breath.

"I'm so sorry," I said, letting my concern show on my face and in my voice. I was amazed she would be willing to help Missy so much after going through such an ordeal.

"Well, I'm not too happy about it. But it doesn't do me any good to sit around and feel sorry for myself like I was before you called that morning. I was praying when you called, you know. I was praying for guidance and a way to get on with my life."

"You don't have to give birth to be a mother," I replied, seeing why Jane was so willing to help. She had the instinct, and she couldn't stop caring about people even when she wanted to.

"I know. But it's different. I'd still like to give birth. I'd like to feel a baby fluttering inside of me. I'd like to nurse. I'd like to participate in the miracle, you know?"

I nodded. It was definitely a miracle. A painful one, but still a miracle.

She shrugged her shoulders. "Oh well. I guess we all need to learn how to be happy with what we've got."

"Yes, we do. And that's not always easy," I agreed.

I thought of Alexis struggling with her twins and her husband in rehab every day. I wished she'd let me help her.

Call Alexis. The words whispered in the back of my mind.

Jane climbed in her car. "Can I give you a ride home?"

"Oh, no. It's just around the corner. I'll be fine. Thanks though. It was really good to see you here."

Jane nodded and pulled away.

I walked home as quickly as I could and went straight to the phone to call Alexis. The line rang but no one picked up. I hung up and dialed the number again, in case I'd made a mistake the first time. On the eighth ring, I finally ended the call and placed the phone on the counter.

"Hey, you. How did it go?" Mom came down the stairs with a dirty diaper in her hand.

"Great. We got a lot done," I said as I hugged her.

"Katie's been full of it this morning. What do you feed that girl?"

"Just food, Mom."

"Well, I'm glad you got here. I've got stuff to do." Mom grabbed her purse and kissed my cheek.

I followed Mom out to her car, leaving the door open in case the kids wanted me.

"Your dad wants to start remodeling the front room today."

"Really?"

"Yes. Can you believe it?" Mom looked at me with a wide grin, and her eyes sparkled with anticipation. "He wants me to go with him to pick out wallpaper and borders."

I'd hoped she could stay with the kids a little longer while I went to Alexis's house, but I knew asking her after that wouldn't be the best idea.

"You look disappointed," Mom said. She could always see through me.

"No, I just have some other visits to make. It's just hard to do everything with the kids clinging to me. But you go do your thing. Have fun." I was surprised by how sincerely I felt what I said.

Mom hugged me. "I know it's hard, but every mother in the world has to do it. And eventually, you'll have a sweet, grown-up daughter who encourages you to do your own thing."

I nodded again. A sense of urgency rose in my throat. I knew Alexis needed me as soon as possible.

"Well, Mom, I've got to go. Thanks so much for watching the kids. I love you!"

I ran back into the house and picked up the phone to dial again. But no one answered. I debated leaving it at that. I'd called with no success. No answering machine clicked on. She obviously didn't want to be reached.

She needs you. Go to her. The voice was gentle, but persistent, and I knew what I had to do.

"Okay, kids. Let's get in the car. Come on, let's go." Emily and Jacob ran upstairs to look for their shoes, and I tied on Katie's tennis shoes and buttoned her jacket.

With everyone strapped in their seats, I sped to the apartments. What I was doing didn't make sense, but urgency pushed me until I rang Alexis's doorbell.

One of the twins opened the door just a crack. The chain lock prevented her from opening it any farther.

"Hi. Is your mommy home?" I asked the little girl peeking at me through the cracked-open door.

"Mommy's sick and she's sleeping," she said.

"She is? Can you wake her up and tell her she's got company?" I asked. Katie pushed on the door, trying to get into the house.

"She says no."

"Well, honey, go try anyway, okay? Go wake up Mommy."

The little girl ran back in the apartment and opened one of the doors. I listened for Alexis's voice, but could only hear the little girl.

We waited for a few minutes. Through the crack in the door I could see the other twin on the couch, transfixed by the television.

Finally, the little girl came back.

"Mommy won't wake up. She's too sleepy."

"She won't wake up at all?" I asked to clarify.

The little girl shook her head.

Panic grew in my chest. I knew the Lord sent me there to help Alexis. Never before had I received a prompting so strong.

"Now, tell me which twin you are." I tried to take control of the situation.

"I'm Evey."

"Okay. Evey, can you pull a chair over from the kitchen and unhook this chain so I can come in and check on Mommy? It could be very important."

Evey nodded and pulled a chair up to the door.

"Okay, sweetie. I'm going to shut the door, and when I do, you slide that chain out, okay?"

I closed the door. I heard the chain rattle, and when the noise stopped, I tried to open the door again. But the chain was still locked.

"Evey, honey, it didn't work. You've got to try again."

I peeked through the crack in the door, and Evey sat next to her sister on the couch, shaking her head.

"I can't do it. It's stuck," she whined in frustration.

"No, Evey. You've got to try again," I pleaded.

She sighed and stomped over to the door. I shut it and listened to the chain rattle.

I tried to open the door again, but it was still locked.

"Okay, Jaqueline, you try." I felt anxiety growing in me. I needed to get to Alexis.

The other girl shook her head.

"Come on, sweetie, your momma may be sick. She might need some help."

The girls stared at the television.

"Alexis!" I yelled, banging on the door. "Alexis, wake up and open the door!"

But Alexis didn't come to the door.

The neighbor across the hall opened her door and came out of her apartment.

"Is there a problem?" she asked as she wiped her hands on a dish towel.

"I think Alexis is sick," I explained. "Her girls can't wake her up, and she won't answer the phone or come to the door."

The neighbor called Alexis's name, but there was still no answer.

"Bring your kids in here," she said, "and let's call 911."

I led my kids into the neighbor's apartment, and she picked up the phone to dial. But that wasn't enough for me. I ran out into the hallway and rammed my shoulder into Alexis's door. It hurt like crazy, but the door stayed put. I rammed it again, and the chain gave way. The twins screamed and started crying as I ran into the apartment and made my way to Alexis's room.

Simple Things

Alexis lay on her side, her dark hair spread across the forest green pillowcase like tree roots. An ivy-colored comforter hugged her face, like she'd been freezing when she fell asleep. Her hands clutched the comforter at her throat. I rested my hand on her shoulder and felt it rise and fall slowly with her breath. With a sigh, I sat down on the bed.

"Father, I thank Thee that she's alive." Relief swept over me, and the thumping in my chest slowed almost to normal.

But why wouldn't she wake up? I held her shoulder and shook her. "Alexis. Wake up."

She didn't respond.

"Alexis!" I said, a little louder. "Alexis! Wake up!" I shook her harder.

But she lay there, breathing slow and shallow.

"You shouldn't wake Mommy. She'll get mad at you." One of the twins walked into the room. Her long dark hair was tangled, and she still wore a nightgown, even though it was about one in the afternoon. She wiped tears from her eyes.

"It would be okay if she got mad at me," I said calmly as I motioned for her to sit on my lap.

"Now, which one are you?" The twins looked so much alike, I couldn't tell.

"I'm still Evey." She rolled her eyes.

"I'm sorry, you just look so much like your sister, and I can't tell you apart. I guess I need to spend more time with you." I smiled.

She stared down at her mother.

"Does Mommy sleep like this very often?" I asked.

"No. She's really tired today."

The neighbor ran in the room with Katie in her arms. Katie reached for me immediately. "I called 911, and they're sending an ambulance. They want me to wait in the parking lot so I can direct them to the apartment."

"Okay. Are the kids in your apartment?"

"No, I brought them all in here."

She looked at Alexis, then looked at me.

"Is she breathing?"

"It seems shallow, but yes, she's breathing." I watched Alexis's chest rise slowly.

"Oh, good. They asked me if she was breathing, and I said I didn't know. You can't wake her up though?"

"Nope. Nothing," I said.

"Okay. Well, I'll go wait for them. Hopefully, they'll get here soon."

I took Evey and Katie into the front room. Evey, Jaqueline, Katie, Jacob, and the neighbor's little boy all sat in front of the television. Emily stood and came to my side. "Is everything okay, Mommy?"

"I don't know yet, sweetie."

"Is their mommy sick?" Emily stood away from the bedroom door, too nervous even to peek into the room.

"I think so." I nodded and put my arm around Emily's waist.

Emily walked over to the twins and sat between them. She put one arm around Evey and one around Jaqueline. They each leaned into Emily, resting their heads on her shoulders. It amazed me how quickly children changed their ways. According to Alexis, Emily had teased the twins on many occasions. But there she sat, comforting them like they were her sisters.

Forever passed before the paramedics came.

"Who found her?" a young woman asked as she led a gurney into the bedroom.

"I did." I raised my hand.

The young man that followed the gurney motioned for me to follow him.

"Did she take any medications or drink any alcohol?"

"I don't know," I said, wishing I could be of more help.

"Did she pass out, or was she like this when you found her?"

"She was lying here in bed, just like she is now."

The young woman took Alexis's pulse, then pried each of her eyes open and moved a pen light in front of them. "Bag her. She's comatose."

The young man put an oxygen mask over Alexis's face.

"Did you say she's comatose?"

"Yes. Her pupils don't respond to light. We've got to get her to the hospital."

"Oh," I said, wondering what to do next.

I went back into the front room where the kids were, and held them out of the way as the EMTs pushed Alexis out of the apartment on the gurney.

"Are you the next of kin?" the woman asked me.

"No. Her husband is in a rehab center right now. He got in a bad car accident a while ago," I said.

"You need to notify her next of kin for the paperwork and stuff."

"I will."

"We'll be at the University Hospital."

I nodded. I knew Alexis's mother wasn't too far away, because she had the twins with her the last time I visited Alexis.

Jaqueline stood from the couch and started following the gurney out the door.

"Mommy! Don't go, Mommy!" I wrapped my arm around Jaqueline's waist and held her. She kicked and screamed, fighting with all her strength to get away from me and follow her mother.

"Shh, it's okay, Jaqueline. Mommy's sick, and they're going to make her better. They're going to help, okay?" I tried to hold and comfort her.

"No! I want Mommy." After a while, she settled and cried in my arms.

I looked up at Alexis's neighbor. "Do you know where Alexis might keep her phone numbers?"

The neighbor shook her head. "I actually just moved in last week."

I snorted and cocked my eyebrows. "Welcome to the neighborhood."

I found a rehab center magnet on the fridge and called the number. They directed me to Isaac's room.

"Hi, my name is Lia Tucker. I'm from the ward," I introduced myself.

"Yeah. What can I do for you?" His voice was cold, much as Alexis's had been during our phone conversations.

"Well, I'm at your apartment, and something's wrong with Alexis. We had to call 911, and she's on her way to the hospital."

He was quiet for a moment, then he cleared his throat. "What's wrong with her?"

"We're not quite sure. She was asleep when I got here, and I couldn't wake her up," I explained.

"She probably took too many sleeping pills or something. What can I do about it? I'm kind of stuck here." He sounded put out. I couldn't tell whether he was more upset by my phone call interrupting him or by the fact that he was obligated to listen to me.

"Sleeping pills. Why would she do that?" I wondered aloud, disbelieving.

"She's been really unhappy lately. And yesterday I asked her for a divorce. It might have pushed her over the edge."

I couldn't believe what I was hearing. And he said it so matter-of-factly, like it was no big deal.

"Why would you ask her for a divorce when she comes to you every day and helps you with rehab? Don't you think your timing's bad?" I probably shouldn't have pried, but he was irritating me, so I did.

"Because she doesn't help me with rehab. She sits there and cries all the time. She's a whack job. I waited too long to get rid of her."

She's the one who waited too long, I thought. He completely disgusted me. I couldn't talk to him anymore.

"Okay, just tell me her mother's phone number please. Or tell me where Alexis keeps her numbers or something." I wanted to call him a few choice names, but I held my breath instead.

"She keeps her numbers in the top drawer in the cupboard by the fridge. But I doubt she wrote her mother's number in there. She calls her every day."

"Does she live in Salt Lake?"

"Bountiful."

"Okay. Tell me her name." I held my breath again.

He sighed. "Patricia Woods. Her dad's name is Kent."

I hung up the phone without so much as a "thank you."

"What a jerk," I said.

Sarah, the new neighbor, sat in the front room with all the kids. She'd pulled out a bunch of toys and sat on the floor, having just as much fun as the kids were.

"Who?" she asked after my comment.

"Alexis's husband. He thinks she took too many sleeping pills . . . on purpose." I glanced at the children playing with dolls on the front room floor. "After talking to him, it wouldn't surprise me."

I knew that Isaac had cheated on Alexis, too. Why did she stay with him after that? I guess when you're blessed with a good marriage, it's hard to understand why women stay in a bad one.

"When is Mommy coming home?" Evey asked.

I looked at her young face. What a horrible thing for this child to go through. I put my arm around her.

"I don't know, sweetie. The doctors need to figure out what's wrong so they can make her better."

"Is Daddy coming home?"

"No. Daddy's still sick too."

I smiled at the innocent little face looking up at me hopefully. That was why she stayed with him. That face and its twin. I thought of Missy and Ethan. It occurred to me that just like Ethan, these two little girls needed a daddy.

"Who will watch us?"

"I'm going to call your grandma, sweetie. Everything will be okay."

The afternoon slipped quickly by while we waited for Alexis's mother to come pick up the girls. I called the hospital and left Mrs. Wood's phone number with them as the next of kin. I asked how Alexis was doing, and they said she was still sleeping.

We bathed the twins and got them dressed, then foraged through the cupboards and found a box of mac and cheese. Sarah went to her apartment and brought over a pack of hot dogs. The kids were thrilled with the feast.

"Do you like the neighborhood so far?" I asked with a sly grin.

"Oh yeah. Never a dull moment." Sarah rolled her eyes.

"When did you move in?" I asked.

"Two weeks ago tomorrow."

"Wow. Can I ask if you're LDS, or would that offend you?"

"I'm LDS. I haven't been to church yet though. We're actually buying a house in the ward, but we can't move in yet. We're between residences."

"Cool. So why unpack, right?"

"Right. But it makes it hard to live comfortably. Half of our stuff is in storage." Sarah scooped another serving of mac and cheese onto Jaqueline's plate.

"Alexis is in our ward too," I said. "She's had a really hard life. I know a lot of people going through tough times right now."

"Yeah, don't we all. I'm amazed at the stuff people live through. And it seems like the tougher things people survive, the better people they are. I just don't know how they do it."

"Well, if Alexis survives this, she'll be a true saint."

"What brought you here anyway? I haven't seen you around since I moved in. And you don't really know the kids. I mean, you don't seem like a close friend."

"Honestly? I was prompted to come. The strongest prompting I've ever had."

She smiled at me. "See, the Lord wants Alexis alive and kicking. He wants it so much He sent one of His servants to make sure."

I nodded. "I'm glad I listened."

"Me too." She nodded at me and smiled.

After the twins were with their grandma, who couldn't stop thanking me for breaking the lock on the door and not just walking away, I loaded my kids in the car and went home. It was dark, and the porch light was on.

My heart swelled with the thought of seeing Jon's face and holding him. I hurried into the house.

"Where have you been?" he asked. "And why didn't you call?"

"It's not even six yet," I teased, since he usually came home just after six.

"Well, I came home early today. You usually leave a note or something."

I held his stubbled face in my hands. "You're so sweet when you miss me."

He wrapped his arms around me, and I hugged him close.

"The Spirit told me to go to Alexis, and I went."

"Really? Did you patch things up?"

"I may have saved her life actually."

I told Jon about the events of the day as we fixed dinner together, and I couldn't stop staring at him as we ate. How lucky was I to sit across the dinner table every night from a man who really did want me to be happy! He didn't come home early very often, but once in a while he did. And he missed me when I wasn't there. It was simple, and it appeared to be insignificant, but it made me love him. And those simple things added up.

It reminded me of the day after our argument, when he bore his testimony. He said he could have gone to confide in someone from work, but instead he confided in the Lord. It was a simple decision, I thought, but the outcome was very important. Maybe if he had confided in someone from work, Jon wouldn't have been so patient with me or so forgiving. And if he had been more aggressive, my reaction may have hurt our marriage even more.

My decision to see Alexis that day was a simple one, but it may have saved her life.

Through small and simple things are great things brought to pass, I thought.

"I love you, Jon."

He smiled at me as he scooped up his last bite of potatoes. "I love you too."

Waking Up

Missy came home from the hospital on a cold windy day. She pulled her jacket close around her neck and hugged herself. I waited on the front porch with a bouquet of balloons held tightly in hand. Emily held a rose for Missy, Jacob held a wrapped gift for Ethan, and Katie played with an extra balloon I'd tied to her wrist.

She smiled and clapped her hands, looking at the kids. "Yay! Thank you! How sweet you all are!"

She looked pretty much like the same old Missy but she couldn't quite stand up straight. She walked slowly up the front steps, and her eyes seemed darker, older, and much sadder.

When we went in the house, I let go of my balloon bouquet, and it joined several more balloons on the ceiling. Mary pulled out a big plate full of chocolate chunk cookies and a two-liter bottle of pop.

"You guys! You shouldn't have done this," Missy exclaimed.

"Why not?" Mary asked.

"Because it's like a hero's welcome. I didn't do anything worth celebrating."

"You survived a month in the hospital," I said.

"Yes, and you gave us our first grandchild," Mary said.

Missy looked away from her mother, shook her head, and took a deep breath.

"Did you expect us to punish you or be ashamed of you?" Mary asked with love in her eyes. "You've punished yourself enough. It's time to start healing and get on with your life."

"I haven't even had my first appointment with the bishop yet. I'm sure he'll at least disfellowship me. I haven't even started my punishment." Her voice was so solemn it made my heart break.

"Yes you have, Missy," Hyrum said, helping Missy toward the couch in the front room. "You've been punishing yourself for months. Besides, repentance isn't necessarily about punishment. Remember, the Lord took our stripes that we might be healed."

Missy shook her head.

"Don't you believe it?" her father asked.

"Yes, I believe it, but it's not working. I mean, I . . ." She shook her head again. She looked tired.

Hyrum put his arm around Missy and kissed her forehead. "Have faith, little one. Everything will work out for the best."

We brought Missy up to speed on everything that had happened while she was away. Her brother had twelve baptisms in one month, a new record for him. They shared his letters with Missy, and she cried as she read them. Her sister from BYU was doing well, dating a different guy every weekend, studying hard.

And Missy got stacks of get-well cards from friends at school and from the young women in the ward. Her best friend, Tonya, sent a huge bouquet of flowers. But there was nothing from Ethan's father.

"I got to hold Ethan before I left the hospital," Missy said wistfully.

"Really?" I asked.

Mary and Hyrum smiled and hovered around Missy for the details.

"Yes," Missy continued. "He's so unbelievably soft. And he's so tiny, you can barely tell you're holding him."

"Stop it, you're making me baby hungry," I said with a smile.

"I can't believe I'm a mom. I mean, wow." Her voice didn't portray the excitement her words implied.

Katie ran up to me with a half-eaten cookie in her hand. Chocolate covered her face, hands, and eventually the front of my shirt.

"No more white shirts for you, Missy," I teased.

"And no more restful nights," Mary added.

"Lots of worrying, like when they're up all night with a fever," I said as I dabbed at the chocolate on my shirt with a wet wipe.

"And you worry constantly about their development. Are they doing what they should be doing, when they should be doing it? Are they okay? Will they do well with friends, or at school?" Mary stood beside Missy and rested her hand on Missy's shoulder.

"But it's all worth it," I said.

"Yes, it's all worth it." Mary kissed Missy's forehead as she spoke, and tears blurred her eyes. She and Hyrum disappeared into the kitchen, leaving Missy and me alone.

"I wish he was here now. It was so hard to leave him." Missy looked up at me.

"I'm sure it was. I've never left my kids, even for an overnighter," I said.

"Hey, where's Jane?" Missy asked.

"She said she had something else to do today, but she'll try to visit you tomorrow." I smiled. I was proud of Jane. She was amazing.

"Mom said she had an in vitro, and it didn't take." Missy was thoughtful, and spoke quietly.

"That's right," I said.

Missy folded her arms across her stomach. "So, is that it? Are they going to try again?"

"I don't think so. She told me this was their last try."

Missy slowly sat back in her chair. "I feel so bad for her. She's been so great through all of this, but she must hate me."

"Trust me, she doesn't hate you." At that point, I thought Jane was incapable of hate.

"Do you know, she went with me to the nursery once, and explained to me what all the machines were that Ethan is hooked up to. She talked to the nurses there for a while, and they were talking about some of the possibilities for Ethan's future. He's had a really hard time breathing. His lungs keep getting fluid in them, and they have to pound his back a lot to help him breathe. I hate it when they do that. But Jane knows just what to do. She taught me how to handle those times when Ethan can't breathe. I guess it might cause problems for him all his life."

"Really?" I interjected. "I thought everything was going well."

"Oh, it is. But he was twelve weeks early. Think about it, that's a lot."

"Very true."

"And the problems he'll have all his life may be something as simple as asthma. But that can be a big deal. You always have to have medicine around. His activity will be limited. And I remember teasing kids in elementary school when they pulled their inhalers out." Missy rubbed her arm thoughtfully. "Kids can be so rude, you know?"

"I know." I thought of Emily teasing Alexis's kids. Then I remembered Emily putting her arms around Alexis's twins and comforting them. "But they can turn around and be the sweetest friends too."

"I don't know if I'm ready to deal with all this, you know? I mean, I hated leaving Ethan, but once I bring him home, my life will never be the same again."

"Motherhood does that to you. But your mom said they made arrangements for you to go back to school. They said you can even graduate with your class."

"Yeah, but I feel like I've done enough to my mom. She'll have to take care of Ethan while I'm at school and while I study."

"Well, you're talking about her grandson. She loves him too, so she's probably willing to do whatever she can to help you get an education. You'll need an education to be able to support him." I watched as reality began to reveal itself to Missy.

Missy shook her head, and tears slipped down her cheeks. "I'm not sure I can do this."

I wiped chocolate off of Katie's fingers for the fifth time, then I wiped her face as she squirmed. "The question is, do you have a choice?" I felt Missy's eyes on me as I spoke, but I concentrated on Katie's fingers. Missy did have a choice, and she knew it.

I called the hospital to check on Alexis, and they put me through to her room. Alexis answered the phone, and she sounded so weak I couldn't tell whether she was happy to be awake or not.

"You can come see me, Lia. I'd love to talk to you." Alexis sounded sincere.

"Okay. I'll come tonight after Jon gets home. Is that soon enough?" I asked, amazed that she was so willing to see me.

"Yeah," she replied. Then she hung up without a good-bye. I couldn't figure Alexis out, no matter how hard I tried.

Jon came home and took charge for me, so I drove to the hospital. I'd been there so many times that I knew all the parking secrets and got a space close to the entrance.

Alexis sat alone in her room. The room was empty except for one small flower arrangement. A small card among the flowers said, "We love you! Love, Mom, Evey, and Jaqueline." I wished I had brought something for her.

The room was quiet, and Alexis looked like she was sleeping. They'd taped an oxygen tube to her face and she had an IV.

I sat next to her, trying not to wake her, but she opened her eyes and looked at me. She didn't smile.

"How are you feeling?" I asked with a smile.

"Like I wish I were dead," she replied with a grimace.

"Alexis, you can't wish that."

"Yes, I can. What do you know anyway?" If she'd had the strength, she probably would have yelled at me. It wasn't the reception I'd expected.

"I know you love your daughters. But you almost died, locked up in the apartment with them. How do you think they feel through all of this, Alexis? How will they remember this? And what if you had died? What would they have done?"

"I didn't really think I'd die. I didn't even take the whole bottle. I just wanted to scare Isaac. He wants a divorce, you know."

"I know. He told me," I said.

"After everything I put up with, he wants to leave me. What a jerk."

"Funny, I said the same thing," I told her.

Alexis closed her eyes again.

"You know what though?" I said. "It's going to backfire on him when he tries to leave that rehab center and doesn't have anyone to go home to."

A weak smile spread across Alexis's face and her eyes opened a slit.

"Let him experience life without someone who loves him and takes all the garbage he throws. It will be good for him," I said.

"Yeah. Maybe he'll come crawling back, or at least rolling back in that wheelchair of his," she chuckled.

"What would you do if he came rolling back?" I asked.

A lost look flashed across her face. "I don't know."

"Maybe you need to find a way to take care of yourself and your daughters without him. You deserve better."

Alexis stared at me with a hint of hope in her eyes.

"Have you talked to your mom?" I asked.

"Yes. She's got the girls. She said you broke down my front door to get to me."

"Just the chain."

"Why? I haven't been very good to you." She avoided my eyes.

"Well, I haven't been very good to you either. But I believe in repentance."

She smiled weakly again.

"So how long do you have to stay in the hospital?" I asked.

"You mean purgatory?"

"Okay. If that's what you want to call it."

"I don't know. They say I'm suffering from depression and anemia and a whole slew of things that just mean I haven't been taking care of myself." She closed her eyes again.

"Well, I hope you heal here in purgatory," I said.

"They've got counselors coming, they're putting me on antidepressants. Maybe they'll send me to the loony bin for a while."

"Well, if they do, I'll come visit you in the loony bin, too." I smiled at her with all the love and support I could muster.

She looked at me through the corner of her eye as her countenance changed. I wasn't sure what I said wrong, but she blustered before my eyes like a winter storm. "Why? Because you're the compassionate service leader? Don't visit me out of obligation. If that's why you're here now, you can leave. You've done your service for the day."

She said "service" with such contempt it made the hair on my neck and arms stand on end.

"I'm not here out of obligation, Alexis," I said. "I'm here because we should be friends. And we should have been friends a long time ago. We were the only two girls in Stargazers. Why weren't we friends?" I asked with sincerity. "It really doesn't make sense."

Alexis tried to sit up in bed and looked at me with flaming gold eyes. "I'll tell you why. I was awkward and shy and ugly. Do you know that Derek was the only guy who would go out with me until I met Isaac? And Derek wasn't interested in me, he only went out with me because he was nice."

"Is that such a bad reason to do something? You act like being nice is something bad."

"There's a difference between being nice and being sincere. Take you, for instance. You're here because you feel guilty or because you feel obligation. You're here to serve your own interests, not because you care about me. It makes your visit a slap in the face, because you're here to serve yourself in the end. Just like Derek going out on that date with me. He went because he was known as the nicest guy in the school. He had a rep to keep. But he didn't really want to be there with me. It would have been better for me if he'd said no and left me home so I couldn't watch the two of you flirt over my shoulder."

I sat back in my chair and wondered why I was visiting the venomous woman. She got mad at people who were nice to her. How could anyone win? It made me angry, and I stood to leave. But I couldn't leave with her harsh words hanging in the air.

"There's nothing wrong with wanting to do the right thing, Alexis. Do you know why I broke down your door? I didn't know you'd taken too many sleeping pills. I didn't know you were depressed or sick or anything. I did it because the Spirit told me to. The Spirit practically shouted at me to get to you. I broke your door down because God wants you alive. So what if my initial reason for serving you is a selfish one? My initial reason for serving God is selfish too. I want eternal life. I want my family to be mine forever. But you know what? In the process, I'm learning to love the Lord. I'm learning to serve Him for the right reasons. And if you let me serve you, I'll learn to love you too."

She looked up at me with sallow eyes, heavy with hate.

I smiled at her sour expression. "You know what, Alexis? Go ahead and hate me if you want to. I'm going to love you anyway." I pulled on my jacket and headed for the door. "I'll see you later."

Alexis's attitude bothered me all the way home. Her contempt for me hung so thick in the air of her hospital room that my lungs still burned from breathing in there. I couldn't figure her out. One minute we were almost joking together, enjoying one another's company. The next, she was hateful. When I saw her on Halloween night, I thought she was willing to bridge the gulf between us. I had hopes to form a friendship with her, maybe even make up for lost time. But with the mere mention of anything to do with helping her, serving her, or loving her, she nearly bit my head off.

She's sick. Be patient with her. Love her anyway. The words came quietly to my mind then eased from my mind to my heart, and I thought of her there in the sterile, empty hospital room until my heart broke. She was sick. She was depressed, maybe even manic too. And through it all, she pushed away everyone who would love her. Maybe Isaac wasn't as much of a jerk as I thought he was. Maybe life with Alexis, a tortured woman he didn't understand, had been so unbearable that he searched outside of his marriage for comfort. Granted, he searched in the wrong direction; instead of turning to the Lord for answers, he turned to the world. But his life with Alexis must have been very lonely if she treated him anything like she treated me.

I pulled into the driveway of our little home. I loved the deep red bricks, the light glowing in the front room window, the smell of cookies coming from the kitchen. The kids were covered with flour, and the counter was a mess. Jon laughed and dumped a handful of chocolate chips in his mouth.

"Save some of those for the cookies," I said as I hung my keys on the key rack.

"I bought two bags on purpose." He smiled. The kids all had chocolate faces too.

"Clever." I grabbed a handful of chocolate chips from the open bag and raised my fist to Jon before I filled my mouth.

"So, how is Alexis?" Jon asked.

"I think she'll be all right. You know, I think she's a manic-depressive. She's probably gone without treatment for a long time, too."

"You did a good thing, Lia. I'm proud of you. I think most people would have walked away."

"Well, I couldn't shake the feeling that she needed me. And when I got to her place, and she wouldn't wake up, I got really nervous. You know, that was the clearest prompting I've ever received. I would never have gone over there if the Spirit hadn't persisted. I feel so bad for her, Jon. She thinks I'm only visiting her out of guilt or obligation. She doesn't think I care about her at all."

"Well, all the more reason to see her again. Prove her wrong. Let her feel your love for her."

I nodded and filled a glass with water. "Maybe we can take her a care package after you're done with the play. What do you think?"

"I think that's a great idea." He smiled.

Jon distributed more chocolate chips to everyone.

"How is your book coming by the way? You've been coming home early a lot lately. Are you going to meet your deadline?"

"I'm almost done with it actually. We should have a Christmas break this year without any distractions."

"Oh, Jon. That would be great!"

"Yup. Opening night is my last night for interviews and stuff. Hopefully you won't get bored during the interviews. Actually, we thought we might have an open forum for the audience so they could all ask questions."

"If I'm with you, I won't get bored," I said. Jon leaned across the messy counter and kissed me. "I love you, Jon. I'm so glad I married you."

"Really?"

"Yes." I smiled and winked at him. "You know what my favorite thing to do is?"

He shook his head.

"I love Sunday mornings when I wake up and you're there next to me, still asleep. Sunday's my favorite day of the week because my day starts with you."

He kissed me again over the warmth of fresh chocolate chip cookies.

Sigh No More

———⊗———

"Experience has taught me that you get a lot more out of the arts, the opera, ballet, Shakespeare, even the symphony, if you go a bit prepared." Jon stood before the bathroom sink, carefully shaving his foamy face as he spoke.

I rummaged through the closet for my best dress, hoping it would still fit me.

"See, in *Much Ado,* there's this prince, Don Pedro, who's leading his troops home after some war," he continued.

"Some war?" I asked.

"Yeah, the war really isn't integral to the plot."

"Okay." I thought it funny that something like a war and the cause of it wouldn't have anything to do with the plot of the play.

"Anyway, Don Pedro has a brother, Don John, the bastard."

"Jon! Watch your language."

"Sorry, but all the bad guys in Shakespearean plays seem to be illegitimate heirs to the throne. It's symbolic."

"Okay. And this stuff is performed all over, even though half the population is offended by it."

"Come on, Lia. I didn't write it. Think sixteenth century, okay?"

"Sorry. I'll keep my mouth shut."

"Anyway, John is a miserable guy. And like most miserable guys, he wants everyone to be miserable with him. So he decides to cause some problems and break some hearts while he sits back and laughs at his mischief." He patted his face with aftershave and walked over to the closet.

"It will be quite a stretch for me to think of someone named John as a bad guy," I teased.

Jon wrapped his arms around me and kissed me softly. I loved it when he kissed me with a clean-shaven face. I held him close and made the kiss a long one.

"You're distracting me. How can I prepare you for the play if you distract me?"

"Sorry. I know how you hate it when I do that," I teased.

Jon returned my kiss with a smile.

"Okay, okay. Tell your story." I turned back to the closet and found the dress I was looking for.

Jon cleared his throat. "Anyway, Don Pedro has two guys who work for him named Claudio and Benedick. On their way back from the war, they stop in this place called Messina. A guy named Leonato is the governor of Messina.

"Well, Claudio falls in love with Hero, Leonato's 'short' daughter, as Benedick puts it," Jon chuckled as he quoted the play. "Don Pedro agrees to court Hero in Claudio's name so that Claudio can marry Hero. In the meantime, Benedick and Beatrice, that's Ashley's character, hate each other. They throw insults at each other constantly. But there are a few hints in the play that they once had a relationship that ended badly, and that's why they're so terrible to each other. Watch the way Ashley portrays Beatrice. She makes her such a deep, wonderful character."

The realization that it didn't bother me when Jon praised Ashley filled my heart with joy, and I couldn't stop smiling.

"What?" Jon asked as he buttoned his shirt.

"Nothing, I just love you."

Jon's eyes glinted in the light of our bedroom. My heart fluttered as I looked at him. It was like the past years we'd spent together melted into moments, and he looked at me the way he used to. The shy, curious spark in his eye, the slight quiver of his lip as he flashed a lopsided grin. It thrilled me and pumped my blood quickly through my body.

"I'm never going to finish this story, am I?"

"Okay, I'm sorry. No more distractions." I meant it that time.

He nodded. "All right then." But the spark didn't leave his face.

"Well, Don John decides to mess up the intended marriage and make Claudio think Don Pedro is really wooing for himself. But that misunderstanding straightens out quickly and all is well. So Don John takes it a step further and arranges a rendezvous at Hero's window that misleads Claudio to think that Hero is cheating on him. It hurts Claudio so much that he meets Hero at the altar and accuses her of infidelity in front of everyone."

"Ouch," I said.

"Exactly. Well, Beatrice knows she's innocent, and it's all just a misunderstanding, so she gets really upset at Claudio. Meanwhile, everyone has plotted to get Beatrice and Benedick together. They stage these conversations where they gossip about how much Beatrice loves Benedick in such a way that only Benedick will hear it. They make Beatrice think that Benedick loves her with the same type of trick. So, since Beatrice thinks that Benedick loves her, and Benedick thinks Beatrice loves him, they realize they really do love each other."

I concentrated on his words so I could follow who was in love with whom and why. "So what you're telling me is that this whole play is based on a couple of misunderstandings?"

He smiled and cocked his head as if he were surprised I got it. "Exactly. It's *Much Ado About Nothing*. I knew you could get Shakespeare if you tried."

"Well, you are here to explain the story to me. That makes a difference," I admitted.

"Yeah, so all you needed was a nudge in the right direction. You get the rest on your own." He smiled.

I rolled my eyes and went in the bathroom to put my face on.

"All the misunderstandings get cleared up in the end." Jon tightened his tie and stood in the doorway between our bathroom and bedroom.

"So does that mean Benedick and Beatrice aren't together at the end?"

"No. I think their misunderstanding happened long before the play, when they broke up in the first place."

"Oh. And the other couple, do they get married?" I asked.

"Yep, and live happily ever after. It is a comedy, after all. If it were a tragedy, they'd all die."

"Sounds like maybe Shakespeare is a little predictable."

"Yeah. But it's all about the journey."

I looked up at his handsome face. I knew I could never get tired of that face.

"Do you have any idea how beautiful you are, Liahona Tucker?"

I wrapped my arms around his waist so I could hug him close and avoid his question. I couldn't look half as beautiful as he made me feel.

"So tell me, Mr. Shakespeare. Do we have a predictable, happy ending?"

"Of course not." He leaned down and kissed me again, soft and tender. "We don't end."

I couldn't imagine a more romantic thought.

The small Babcock Theater was full. Jon and I sat on the back row so that the other patrons could get the full experience from the best seats. The small stage had been transformed into a garden, with ivy growing up marbled walls and planters hanging from the ceiling, overflowing with vibrant flowers and ferns. The boy with shoulder-length blond hair and brown eyes, who played the part of Benedick, was in rare form, throwing the audience into gales of laughter. Ashley was great too. Her dark eyes burned into him when they needed to and grew soft like velvet in her occasional moments of tenderness. They had a strong chemistry between them, and in the moments when their characters exchanged loving words, I totally believed they loved each other. Ashley was everything Jon said she was.

After the predictable happy ending, most of the crowd left, moving en masse to their cars. Jon and I moved closer to the stage as the question-and-answer period began. The whole cast sat in chairs lined up along the stage, Ashley sitting in the middle. Every eye naturally fell on her, and most of the questions were directed toward her. I wondered if she ever grew tired of the spotlight.

"Neil, I was wondering, what is your favorite line that Benedick speaks, and why?" Jon asked.

Neil smiled. "Well, that would have to be 'the world must be peopled.'" He spoke the line with a flourish and everyone laughed. "It's such a funny excuse for love.

"I also like it when Benedick says, 'Peace! I will stop your mouth.' He gets a kiss with that line." Neil reached to Ashley, who sat next to him in center stage. She took his hand with a quizzical look on her face.

"And with that, I'd like to announce something." Neil stood and pulled Ashley up with him. Her face went white.

"Ashley and I are engaged to be married." Neil lifted Ashley's hand into the air, smiling broadly as he displayed his trophy. The boy who played the part of Claudio looked like he might become sick. Ashley just smiled demurely and avoided Claudio's eyes.

I leaned to Jon and whispered, "It looks like there was a play within the play."

Jon tried desperately to stifle his laughter.

Jon and I left the theater, hand in hand. The night was chilly, with a clear November sky.

"I thought we'd go downtown for dinner," he said. "It's late enough we should be able to get in."

"Really? Where?" I asked.

"Oh, I'm not telling you. It's a surprise. But let's just say it's someplace you've always wanted to go."

I wondered if we'd eat at The Roof restaurant overlooking Temple Square. I smiled at the thought.

"Why don't you wait right here, and I'll go get the car."

"Oh, I can walk with you, it's all right."

"No, you're cold. I can tell. Go wait in the lobby, and I'll be right back."

He took off toward the car as I turned to wait in the lobby. But the stars were so bright, glowing in the velvet sky, I could stand shivering for a moment to look at them.

"Hi, gorgeous."

I turned to see Derek smiling down at me. His breath chilled and hung in the air.

"Hey, what are you doing here?" I was surprised to see him. My first thought was that he was violating the restraining order.

"Enjoying the arts."

"You shouldn't be within five hundred feet of me."

"I shouldn't be within five hundred feet of your house," he corrected.

"Oh," I said. I didn't know the specifics of the restraining order, but apparently Derek had done some research. "Well, did you see the play?" I tried to smell alcohol on his breath and I looked for the hollow glaze he'd had in his eyes on Halloween. But he looked and smelled fine.

"Yeah. It was pretty good too. That redhead has some talent."

I chuckled.

"I saw you and your husband here, and I waited to talk to you. I need to apologize for Halloween." He cast his eyes to the ground then looked up at me. His green eyes looked exposed and vulnerable as he waited for my forgiveness.

"What happened there Derek? I thought you were sober."

"I was, for five years. But I relapsed."

"Why? I thought you were doing so well." I shivered and looked toward the circular driveway as Jon pulled up. It was cold, and I was sure Jon had the heater cranked.

"I had an insight into myself that night, and I couldn't handle what I learned."

I furrowed my eyebrows quizzically. "What do you mean?"

Jon parked the car and hurried over to me. He put his arm around me and pierced Derek with his gaze.

"What are you doing here?" Jon's question wasn't as kind as it had been when I asked it. "I've got a restraining order out against you. I could press charges."

"I came to apologize for Halloween. Actually, I went to your house as you were leaving and I followed you here."

"You followed us?" Jon's breath hung in the cold air in great, angry puffs.

"The play was wonderful." Derek smiled weakly as Jon's face turned red.

"Come on, Lia, we're leaving." Jon pushed the small of my back lightly and led me to the car.

"Wait," Derek exclaimed as he started to follow us.

"I just wanted you to know I'm putting the house up for sale. I can't stay in Salt Lake anymore."

I stopped and looked over my shoulder at Derek. "You're selling the house?"

"Yes. I thought you might like to see it first."

I looked at Jon. His brow furrowed with a warning, but I pleaded with my expression. I wanted to see the house. Part of me needed to see it.

Jon's eyes softened as he looked at me. He looked cautiously at Derek, but Derek couldn't return Jon's steady gaze. He glanced at me, then at the ground.

"Why don't we all go?" Jon asked.

Derek looked up at him with surprise.

"Oh. Umm, sure," he stammered. "I'm parked there on University Street. The black BMW. Do you want to ride with me, or . . ."

"We'll just follow you." Jon slipped his hand into mine and started leading me toward our waiting car.

"Okay." Derek gave me another look. He seemed apprehensive, like something was very wrong.

Jon helped me into the car.

"We'll be right behind you," Jon said, and he waved at Derek.

When he'd joined me in the car, he scoffed as Derek turned to look at us before he disappeared down the slope to his car.

"He wanted to see you alone," Jon growled and his lips curled in defiance.

"Come on," I scoffed.

"Didn't you notice the way he looked at you?"

"Now who's imagining things?" I looked out the window as we pulled up behind Derek on University Street.

After navigating the neighborhood around campus, Derek turned onto Foothill Boulevard and headed toward the freeway. Jon stayed close on his tail, looking at me occasionally.

"I hope seeing this house will be enough."

"What do you mean?" I asked.

"You can live in your past or in your present, Lia. Right now it looks to me like Derek is pulling you back about eight years. I prefer having you in the present."

"Jon, I'm just curious. Whether we like it or not, Derek was a big part of my life. I'm not going to be rude to him just because you're jealous."

"I'm not the one who's jealous. I got the girl. He's the one I'm worried about. I don't like the way he looks at you, like he still dreams about you. And building this house of his gives him ample opportunity to waste time fantasizing about something that can never be. What does that do to a man?" he asked with good reason.

I folded my arms and looked out the window. I had no way of predicting what was going through Derek's mind. After all these years I wouldn't have bothered to build our house even if I had the means. As I remembered it, the house was impractical and unsuitable for children, nothing like the type of house I would want as a wife and mother. But to me as a teenager, it was grand and romantic.

"He's putting the house up for sale, Jon. It's my only chance to see it and walk around inside. I may as well take the chance while I have it. Unless you want me to go with him alone during the day." I looked at Jon through the corner of my eye and grinned.

Jon glared at me. "That's not funny."

Derek exited the freeway and headed toward Olympus Cove on the east bench of the valley. The moon rose just above the mountain, and the higher we climbed, the bigger the moon seemed. I wondered if Derek remembered every detail of our plans, and as I looked up at the moon, I desperately hoped he had.

Jon started humming a tune I was familiar with. It was the song from *Much Ado,* the one that chased me from the rehearsal weeks before.

"Don't hum that. It's degrading to women." I folded my arms across my chest in defiance.

He snorted. "Degrading to *women?*"

"Yes, telling them to stop caring about their men being deceivers."

"Funny, that sounds more degrading to men than it is to women."

True, it did degrade men too. "Then why sing it?"

"Because it's in my head," he retorted. Then he took a deep breath and changed his mind. "Because it's about relaxing and not being too emotional about life. Don't let your emotions confuse you. 'Sigh no more.'"

I could tell Jon was miffed, and I caught his mood like a virus. I wouldn't have gone to Derek's house if Jon hadn't offered to take me there. I didn't know what he was getting at with the song anyway; I didn't feel confused about anything.

He insisted on humming the song though. He hummed until city lights faded behind us and darkness closed in.

Memory Lane

———⊗———

We passed several mansions as we drove farther up the winding road. Occasional patches of snow gradually became blankets until the road was a streak of brown slush on white cotton. We reached the end of the developed road and our car lurched up a frozen pitted driveway toward a house shrouded in darkness. I could barely see the outline of the home, penned by moonlight.

"It's huge," I whispered.

The rear of the home faced the valley, and the large double front door faced the mountain. There was no lawn, and though a place had been cleared for a driveway, it was still unpaved. Derek stopped his car in front of the home's entrance, and we parked behind him.

Derek climbed from his car and walked to the front door. I couldn't wait for Jon to open my door for me, so Jon was the last of the three of us to reach the front porch.

"As you can see, there's still a lot of work to do. Whoever buys the house will have to put in a lawn in the spring and have the driveway paved. There's not much furniture in here because I'm used to a studio apartment in New York, and there's six thousand square feet of space in this house. I've got most of my furniture on the top floor."

With his last sentence, Derek looked at me. It was hard to discern his expression in the dark, but the tone of his voice told me he was flashing a toothy smile. I remembered that the master bedroom and the library, my two favorite rooms in the house, were on the top floor.

Derek unlocked the entrance and we followed him in. Jon slipped his hand into mine as we stepped over the threshold.

I was stunned before Derek turned on the light. The ceiling was three stories high in the entryway and in the ceiling was a ten-foot-wide skylight. Moonlight flooded the room, reflecting off the hardwood floor.

When Derek turned on the light, I gasped. My home could fit in the space that spread before me. There wasn't a piece of furniture in the sprawling room, but the soft peach tones of the walls and the gentle oak grain in the floor made the room soothing even though it was empty.

"So, Lia, what do you want to see first?" Derek smiled softly at me. His voice echoed, bouncing gently off the walls.

"Show me all of it, Derek. I want to see the whole thing."

He smiled. I could see in his face that he was pleased with my reaction. Derek kept his eyes on me as if he were pretending Jon wasn't holding my hand. I looked up at Jon and smiled, hoping to remind Derek that he and I weren't the only two people on earth.

We started in the basement. The strong smell of new carpet met us at the bottom of the steps.

"This will be an entertainment room. It's wired for surround sound and it's soundproof, so you can have a theater experience here. And over on that side of the room you could have a pool table or whatever. Around the corner there's a hot tub, but it doesn't have any water in it."

Derek's big screen TV sat against the wall with one beanbag tossed in front of it.

"Here's my DVD collection. Remember this movie, Lia?"

Derek pulled *It's a Wonderful Life* from the top of the stack.

"Yes! How many times did we see that together?"

"I stopped counting after twenty."

We both laughed.

"I don't want to get married. I want to see the world." Derek's voice lilted like Jimmy Stewart's.

"Oh my heck! I forgot how well you do impressions."

"Well I had plenty of opportunities to practice. When I was in rehab, we watched old movies all the time. This one was my favorite."

"That doesn't surprise me." I smiled. I had to admit it was fun to be around him. As I looked at his face, I glimpsed the young man I'd known so well, and I felt a little younger too.

"We could watch it if you'd like. I've got another beanbag upstairs."

I looked up at Jon. He wasn't having near as much fun as I was. A scowl creased his face.

"No, Derek we'd better not."

"We've got our family to get home to." Jon put a little too much emphasis on the word *family*.

"And we were going out to dinner," I added.

"Yes, we've got plans." Jon smiled.

"Well, I could order out if you'd like. Is Chinese still your favorite, Lia?"

I smiled, amazed that he remembered. "It is my favorite, but . . ."

"We're not hungry yet, thanks," Jon said firmly. My stomach growled in the silence. "Let's just see the rest of the house," Jon prompted with a wan smile on his face.

Derek cleared his throat and I looked at him. "Should we move on then?" he asked. His face wasn't glowing like it had a moment before. He threw a simmering glare at Jon.

Jon and I followed Derek up to the main floor. We walked through the kitchen with its oak floors and cabinets and enough counter space to impress a chef. The whole place was spotless, as if Derek barely lived there. A small table and one chair sat in the dining area.

Seeing the one chair at the table tore at my heart. My life bustled, with Jon and our children, with the sisters from the ward I loved and worried about, with the parents I spoke to every day. My life was full. But Derek was alone in an empty home much too big for him.

Tears stung my eyes as we climbed the winding stairs to the second floor. Derek showed us a laundry room, bathroom, and three bedrooms, each large enough for most people to use as a living room.

"You could use these for children or guests, or storage, I guess," Derek said. It was obviously his least favorite floor of the house.

"Now for the best part," Derek said as he looked at me.

At the end of the hall was a narrow spiral staircase. I remembered loving them for their elegance when I was young, but as I looked at the stairs, my first thought was how dangerous they would be for Katie to try and navigate.

We climbed the stairs single file and finally reached a part of the house that looked lived in. At the top of the stairs was the library. The walls were lined with row after row of books. A fireplace and an elegant sofa sat at one end of the room. At the other end, Derek had set up an office, complete with all the necessary equipment. Thick reference books lined the shelves near that end of the room.

Jon's eyes widened at the sight.

"You didn't think I would be the type to like books, Professor?"

Jon walked to the shelves and read the spines. His face glowed like Jacob's did on his birthday.

I glanced at the door to what I knew was the master bedroom, my favorite room in the plans. Derek smiled.

"It's got everything you wanted it to have."

"Really?" I asked, my excitement growing as I waited.

"I added a few things too. I think you'll love it."

"If I remember right, there's a balcony in here that I'm dying to see," I said as we headed toward the room.

"I'm right behind you," Jon said, and he was true to his word. He clasped my hand and tore his eyes from the books. He wasn't about to let Derek and me go on a lonely walk down memory lane. I was relieved to have him clutch my hand, even though I was still a little peeved.

Derek strode to the bedroom door and opened it.

The Dream House

———————⟨∞⟩———————

The gibbous moon shone brightly through a wall of glass wrapped around a marble balcony. White translucent fabric collected the moonlight around a mahogany four-post bed, covered in a white, pillow-top quilt and matching throw pillows. And the stars! The stars winked through the windows, as bright as lights in a planetarium. I'd forgotten how bright the stars were in the mountains.

A telescope stood in the corner of the balcony, bathed in moonlight.

Derek turned on the lights. The whole room was white from the smooth walls to the thick carpet. The bathroom door was open, but the room itself was encased in translucent walls. There was a double-headed shower and a hot tub. Two white robes hung on the white tiled walls next to the hot tub, and white billowy towels folded across mahogany racks.

It looked like a little bit of heaven.

"This is the master bedroom. Do you like it?"

I was speechless.

"This is my favorite room in the house. I spared no expense."

"I can see that."

He ran past the bed, giddy as a boy at Christmas. With the press of a button a fire blazed in the glass-encased fireplace.

"This is the best part though." He walked out on the balcony until he stood right against the windows at the balcony's edge. "See how you can go out on the balcony and get a spectacular view even in the winter?"

I nodded.

"Well, these windows aren't really glass. They're a pliable plastic that rolls up in the ceiling there." He pointed to what looked like a huge awning over the marble balcony. "And a railing comes up where the windows are now, right along the balcony's edge. Plus a mosquito net comes up right at the edge of the carpet there, to keep the bugs out of the house." He pointed at a narrow gap between the carpeted floor and the marble of the balcony.

Derek ran back to the panel on the wall and pressed another button. A net rose from the floor between the balcony and the rest of the room and the windows retracted into the awning. Derek pushed aside a section of the net, and led Jon and me to the balcony. The net popped back into place after we stepped through it.

"I've never seen anything like that," I said.

"Spared no expense."

We walked to the balcony's edge and I leaned against the railing. Jon leaned next to me and looked at me with mild impatience. But I was fascinated by the view.

"Look, honey. It's beautiful!" The Salt Lake Valley spread out before us. Lights blinked from Draper at the south end to the bright cluster of lights where Temple Square stood at the north.

Derek led me to the telescope. "Want to look around?"

I couldn't resist. I adjusted the telescope and looked through the eyepiece. The moon filled the lens. It thrilled me to see the details of the moon again, the high ridges and deep craters, the dark seas. I remembered dreams of walking on the moon's surface, leaping in the low gravity, and watching Earth rise.

"Oh, wow," I said. "I forgot how many shades of gray there are on the moon. You can't really appreciate it until you've stared at it up close for a while."

"Like seeing an old friend?" Derek whispered. I hadn't realized how close he stood, close enough that I could smell his musky cologne.

I smiled at him, but my smile faded as I saw his expression of love. Jon had been right all along. I felt a sudden need to get out of Derek's house, like Joseph fleeing before Potiphar's wife.

Jon saw it too and cleared his throat. "Okay, I'm ready to go."

"Yeah. We really do have to go. You've done a beautiful job, Derek," I said, falling in step behind Jon. Derek walked beside me, trying to look me in the eye.

Jon walked ahead of us, holding my fingers loosely in his hand. As we neared the bedroom door, I turned for one last look at the balcony and the huge moon. Jon's hand slipped away from mine.

Derek must have been watching for his opportunity to separate us, and when I looked back, the opportunity arose. Jon continued out the door and before I could join him, Derek pushed Jon out of the way, closing and locking the door behind him. Derek and I were alone in the bedroom and Jon was banging on the door.

"Derek!" I protested.

Derek kept his eyes on me and whispered, "Why did you bring him? I wanted you to come alone. How can we talk if he's hanging around all the time?"

"Derek, he's my husband," I scolded, stating the obvious. "He wouldn't be too keen on the idea of you and me spending time alone. Can you blame him? How would you feel if you were in his position?"

Derek's eyes locked onto mine. A glint in his eyes told me he'd wondered how he would feel if he were my husband instead of Jon. I regretted the question.

"Well, I'm not in his position, am I?"

Jon banged on the door behind Derek.

"Lia! Lia, let me in! Derek, you keep away from her," Jon exclaimed through the hard wood.

"Derek, let him in," I said, anger rising in my throat.

"If you were my wife, I wouldn't let you out of my sight."

His words sent a chill down my spine, and I wasn't sure what to think. Derek's eyes were full of desire as he looked at me. There was a sense of desperation in Derek's voice, like he was holding onto the last thread of me that he could grasp, and he felt his grip slipping.

Derek stood there, looking at me. I couldn't tell what he was thinking, and it made me nervous. And as I looked at him, it occurred to me that he'd planned to have me there alone, just like Jon suspected. He'd planned to flatter me, tell me his life story to get my sympathy, stir up old feelings, tempt me until I gave in. He planned to manipulate me with my memory, and make me give up everything I had for him. He was miserable, and he wanted me to be miserable too. He was Don John.

Derek stood with his back against the door as Jon continued banging against the wood.

"I just want to talk to you, Lia. I want to be alone with you, just for a little while."

"Derek, please let me go."

"I'll find the phone out here and call the police," Jon said, more to me than to Derek.

"That will be hard, old man. I never installed a ground line," Derek called with a smile, knowing he had the upper hand. He had me just where he wanted me.

Derek looked at me with soft eyes. "All it takes is money to get to the moon. Did you know that? If you'll stay with me, I'll give you the moon."

I felt sorry for Derek, but maybe his marriages failed for reasons other than alcohol. The fact was that I knew very little about what Derek had done during the previous years. I didn't know him anymore. And as I saw the possessive look in his eye, I realized I didn't trust him. My stomach knotted in fear.

"I'll break this door down, Derek. You let my wife go!"

"He can break it down. He has a temper," I said.

"If he breaks it down, he'll regret it, I swear." Derek walked to the bedside table. Slowly, he pulled a small handgun from the top drawer and stuck it beneath his waistband.

It was the last thing I ever pictured happening in my dream house.

Trading the Moon

I ran to the door and banged my hands against its hard surface. "Jon, don't break down the door. I'm all right."

"You don't sound all right," Jon pointed out. He didn't sound all right either.

The sound of his voice vibrated against the wood and told me he stood as close to the door as I did.

"He's got a gun, Jon. Let me talk to him," I said in a low voice.

Jon hit the door not far from my face. I pictured him slamming his fist against the wood with an expression of concern and anger.

"I'll be okay. Say a prayer out there and give me a few minutes." I prayed silently as I spoke.

"I'm not going to hurt you, Lia. I promise I won't hurt *you* at all." Derek sat on the bed and watched me lean against the door. When I turned to face him, my cheeks were wet.

"If you hurt Jon, you'll hurt me."

I slid down the door and sat as close to Jon as I could get.

Derek looked at me with sympathetic eyes. "I'm sorry if I'm scaring you. This isn't going at all the way I planned it."

"Did you expect me to leave with you and ditch Jon?" I asked in disbelief.

"I don't know what I expected. But this wasn't it."

Derek walked toward the balcony, running his fingers through his hair. I watched him walk away and wondered what to do. If Derek didn't have the gun in his belt, I would have taken that opportunity to bolt from his house. But I couldn't risk any hurt to Jon. Derek turned and looked at me again.

"Why did you come here tonight?" Derek asked.

"Because Jon brought me here."

"He only brought you here because he knew you wanted to come. So, why did you want to come?"

"I was just curious," I said, trying to discover why I was there.

"Curiosity isn't enough of a reason. You're too deep a person for that. You're too emotional." He grinned and wagged his finger at me as he spoke. "Don't forget, I know you. I can tell when you're not being completely honest."

Anger flared in my heart at his arrogance. But I didn't want to do anything rash. I slipped my fingers under the door and wiggled them until Jon stroked them gently.

"I'll tell you what I think. I think you still have feelings for me. I think you wanted to see this house that we dreamed of, to try it on and see if it still fit you." Derek turned off the light and walked to the balcony's edge.

"You can see the city so much better in the dark. Do you realize how much this city has grown in eight years? I hardly recognize it." He gripped the railing.

"A lot has changed in eight years—not just the city," I said, hoping he'd see the multiple meanings of my statement. I'd changed. He'd changed. Everything had changed.

Derek turned to look at me. He stood there, a dark shadow against the moonlight and the sparkling valley.

"But you haven't, Lia. I can see it. You miss me. You love me as much as I love you. You just won't admit it." He turned his face back to the city lights.

I concentrated on Jon's gentle touch against my fingers under the door.

The sweet voices of my family played through my mind: that Sunday morning as Jon woke Emily and helped her get dressed, Emily's excitement as she ran to the desk with her name on it, Jacob's loving whispers after a hard day at Primary, Katie's squeals and wet hugs after running through the sprinkler. How could I ever have felt that any of that was dull or mundane? I played the moments over repeatedly as I sat in the dark, staring at Derek's silhouette.

Derek walked to the CD player and slipped in a CD. He pressed a button to advance the track and a beautiful melody filled the room. It was "In the Wee Small Hours of the Morning."

"Remember this song? *Sleepless in Seattle* came out around the time we went on our first date, remember? And they played the sound track over the loudspeakers when we went to the county fair. It rained. We danced in the rain." He started to sway with the music and hum the tune. "I love this song. I hear it and I can almost feel you in my arms again. I can almost feel your soft kiss."

I felt nauseated. "Are we done talking now? Can you let me go?"

"What would you do if I kissed you, Lia? Remember how it felt? Remember the adolescent thrill? Would you kiss me back? Or would your fears take over and would you push me away?"

"Derek, please don't talk like that."

"Are you okay, Lia? What is he doing?" Jon spoke through the door, his voice high and tense.

Derek stopped swaying and saw me sitting by the door, talking to Jon. "Come away from the door, Lia." Derek's voice was firm. "Come here, where he can't hear you."

"No, Derek."

"Lia," Derek's voice was firm, "please do as I ask, or I won't let the two of you leave my house."

I pulled my fingers from beneath the door, Jon's touch slipping slowly away.

"Lia, are you all right?" Jon asked.

"I'm fine," I said, though I didn't believe my own words.

I walked far enough away from the door that Jon couldn't hear me speak, but I stopped at least ten feet from Derek.

"What would you do if I kissed you?" Derek asked again.

I looked at him defiantly. I needed to prove a point to him. He didn't know me anymore. I wasn't the girl he loved. The only way to get Derek to leave me alone was to prove to him that he didn't want me anymore. I had to help him see the truth. "If you know me so well, Derek, why don't you just answer that question for me."

He looked happy to tell me his fantasy. "I think you'd kiss me back. Maybe not at first, but eventually. You'd remember me and you'd kiss me back."

"Well, Derek, the city isn't the only thing that's changed in eight years. I'm not the little flirt you knew. If I saw you dancing with someone else right now, I would leave you alone and let you be with your date. I'm here with someone else, Derek. I'm not going to flirt with you over his shoulder."

"Why are you doing this to me, Lia? I know you're not really happy with Jon. I can see it. I know you're still attracted to me. I can see that too. Are you doing it because of the Church? Because of your testimony? How can you really know what's true, Lia? You're so sheltered in your little home in Salt Lake. You've never experienced anything. Plus, if you really knew the gospel was true, if you really had all the answers, you'd be happy all the time. You're such a hypocrite, Lia. You're just scared of what everyone will think if you do what you really want to do instead of what you've been told. If you come with me, like I know you want to, you won't ever have to do anything you don't want to again. Don't care about what they think. Do what you want to do."

"You don't know anything about me Derek, so just be quiet." I raised my voice and walked back to the door to flip on the light. "Look at my face, Derek. I want you to see me so you won't have a shadow of doubt." He'd insulted my commitment to my church, my God, and my vows. Indignation swelled in my heart and spilled over into my voice.

Derek stared at me from across the room. He'd never heard me speak with such conviction, and surprise flickered across his face.

"I may have been unhappy for a while," I said, my voice strong, "but I discovered that it was my fault, not Jon's. I'm responsible for my happiness, no one else." I went over to the stereo and turned it off. "This music is driving me nuts!" I shouted.

Derek looked at me with shock on his face. I liked seeing him speechless.

"I may have had some lingering feelings for you, but you've certainly helped me get over them," I continued. "And even if I hadn't gotten over them, they wouldn't have led *us* anywhere. You may offer me the moon, Derek. You may offer me money and what might seem like freedom and all the things I thought I wanted, but it would all be empty without the gospel. I do know the gospel is true, Derek. But I'm an imperfect person who's learning bit by bit how to live it. And I'm learning how to live it with Jonathan Tucker." I pointed at the door.

Derek looked wounded, but he didn't take his eyes off of me.

"You may offer me the moon, Derek, but Jon has offered me worlds without end—an eternal marriage, and an eternal family. We've already started our journey together, Derek, and our journey will never end." I spoke the last words with such finality that I surprised even myself. I hoped Jon had heard me from the other side of the door. But even if he hadn't heard me, I was pleased with what I'd said, and I knew it was true.

Derek nodded and gripped the gun in his waistband. He stood there with downcast eyes, holding our lives and my breath along with his weapon. The moment stretched on as I looked in the face of the stranger I once knew, trying to guess what he would do when the moment finally passed.

He pulled the gun from his waistband and walked closer to me. Slowly, he pressed the play button on the CD player with the muzzle of the gun. The familiar opening chords of our song sounded distorted to me, far different than I remembered them as he put his arms around me and pressed the cold steel against my back. He held me to him and kissed my cheek.

I felt myself grow nauseated, and darkness bled to the corners of my vision.

Derek caught me as he backed away. He steadied me and looked me in the eye.

"Go back to your husband," he whispered, looking at me with moist eyes.

I steadied myself against the stereo as Derek walked over to the nightstand and placed the gun in the top drawer. I drew deep breaths until my vision cleared.

Derek lifted a small black velvet bag from the same drawer where he kept his gun.

"I want you to have this, Lia," he said as he walked toward me and placed the bag in my hand.

He lifted my hand to his mouth and kissed the fingers I'd wrapped around the ring.

"And if you don't take it, it will remind me of you again, and I'll have another reason to come back and see you. You'll never get rid of me if I have an excuse to come back." Derek tried to smile, but his chin twitched and his lips curled in a frown.

I stared at Derek. He was letting me go. He was finally saying good-bye. And I could finally say good-bye too.

"Turn out the light as you go, please." Derek turned his back to me and walked out onto the balcony.

Without a word, I unlocked the door and opened it. Then, I turned off the bedroom light. Light from the library flooded the bedroom and Jon stood from the spot just in front of the door where he'd been kneeling.

We both looked at Derek's silhouette against the night sky, then we turned and left Derek's home.

We hurried down the spiral staircase, then down the hall to the main stairs. As we moved through the open entryway, my heart said good-bye to Derek, to the dream house, and to the moon. I'd traded it all, finally, for something much better.

Better Than Innocence

—————⟩⟨⊱—————

Jon held my hand all the way to the car. In his hurry, he fumbled for his keys and jammed them in the ignition as soon as we were both seated. The car weaved a bit on the snow-covered gravel as he pushed the gas too hard.

I fastened my seat belt and looked at him. Small beads of sweat gathered on his forehead, and a tear graced his cheek. The extreme emotions of the night gathered inside of me and came to a head. The tears fell fast and I couldn't catch my breath.

"Are you okay, Lia? What can I do?" Jon glanced at me as he steered the car through the winding path down the mountain. His concern touched me so much I couldn't look at him anymore.

We reached the bottom of the weaving road and Jon pulled into the dark corner of a strip-mall parking lot. He turned to me and rested his hand on my shoulder. I collapsed in his arms and cried until my head ached.

Finally I was able to calm myself, and I looked at Jon. His forehead creased with worry and his eyes were wet. He'd never seen me so emotional. In fact, I couldn't remember a time when I'd been so emotional.

"Are you okay?" he asked gently.

"Why do you love me?" I gasped.

"What do you mean? You really told him off. I don't think we'll have to worry about him ever again."

"You know what I discovered while I was telling him off?" I asked, my voice filled with desperation.

He slipped a lock of my hair behind my ear so he could see me. "What did you discover?"

As I looked at Jon's sweet face, I couldn't admit what my discovery was. Not yet. "Why did I want to see that house anyway? I mean did I *have* to see the house? I'm certainly not any better off for having seen it. And I'm starving, to boot."

"Maybe you did have to see it, to help yourself say good-bye."

I couldn't believe how well he knew me. He spoke my thoughts as if he'd thought them himself. I shook my head. "I shouldn't have to say good-bye. I said good-bye eight years ago."

"Apparently you weren't finished."

"I wonder what I would have done if you weren't there," I said quietly.

"Well, maybe next time you're chased by a possessive ex-boyfriend you won't let him get close enough to give you the opportunity to find out," he chided.

I nodded. I should have told Derek off instead of sending the letter and the ring back without a reply. I shouldn't have let him in my house that day while Jon was at work. It dawned on me that sin, just like salvation, has a path that leads to it. With a flash of fear I understood that I was farther down that path than I ever should have been.

I chuckled. "How ironic," I said, looking at Jon's face in the moonlight.

"What's ironic?"

"I thought you were in danger . . . with Ashley. I thought you were in danger of . . . I don't know, emotional adultery. I knew all along it would never become anything physical because that's too obvious. But the emotional stuff happens when you aren't looking. It sneaks up on you." I looked at him. I felt vulnerable, raw, like I was revealing more of myself to Jon than I'd ever revealed to anyone. But it felt good. I felt safe.

"I thought you were in danger," I continued, "but it wasn't you. It was me."

Jon cried softly, then embraced me. He knew what had just happened. He knew I'd opened up far beyond my predicted ability. I was more his wife at that moment than I'd ever been. We were one.

"I'm sorry, Jon," I cried. "I'm so sorry."

He kissed me despite my wet face.

"I *love* you, Lia." He held my face in his hands and looked me in the eye. His eyes communicated so much to me that the words he spoke meant more than any other words I'd ever heard.

We held each other until the tears subsided and we felt tired enough to go home.

The strong emotions of that night faded. We resumed our routine. But our relationship had new life, as if it had been born again through fire like a phoenix. After that, I got butterflies when Jon called me during the day. Everything felt new and exciting. A simple kiss thrilled me to my toes. It was like innocence, but it was better.

Rings and Revelations

Jon and I had filled a ten-gallon tub with things from our past: yearbooks, old pictures, old letters. We didn't want to throw them away because they did tell something about us, hopefully something our posterity could learn from. But we didn't need reminders of anything except the gospel and our beautiful family.

"Sweetheart, what should we do with this?" Jon tossed me the velvet bag.

I took the bag in hand. "Actually, I have a couple of ideas, but first, we have to go to a pawn shop."

We sold the ring, and I bought a simple telescope with some of it. In a way, Derek did give me the moon that night, because he reminded me how much I loved to look through that lens. My telescope was nothing like the one on the balcony, but it was enough.

I put the rest of the money in an envelope and handed it to Bishop Ames with strict instructions not to tell Alexis who it was from. I knew she'd need the money, especially once she started getting hospital bills. Plus, I figured Derek owed her as much as I did.

We had a wonderful Thanksgiving. I helped Mom with the food, so my home filled with the spicy smell of pumpkin pies and the warm, comfortable scent of baked bread. The turkey was juicy, and we ate until Jon had to undo the top button of his jeans and throw himself across the couch to digest while we watched football all afternoon.

Watching the Lions lose was almost fun as we wrapped up in blankets and snuggled with our children in front of the television. Snow fell in family-sized chunks as several flakes stuck together and covered the ground. We were truly thankful that day, for every blessing.

Missy called the day before Ethan's homecoming. She asked me if she could come and visit because she wanted to talk, but not over the phone. I told her my door was always open.

"Hi, Lia," she said as she stomped her feet on the welcome mat to shake the snow from her shoes.

"How are you, Missy? On the phone you sounded like something was wrong."

"Oh, no. Nothing's wrong. I'm just really sensitive right now," she explained.

"How is Ethan?" I asked.

"He's great. He's beautiful. How's Jane?" Missy sounded concerned.

"Fine, as far as I know. I haven't talked to her for a while. Can I get you some hot chocolate?"

"Oh, no. I'm fine. Thank you though," she said.

I sat down next to her and looked her in the eye. "What's going on?"

"I've had my meetings with Bishop Ames."

"Oh. What did he say? I mean, if you don't want to talk about it you don't have to." I felt suddenly embarrassed about asking such a personal question.

"Well, I had a disciplinary action, and I've been put on probation." She folded her hands in her lap.

"What does that mean?" I asked.

"I can't take the sacrament for a year, and I have to visit with the bishop once a week during that time."

"Oh, well that's not too bad, is it?" I'd never thought of what it would be like to not be able to take the sacrament.

"I've missed the sacrament for two weeks now, in addition to all the time I was in the hospital, and it's bad. I never realized how important it is. That sounds crazy, even while I'm saying it, because that's really the main reason we meet on Sunday. But when you can't take it, especially because you know you're not worthy to, it's . . . well it's a lot worse than you think.

"I still feel the Spirit, and I still have a testimony of the gospel, but every week that goes by, I feel more and more guilty. I'm so aware of all the little things I do wrong, the things I say that I shouldn't say, and the things I do. All I feel is guilt, and it's killing me."

"Have you told Bishop Ames this?" I asked. "Are you supposed to be feeling this way?"

"He's such a wonderful man, you know? He told me to be patient and hold on. He said forgiveness will come, and comfort will come."

Missy's eyes filled with tears that spilled quickly down her cheeks. I put my arm around her and let her cry on my shoulder until the tears subsided.

"Anyway, that's not really why I came over." She broke our embrace and sat up, wiping her cheeks. "I want to talk to you about Jane."

"Oh. Okay. I really don't know much more about her than what I've told you."

"Do you think she'd make a good mom?" Missy asked, her face intense like she was putting a lot of trust in my answer.

"Based on what I know of her, she'd make a fantastic mom. She knows how to handle children, and she's got a strong testimony of the gospel. She realizes when she makes mistakes, and she works hard to fix them if she can. I think she might be a little overprotective, but that's not necessarily a bad thing in the world we live in."

Missy nodded. "And what about her husband? Have you ever met him?"

"I've seen him at church. He spoke in sacrament meeting while you were in the hospital. He seems like a neat guy. I know he served a mission in France."

"Do you think he'd make a good dad?"

I blinked quickly as hope for adoption raced to my heart. "Missy, why are you asking me this?" I asked.

She smiled and looked at her hands resting in her lap. "I never could hide much from you, Lia." She looked back up at me. "I'm thinking of letting Jane take Ethan home with her."

My heart quickened in my chest, and my mouth felt suddenly dry.

"It's going to kill me, but I want Ethan to have the best parents he can have. I want him to have a mom and a dad. I want him to have more than I can give him." Tears rolled down her young face. "Besides, I think it's time I started doing what's right."

Tears slipped down my face too. I couldn't imagine anything harder than giving up a baby. And I knew how much Missy loved Ethan. Missy was already in anguish, but out of love for her child, she was prepared to cause herself even more pain. Words of compassion crowded in my throat until I couldn't speak. I wrapped my arms around Missy instead.

After I pulled away, I went to get a box of tissue from the end table.

"I hope you're not asking my advice, Missy. I don't think I can tell you what to do in this case, beyond what I've already told you."

"I know. I've prayed about it for a while now, and I think the Lord approves of my decision. Mom and Dad are going to miss their first grandbaby but they think it's the best thing for him. I just wondered what you think Jane will say. How should I ask her? What if she's not even interested in adoption, and she turns us down?"

"All you can do is ask," I encouraged.

Missy nodded and dabbed at her nose with the tissue.

"Well, thank you." Missy stood and headed toward the door.

"For what? I didn't do anything."

"Sure you did. You listened." She smiled at me.

I stood and Missy hugged me.

"You're amazing, you know that?" I said as I squeezed Missy just before we let go.

"No I'm not. But Ethan is. If Jane says yes, will you throw a baby shower for her like you wanted to for me?" she asked. "I'm sure she'll need all that baby stuff."

"I will," I agreed.

Missy nodded and left, walking carefully along the sidewalk to Mary's car. I watched as she pulled off in the direction of the apartments.

Joy rushed through me and I couldn't help but clap my hands. I wished I could be there to see Jane when Missy revealed her hopes.

I Remember You

———— ✦ ————

Blue streamers and laughing women filled my front room on a cold day in December. We passed Ethan around, and when I finally got to hold him, I rubbed my cheek tenderly against his downy hair. He smelled clean and lotioned and was dressed in an adorable pair of denim overalls and a long-sleeved jumper with trucks all over it.

"There's something about a newborn," I said. "You forget how sweet and soft they are until you hold one."

"Well, he's two months old now. You should have held him a couple of weeks ago," Jane said. She couldn't keep her eyes off the baby boy. She made all the shower guests wash their hands before they held him, and she changed his diaper every hour. I kissed his head when Jane's back was turned, and handed him to Mary, who took him gratefully and cooed until he smiled at her.

"How's Missy?" I lowered my voice as I sat next to Mary.

"She's okay. She's staying with my sister until Christmas. This was all too much for her to take. But she's stronger than she thinks. She'll be all right," Mary said with conviction.

"To be honest, Mary, I'm surprised you're here." I put my arm around her.

"I love this little boy. And I love Jane. Why wouldn't I be here? Once a grandma, always a grandma."

I nodded and squeezed her shoulders.

Sarah, the woman who helped me with the children the day I found Alexis at her apartment, stood at the card table in the far corner of the room, picking at the refreshments.

"How are you, Sarah? You all moved in?" I asked.

"Yup. We set up our Christmas tree already because we knew we'd have to move the furniture again if we waited until next week to put it up. So, it's Christmas all month in our house," Sarah explained.

"That's the best way to do it. We're setting ours up tomorrow after I get all this mess cleaned up."

"We should call the young women over and help you clean up. They can make it their service project for the month." Sarah raised her eyebrows.

"See, that's why I called you as my counselor, always coming up with practical ideas." I smiled. Being the new Young Women's president was just as fun as I thought it would be. But I looked at the girls more like a mother, and less like a friend. I'd developed my own themes for my presidency, making sure I taught the girls the importance of treating everyone with kindness, especially the quiet, friendless people at church and school. And I told them to follow the Spirit every time it speaks, to avoid every temptation they could.

"Is Alexis all moved out?" I asked Sarah.

"She moved out the same weekend we did. She seemed really upset about moving back in with her parents, but at least she's going to school. Maybe she'll get her life in order. Did you hear about the stack of money she got from Bishop Ames?"

"Yeah, I heard." I nodded.

"Wouldn't it be fun to give away that kind of money?" Sarah mused.

"It would be." I smiled and nodded, trying hard to look like I had no idea how fun it would be.

When all the gifts were unwrapped, and everyone had run out of endearing interjections about the new clothes and soft blankets, we gathered everything up and helped Jane to her car. She bundled Ethan in his car seat and set him next to Mary.

Jane hugged me tight. "Thank you so much for the shower. You're so sweet. And none of this would have happened if it hadn't been for you. I hope you know that."

"I don't deserve any credit at all," I said. "I'm just trying to be who God wants me to be."

Jane smiled.

"So when are you moving?" I asked.

"We'll go back to Iowa after Christmas. Our social worker said it would be easier on Missy if we're out of town, and my heart is in Iowa."

We looked at Mary, who knelt over Ethan. Mary's smile quivered as she cooed at him, and tears glinted in her eyes.

"But a part of my heart will always be here." Jane put her hand on Mary's shoulder.

"And a part of my heart will be in Iowa," Mary said in a strained voice.

Jane hugged Mary, and they cried together while I filled the trunk of Jane's car with clothes enough to get Ethan through his first birthday.

After the house was empty and quiet, I wiped off the table and put the last of the refreshments in the fridge. Jon came through the kitchen door, dripping and shaking snow from his boots. One by one our children followed him in, leaving their boots outside and sliding across the linoleum in stocking feet.

"Did you hand in your manuscript?" I asked.

"Yep. We're free and clear for Christmas break. Disneyland, here we come! I picked this up at the store, too."

Jon pushed a magazine in my hands, and there was Derek on the cover. I shook my head and turned to the article.

"Derek Sullivan hit the mother lode in modeling over eight years ago, but what is this young man's passion? He's an architect."

The article showed pictures of the dream house, and in one of the pictures Derek reclined on the bed's white comforter holding a single red rose to his smiling face. The caption below the picture read, "Here's to the one who got away!"

"Can you believe that?" I squealed, fighting a shocked grin.

"Oh, there's more. Read the article."

I read on. "After two visits to rehab for recovery from alcoholism, Sullivan says he has finally found the key to staying sober. 'I'll never have a problem with alcohol again. A dear friend of mine reminded me that *I'm* in charge of my own happiness, no one else.'"

I smiled.

"See, you were a good friend to him after all," Jon said with a tender smile.

I winked at Jon then turned back to the article. "Sullivan is quite possibly the most eligible bachelor in the country, and when we inquired about his love life Sullivan responded, 'My heart has been broken, and broken bad. I guess I'm looking for just the right woman to heal me.'"

"Oh brother," I said as I rolled my eyes. "He's never going to find the right girl now."

Jon put his arms around my waist. I flung the magazine to the table and returned his embrace.

"I got you an early Christmas gift, too," Jon said with a grin.

"Oh really? Let me see."

He pulled a box out of his pocket about the size of a pair of eyeglasses. I untied the red-and-green plaid ribbon and opened the box. Inside lay two compact cell phones.

"Now you can always find me, and I can always find you." He winked.

"Wow," I said, "we've officially entered the digital age."

"Yeah. Eventually, I'll start taking my notes on a laptop instead of a bunch of index cards."

"So, do they work?" I asked.

"Well, let's try them out. I've already programmed your number." He flipped down the bottom of his phone and pressed a button. My phone rang.

"Push 'yes,'" he said.

I flipped down the bottom and pushed the designated button. "Hi."

"I remember you." He smiled at me, and his pacific eyes sparked. Our voices echoed in the phones.

"I remember you too."

"Yeah, you're the little girl in my English class, the one who can't keep her eyes off me."

"That's because I love you, Dr. Tucker."

"I love you too."

Jon closed his phone, and I closed mine. He kissed me as he had countless times before, but it was better than the first kiss. It flooded me with more than infatuation, attraction, or even love. It was a kiss of commitment, of promise. It was solid, dependable, consistent, eternal. It was the kind of kiss I'll always remember.

About the Author

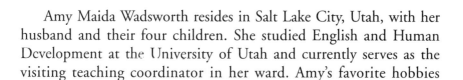

Amy Maida Wadsworth resides in Salt Lake City, Utah, with her husband and their four children. She studied English and Human Development at the University of Utah and currently serves as the visiting teaching coordinator in her ward. Amy's favorite hobbies include singing, cooking, and watching movies.

CROSSROADS

Beth was barely able to control the scream rising in her throat. "Grant! You're scaring me! Please slow down!" She clutched the dashboard of the dark green, older-model Camaro.

The good-looking blond seated behind the wheel laughed. He was handsome, but to the close observer his face was full of hard lines, and he looked older than his twenty-three years. He held the leather-covered steering wheel carelessly, turning his sharp blue eyes toward his passenger.

"What's the matter, babe? Don't you like my driving?" He laughed again and his white teeth flashed in the darkness. "We're going for a little ride, so sit back and enjoy." He glanced at the back seat. "Hey, Seth," he called, "Lizzie here thinks I'm driving too fast. What do you think, cuz?"

Beth could definitely hear a slur in Grant's voice now. She gritted her teeth. He only called her Liz or Lizzie when he was mad or wanted to goad her into fighting with him. He knew it reminded her of the dumpy little high school girl she'd been—too recently for her own comfort. Changing her name was the first step she'd taken toward improving herself.

She felt movement against the back of her seat and her nose was assaulted by the rank, sour smell of beer. Out of the corner of her eye, Seth's head appeared and he rested his chin on her headrest. His tousled blond hair was a shade darker than his cousin's, but they both had the same sky-blue eyes, a defining Montgomery trait. Seth, who was a year older than Grant, was actually more immature and always eager to follow his cousin into anything. Beth hated it whenever the two were together.

"Ain't you Miss Perfect, thinking you're too good for us," he sneered, burping into her ear.

Beth shuddered and turned her head toward the window to get away from the smell. When Seth's hand dropped to her shoulder and squeezed cruelly, she pulled away and glared at him.

"Nobody's too good for us." Grant's ice-cold voice sent shivers up her back.

If it had been lighter outside, he might have seen the fear in her dark green eyes. She wished she had waited for a better time to break up with him. She'd been so consumed with being too scared to do it, that the moment he picked her up, she blurted it all out. The expressions that had crossed his face at her announcement should have warned her that trouble was coming, or at least his terse reply of, "We'll talk about this later, Liz," as he'd escorted her out to the car.

On the way to the party he had seemed cool and calm, but Beth had felt the tension building between them. She thought she'd seen the limits of his cruel behavior before, but what followed at the party was worse. He took every opportunity to be spiteful and hurtful, especially in front of others. She tried to stay out of his way, but he never let her get too far from sight before tracking her down, twisting her arm around, and forcing another can of beer into her hand. Pacing herself, she'd sipped moderately on three different cans throughout the evening. She did not want to get drunk tonight. In fact, the whole drinking-throwing-up-headache routine was getting old, and she was finding that she liked having control over herself at times like this.

She almost got to a phone once, but then good old cousin Seth had suddenly popped up and taken it away. Between the two of them, they managed to keep her away from that or any other source of help. Several times Beth had thought about leaving and walking home, but when she stepped outside, the weather had turned nasty, cold, and wet. As she watched the thick heavy raindrops splash against the small dormer window of the kitchen door, she knew she wouldn't last long wearing her thin jacket. She resigned herself to hoping she'd be able to find another ride home when the party broke up.

When Grant finally decided it was time to leave, he grabbed her around the waist, hauled her out through the pouring rain, and practically threw her into his car. She tried to dissuade him from driving, but he got angry and nearly shut the door on her leg. A moment later when Seth—also drunk—had stumbled into the back seat, she knew she was in for a wild ride home.

Beth glanced in the mirror and willed herself to relax, trying not to think about how awful she looked when Grant stressed her out—which seemed to be too often these days. Other than that, she didn't consider herself a beauty anyway, but she worked hard at taking care of herself physically and was satisfied with her classic features most of the time. She'd been pleasantly surprised at how much she'd matured and changed physically in the last two years at college. Her mother had always insisted she keep her dark, red hair short, but now she had grown it long and it was heavy enough to pull into waves instead of curls. Usually she wore it in a braid that hung down the middle of her back. She didn't wear it loose very often, however, because Grant was always talking about wanting to touch it. The one time she'd worn it loose, she was so tired of his pawing and fawning over it by the end of the evening that she'd vowed never to wear it that way again.

The look on Grant's face now was familiar to her and it made her afraid. "Grant, take me home, please." She tried to be firm so he wouldn't hear the trembling in her voice. "Or you can let me out right here."

A flash of movement, glimpsed out of the corner of her eye, was the only warning before Grant's open hand hit her across the left side of her face. She gasped in pain as her head hit the side window. To her dismay, she realized she'd bitten through the inside of her lip. Warm blood was oozing onto her tongue and she raised her fingers to her quickly swelling lip. She wanted to cry, but knew it would only make him more angry.

"Shut up, Liz," he growled at her.

A groan from the back seat turned Grant's attention away from her. "Hey, cuz." Seth sounded groggy. "Pull over, will ya?"

Grant pulled to the side of the road and they waited while Seth opened the back door and thrust his head outside. Beth tried to close her ears to the sound of his retching, but it was impossible and her own stomach flip-flopped. She tried to concentrate on the cool breeze flowing in from the open door and hoped it would help soothe her aching head. Now she wished she hadn't drunk anything.

A large farm truck drove by, throwing clumps of heavy sleet against the stopped car, and slush slapped the windshield violently. Beth wished she'd had the foresight to get out of the car when Grant had first stopped. Perhaps the person in the truck would have stopped for her.

Grant cursed the driver and then turned back to Seth who was still hanging his head out the door. "Get in, Seth. We're going to teach that guy some manners."

Beth knew she needed to get out. She reached a trembling hand for her shoulder belt release and then went for the door handle, but Grant suddenly grabbed her arm and yanked her away from the door. What she could see of his face in the glare of the dashboard lights made her cringe.

"Don't even think about it!"

Beth pulled her arm away from his pincerlike grasp without saying a word and was relieved when he turned his attention back to driving. He angrily shifted gears, and as he sped back onto the highway, the inertia forced Beth's head back against her headrest. She heard Seth tumble against the door and she wished he'd put on his seat belt. She didn't like him much, but she would still hate to see him get hurt if there was an accident. She had undone hers when she tried to get out of the car, but had quickly put it back on when Grant lurched away from the roadside.

It didn't take long to catch up to the truck. "He's going to regret the day he splashed my car," Grant said angrily as he shifted the car into a higher gear.

As he depressed the accelerator hard and pulled out into the oncoming lane, Beth sucked in her breath and tried to ignore the throbbing in her lip and cheek. "What are you doing?" she cried, clinging to the door and digging her fingers deep into the handle.

"Shut up, Liz," he yelled at her.

"Please Grant!" Beth couldn't do anything else but plead with him. "Just pull off, please." Any moment now he was going to lose control of the car, she was sure of it.

"I said shut up!" Grant screamed at her and then let go of the wheel with his right hand.

Even though she saw it coming this time, she didn't have time to move out of the way before he hit her on the cheek—this time with his closed fist—and her head slammed into the window again. Dazed, she tried to focus on the road ahead. The car swerved suddenly to the right, into the side of the truck. The impact jarred her teeth, and she heard the crunch of metal and the shattering of glass as the car slid sideways, tipped as it went off the edge of the road, and then rolled before coming to rest upright.

Beth's world went fuzzy and then black after her head hit the side window for the third time, and she drifted in and out of consciousness. As the blinding pain in her head became more intense, she wondered if she was about to find out what it was like to die. Somewhere in the darkness she heard Grant begin to scream.